THE
BIG HOUSE

THE
BIG HOUSE

LARCHE DAVIES

Matador
9 Priory Business Park,
Wistow Road, Kibworth Beauchamp,
Leicestershire. LE8 0RX
Tel: 0116 279 2299
Email: books@troubador.co.uk
Web: www.troubador.co.uk/matador
Twitter: @matadorbooks

ISBN 978 1789018 240

British Library Cataloguing in Publication Data.
A catalogue record for this book is available from the British Library.

Typeset in 11pt Aldine401 BT by Troubador Publishing Ltd, Leicester, UK

Matador is an imprint of Troubador Publishing Ltd

For Alun and Dafydd.

CHAPTER ONE

"Beelzebub's brats must be brought to justice!" bellowed the yellow-haired man into the phone.

There was a murmured response from head office. The man detected a note of reproof.

"They are no longer my children!" he shouted. "I disown them. The Magnifico disowns them. He will find them and strike them down, and they shall perish in the fire of the melting flesh."

He slammed the phone down and cursed the holy leaders, those long-bearded idiots! They couldn't even be trusted to keep track of a bunch of kids. The fools had lost them. He strode across the room, swearing as he knocked his leg against the corner of the coffee table. Damn this tiny flat! Built for midgets! He pulled his briefcase out from behind the sofa, laid it on the table, and opened it up.

Bad seed must be destroyed. Those who dishonoured their father, dishonoured the Magnifico. That's what it said in the *Holy Word*. His hands shook as he shuffled through the briefcase. Underneath the bank accounts, share certificates and property holdings, he found what he was looking for. He controlled himself and breathed deeply. There were lists of marriages and births and natural deaths, and of the disposals of various unwanted or non-useful individuals.

Memories flashed through his mind as he saw the names of aunts, wives and children that the Good Doctors had disposed of on his behalf. He ran his finger down the list of living children, crossed out two names in angry strokes of thick, black ink, and wrote 'disowned' alongside them. Good riddance. Dorothy and David were no longer his children. It was disposal for them, and for the two Copse kids.

★

The door of the safe house shut behind them. Lucy grabbed Paul's hand, and they ran through the blinding rain. Despite the dribbles of water inside her collar, she could feel the Magnifico's burning breath on the back of her neck. With every step towards the waiting car she breathed *he doesn't exist, he doesn't exist*.

"Choppity chop!" the escort called briskly.

Dorothy was already in the back seat when they reached the car. Lucy pushed Paul along next to her and followed him in. David climbed in after them and the door slammed shut.

The escort settled herself into the passenger seat and pressed the lock. She called over her shoulder, "Hope you're not too squashed back there. I'm Beverley, by the way, and this is Pete."

The driver nodded and switched on the engine.

For once in her life, Lucy was glad she was skinny. Even so, it was a tight squeeze. If they had to sit like this for two hundred and twenty miles, they'd all expire. She studied the back of Beverley's geometric hairstyle, and wondered who she really was. They'd been told they'd be escorted by a trustworthy person, whatever that meant. How on earth could they trust anyone?

Paul wriggled. "I'm squashed," he said, and Lucy hauled him onto her lap.

"We'll take turns with him," whispered Dorothy.

The car nosed its way out of the side road and into the heavy traffic. For the next hour or so it stopped and started, moved forward a few yards and stopped again, until Lucy began to doubt that they would ever reach the motorway. One thing about it though, anyone who grabbed them here wouldn't be able to get them away. London traffic congestion had its advantages.

"Can the Magnifico drive?" asked Paul.

"No," said Lucy, "because he doesn't exist."

Paul squirmed, and twisted himself sideways on her lap as he made himself comfortable. His curly, brown hair was wet from the rain, and Lucy dried it as best she could with her handkerchief. He settled himself ready for sleep. She put her arms round him and held him tight. He was really heavy, but she didn't shift her position. The longer he slept the sooner he'd get there she thought, nestling her face into the top of his head.

It was six months since she had discovered that Paul was her brother, and she could still hardly believe it. She glanced left at David. His eyes were closed, and he was breathing deeply and slowly; in, out, in, out. The pounding of her own heart had settled down a little, but she guessed his was still going strong. On her right, Dorothy sat with her head held high, as bolt upright as it was possible to be in the back seat of a car while rigid with determination to think positive. Lucy smiled to herself. Not only did she have a real brother, but she also had a blood brother and a blood sister. She remembered the oath they had taken, to be a family and never to be separated. For a moment, despite the ever-present fear of pursuit, she felt a flush of happiness.

It was dark when they arrived. The car drew up outside a handsome, three-storey house, and, with a grunt of relief, Pete turned off the engine. He stepped out into the road, stretched his legs and rubbed his back.

"Blimey! I thought the journey would never end," he grumbled, as he shuffled round to the rear of the car. "An' I've got to drive all the way back to London tomorrow. You'd think they could've let me have a couple of days off at the seaside."

Beverley rolled down her window and looked out. "At least it's stopped raining," she said.

Four squashed bodies uncurled in the back seat. David scrambled out and stretched, and ran round to the boot. He lifted out four plastic carrier bags, and lined them up on the pavement. Dorothy crawled out, rubbing the backs of her legs.

"I'm too stiff to walk," she groaned. "Why are you being so efficient?"

David laughed. "It's exciting! Look, we're here!"

The four of them stood in a row, looking up at the house. Its fine, red bricks gleamed in the streetlight, and a soft glow from the downstairs living rooms invited them in.

Paul took hold of his sister's hand. "Lucy?" he said. His voice was anxious. "Is this Wales?"

"Yes," said Lucy. "We'll be safe here."

They thanked Pete politely and followed Beverley up a shrub-lined path to the porch at the side of the house. A lantern beamed overhead, and light from the hall shone onto their faces through panes of coloured glass. Beverley pulled at an old-fashioned bell rope, and the door opened immediately to reveal two almost-middle-aged women, both dressed entirely in grey.

"Good evening, ladies!" chirruped Beverley. "I've brought you four little Londoners." She smiled brightly with Hollywood-white teeth, and turned to wink at the children.

Little! Lucy had often been told she was puny, but she and David were fifteen! Plus he was nearly six foot. And Dorothy was sixteen. Hardly what you'd call little!

As she stepped into the hall, she glanced quickly around. It was big and square, and all the doors leading off it were shut. A wide, mahogany staircase swept up from its centre and curved round at the top. No escape there, unless they jumped out of a window.

The older woman in grey was talking. Lucy remembered the manners Aunt Sarah had taught her, and turned to look at her.

"How do you do?" she was saying. "Do come in, all of you. I am Miss Clements, and this is my sister, Miss Marilyn." Her hands were folded peacefully across her stomach. "Now, my dears, tell me who's who."

Lucy wondered what was going on behind that benevolent expression.

In fact, what Miss Clements was thinking, as Dorothy and David stepped forward, was that they were both too thin. She liked a challenge. With plenty of good food she would build them up in no time.

Dorothy shook hands with both women and said cheerfully, "I'm Dorothy, and this is my half-brother, David."

Miss Clements looked from one to the other. So those were the Drax children, she thought, one dark and one blond, and not at all alike except for their height.

"But we're all four of us blood brothers and sisters," said David firmly, as he shook hands with the two women. "It's best to make it clear from the beginning, in case they haven't explained it to you." The flicker of anxiety in his eyes belied his air of confidence. "We took a vow never to be separated, and have formed our own family, so I hope you can have us all and that there hasn't been some mistake."

Miss Marilyn pursed her lips and twitched them sideways.

"It's alright dear. We've got plenty of room for you all," said Miss Clements reassuringly. "And this must be Lucy Copse."

Lucy stepped forward. The shyness of her smile was tinged with caution. Putting out her hand she said, "How do you do, Miss Clements? How do you do, Miss Marilyn?" She pushed forward a smaller, sturdier version of herself. "This is Paul, my brother," she said proudly. Bending down, she whispered, "Shake hands, Paul."

Christ! thought Beverley, suppressing a little splutter of mirth, the kid was still in the dark ages. She'd be curtseying next.

Paul looked up at Miss Clements and Miss Marilyn with big, hazel-green eyes, and studied their faces carefully. Then, he solemnly put out his hand.

Miss Clements was pleased. She liked children who knew how to behave.

A little white terrier snuffled at Lucy's ankles and she bent to stroke it.

"That's Donald," said Miss Clements. "I suggest you don't touch him, dear. He's fifteen, the same age as you. It's quite old for a dog, so children – young people, that is – sometimes make him grumpy."

Lucy smiled up at her. Soft, brown curls framed a sweet oval face.

Like a little Madonna but without the blue headscarf, thought Miss Clements. But goodness, she was small for her age! Malnutrition probably. Another one who needed building up.

"I've never really known a dog personally," said Lucy, straightening up. "I'm sure I'll love Donald. Perhaps he'll love me back once he's got used to me."

Nice child, thought Miss Clements. "Now, my dears, Miss Marilyn will look after you, while I have a quick chat with your escort. You probably had a meal on the way down, but I thought you'd like a little snack after your journey." She pointed towards the first room on their right. "That's the dining room in there."

She disappeared into the second room with Beverley.

In stern silence, Miss Marilyn showed them where to wash their hands, and then opened the dining-room door and herded them in. Lucy had never seen such a comfortable – and comforting – room. In Father Copse's house, the rooms had been large and high ceilinged like this one, but they had been stark and cold, and so colourless that she couldn't even say they were white. What a difference soft-cream walls and a rose-coloured carpet made! There was a bowl of early daffodils and winter berries on the fine, marble mantelpiece and, in the middle of the room, was a round, mahogany table laid with sandwiches, fruit and home-made cake. She glanced at Paul and almost laughed at the look of surprise on his face.

David's eyes were fixed on the food. "Wow! Call that a little snack?" he exclaimed.

"Shush," whispered Dorothy, nudging him gently with her elbow.

Miss Marilyn made no comment. She served them, but apart from asking if they wanted tea or hot chocolate, she said nothing. Occasionally, her mouth would purse and twitch in a disapproving manner, and the children ate in silence. Even Dorothy's laughing, brown eyes were subdued.

Lucy snatched a sidelong peep. It was strange, she thought, how just one frosty person could make such a lovely room feel cold. She caught Miss Marilyn's eye and hastily lowered her gaze, and tried unsuccessfully to decipher the murmur of voices floating in from the next room.

★

On the other side of wooden dividing doors, Beverley put her briefcase down on the floor, threw her jacket onto a side table, and settled herself into a chintz armchair in front of the fire.

"Hope you don't mind," she said, putting her legs up on a tapestry footstool, "but my ankles swell up after long car journeys."

"Do make yourself comfortable while I just pop out to fetch the tea trolley," murmured Miss Clements soothingly. "Then we can relax. I've had several chats with Mr Lovett about the children, but he told me you'd fill me in with all the details."

Beverley wriggled her bottom back into the cushions and gave a little sigh of pleasure. The long, winding journey from London was already a past discomfort. Old Lovett would have given the briefest and driest of details, typical lawyer – silly old donkey. She could make a far better job of it any day. Her eyes closed, and she had nearly dropped off when the door opened and a tea trolley glided silently into the room, followed by Miss Clements. The gentle sound of pouring tea was so unfamiliar that Beverley opened her eyes again, and wondered who on earth used a teapot these days?

"Now you can tell me all about it," said Miss Clements when she had passed out the cake and settled herself near the fire. "I know someone wants to stop the children giving evidence in a murder trial."

"Two trials, actually, or it could be three," began Beverley. "They escaped from some looney religious sect and have been sent out of London for their own safety." She sipped her tea and nibbled at her piece of cake before continuing. "If the trials do go ahead, it'll cause the collapse of a bunch of crackpots who follow a god called the Magnifico."

"I thought we were supposed to be tolerant of religious beliefs in this country," murmured Miss Clements.

"Yes, but not when they believe in abducting women and keeping them in breeding rooms, and bumping off people who don't obey the rules."

Miss Clements caught her breath. "Oh no! Of course not."

"Mind you, the trial against Father Copse, that's Paul and Lucy's dad, might not go ahead. Mr Lovett reckons he's too crazy to come to court. Mad as a hatter. At this moment, he's in some psychiatric unit being assessed."

"Oh, dear! I do hope it's not one of those inherited madnesses. I'm not trained for that sort of thing."

"No worries. All four kids are absolutely normal, which is a miracle after what they've been through. But if they're caught now, they'll be dead meat – lethal injection by so-called 'Good Doctors'. Almost makes you laugh, giving them a name like that!"

Miss Clements suppressed a gasp of revulsion and reminded herself that one should keep one's composure in all circumstances. She cut another slice of cake.

"There doesn't seem much point to the religion," added Beverley, "like being good or helping others. It's just that the Magnifico says everyone has to be frugal, and uncomfortable, and free from sin."

"Dear me," said Miss Clements. "I never realised that being comfortable could be sinful. I must say, I do enjoy a bit of comfort."

"Well, they think doing without is good for your soul. If you don't toe the line, you're disposed of by the Good Doctors and your flesh melts in eternity."

"How very unpleasant!" Miss Clements glanced at the fire. It spoiled things to think of melting flesh when one had a good blaze going. There was nothing like the dancing colours in a homely hearth to make one feel at peace with the world. She bent over to throw another log on the flames. "How did these poor children get involved?"

"Born into it." Beverley lowered her voice. "The men have God knows how many wives, so as to produce more followers for the Magnifico. Disgusting, I call it."

Miss Clements's hand shook slightly as she poured herself another cup of tea. Beverley noted the rattle of the cup against the saucer and was pleased with herself. She'd always had an effective way with words.

"Most of the kids lived in communes run by aunts," she continued, "but Father Copse kept Paul and Lucy in his own house till his gardener burned it down – a guy called Thomas. They were brought up by an old lady called Aunt Sarah."

"Well, at least Aunt Sarah did a good job on their manners," commented Miss Clements.

"Yeah, maybe, but what they didn't know was that they had a mother, and Copse was keeping her locked up in the attic the whole time. She died in hospital after the fire." Beverley paused out of respect. "Sad!" she said.

Miss Clements took a moment to collect herself. "Would you like another piece of cake?" she asked. "What about your driver? Perhaps you'd like to bring him in?"

"Pete? No. He's OK. He won't need cake. Obesity's his middle name. He's gone to book us into our hotel." Beverley checked her watch. "He said he'd be back in half an hour, and there's ten minutes to go, so I've got time for another slice. Ta." She looked around the room, at the high ceiling, the tall windows and the thickly lined curtains. "Nice place you've got here. Big, isn't it?"

"Yes. We've plenty of room. This will be the children's private sitting room. My sister and I have our own sitting rooms up on the first floor. The house is bigger than it looks from the front. It goes right back almost into the hill behind it."

"Well, they're lucky kids. I don't need to check their rooms, I can see that."

"They'll each have their own bedroom on the second floor, unless, of course, Paul wants to share with his sister."

"He will do," said Beverley. "He's pretty clingy. Follows her around like Mary's little lamb, and hums when he's worried. You don't know what's going on in the mind of a kid that age. He was only four at the time, but he helped Lucy rescue Dorothy and David when they were about to be carted off for the lethal injection." She shuddered. "Can you imagine? Just sitting there in the disposal cells waiting for the grim reaper!"

Miss Clements suppressed her own shudders, while Beverley brushed some crumbs off her natty black skirt and checked her watch again.

"Hell's bells! I'll have to get moving soon. Not that Pete will mind. He's used to sitting in cars waiting for people. It is his job, after all."

"He might not like being on double yellow lines," Miss Clements pointed out.

"No, never mind. He won't have to pay the fine. Anyway, what matters is that the kids are safe now. No one would think of looking for them here."

Miss Clements didn't feel quite so sure of that. The mention of lethal injections had made her feel queasy, and her palpitations had started to give a few skips. She was beginning to think she'd prefer not to have this unaccustomed responsibility – even if it meant turning down a lucrative monthly income.

"It'll be difficult having to keep them indoors the whole time," she said. "I'm not sure that I'm the right person for this. We do live very quietly, my sister and I."

"There'll be no trouble. They're to lead normal lives – go to school, go into town – as long as they keep together and don't go out alone. But if you do see anyone lurking, don't call the police, because the Magnifico has infiltrators all over the country, and you might get the wrong person on the other end of the phone. If you ever see anything odd, ring Mr Lovett and he'll know who to contact."

Miss Clements smoothed her grey lap. She liked smooth things, particularly a smooth life, and was looking doubtful.

"I'm really sorry," she said after some thought, "but I don't think I can do it. We're not used to this sort of thing. The children I normally foster are criminals in the making, but I've never had any who were hunted by criminals."

A little persuasion was going to be needed, thought Beverley. She leaned over the arm of her chair and took a mobile phone out of her very smart briefcase. "Do you mind if I make a call?" she said.

"Not at all. I'll clear the tea things, and you can have the room to yourself while I take them to the kitchen."

Miss Clements bustled about a bit. As she tidied the fine bone china onto a trolley and wiped the crumbs off Beverley's coffee table, she was thinking of her blood pressure and weighing its worth against the monthly fee she would get for fostering four high-risk children. She pushed the trolley out into the hall and shut the door behind her.

By the time Miss Clements returned, Beverley had put her phone away and was rummaging through her briefcase. "I was just talking to Mr Lovett," she said. She extracted two envelopes and peeped inside them.

"Anyway, he's given me the go-ahead to double the fee for care." She paused to give this information time to sink in. "He said the poor little buggers had been mucked about too long. Well, he didn't put it exactly like that, but y'know what I mean. Missing school and all that."

Had Miss Clements been listening she would have said *we don't use that sort of language in this house, oh dear me no*, but her ears temporarily stopped working as soon as she heard 'double the fee.'

A pleasant vision of a little cottage on a Greek island, with no greater disturbance than the lapping of blue sea against snow-white sand, was floating through her mind. There was nearly enough money in the bank to make her dream come true, and a little extra would make it happen all the sooner.

"They insist on being together," Beverley rattled on. "And it's hard to find anyone who can foster all four of them securely for more than a few days. Mr Lovett says they've got to have somewhere stable for a while, at least till the trials."

"Well," said Miss Clements hesitantly, "as long as you can assure me that there's no risk to them while they're in my charge…"

"Of course there's no risk here. No one's heard of this place. I never had until now. What's it called — Aberhyblyg? It's not exactly the hub of the universe, is it?"

Beverley placed her briefcase on the coffee table and closed it firmly. "This is for you," she said, handing one over one envelope, "and Mr Lovett says the rest of the doubling-up will be paid straight into your account."

She checked the second envelope again, and counted four bundles of notes and four packets of small change.

"This is for the children," she said, as she handed the money over. "They've got no possessions except what they stand up in and some night things in those bags, so you'll have to take them shopping. There's enough there for school uniforms and some casual clothes, and there should be plenty over for pocket money. They're not used to handling money, so a little guidance might be needed."

She gave Miss Clements a piece of paper. "That's Mr Lovett's phone number, and that's mine, and the other one is for Mr and Mrs Jones, Paul and Lucy's grandparents. They're local."

"Grandparents?" exclaimed Miss Clements. "I wasn't told they had grandparents here!"

"Yeah, well, I know Mr Lovett meant to tell you, because he was talking to me about it. He said they refused to see the children when they came up to visit their daughter in hospital, so he chose this place in case they have a change of heart. He hasn't told the kids about them yet, because it would be pretty hurtful to know they're not wanted, after all they've been through."

"It certainly would be!" exclaimed Miss Clements, unpleasantly roused from her usual serenity. "But, more to the point, if there's family here, this is the first place the agents will look for them."

"No, it's OK. Apparently, the holy leaders – that's the priests – put a strict ban on keeping records of where abducted wives came from, so that they couldn't be tracked down. The Fathers had to record their own marriages, and the births and deaths within their own families, but there was no background information. So, no one could have known about the grandparents. The only reason Lovett knows is because, when the kids' mother was in hospital, she told the police where she came from."

"Is there anything else I need to know?" Miss Clements spoke a little sharply. "Any more surprises?"

Beverley wrinkled her brow. "I don't think so. I assume Mr Lovett told you that he's changed all four children's surnames to Jones, so they won't attract attention. Everyone's called Jones in Wales. They'll blend in better. And you already know that they're to start school on Monday. I don't think there's anything else."

She shook herself briskly, put on her jacket and pulled down her skirt. "Right! I'll be off." Pausing to check her lipstick in the mirror over the mantelpiece, she added, "The grandparents have been told the children are here. They might get in touch with you, but it doesn't look likely. At the moment, of course, the poor old things are grieving for their daughter."

Oh dear, dear, thought Miss Clements. There was so much sorrow in this world.

"You'll want to say goodbye to the children, no doubt," she said, holding the door open.

Beverley poked her head round the dining-room door. The newly-named Joneses were sitting in silence at the table, looking exhausted, and Miss Marilyn's mouth was furiously pursing and twitching.

"So long then, kiddos," called Beverley. "Holy cow! You look as though you've all got jet lag! You've come from London, not New York! Anyway, you'll be OK here. The back of beyond. You'll be perfectly safe." She waved her hand at Miss Marilyn. "Ta-ta, Marilyn. Take care."

"*Miss* Marilyn," said Miss Clements, giving strong emphasis to the 'Miss', as she showed Beverley out. "Thank you so much for coming. It's been a pleasure meeting you."

What a dreadful girl, she thought, but it was nice about the money.

CHAPTER TWO

Two hundred and twenty miles away, in a flat on the Cromwell Road, Father Drax sat in the dark, looking out of the window. Traffic slowly ground its way along the road below him. Pedestrians wielded umbrellas, and great drops of rain fell into puddles that danced with reflected headlights and street lamps.

London was a miserable city. He was desperate to get away. As soon as the children were disposed of, he'd be off. Mexico City, perhaps, or Brazil. Somewhere big where one could be swallowed up in the crowd. He stood up and closed the curtains before turning and feeling in the dark for the switch on the table lamp. No, not Mexico. He was too tall. It was a handicap being six foot four and strikingly good-looking. People noticed him. The United States would be better – plenty of tall handsome people there – or Sweden. He groaned as he reminded himself there was work to be done before he could even think of leaving. The tedium of being holed up in this flat was beginning to get at him.

A key turned in the front door, a voice called out in greeting and, at the flick of a switch, half a dozen bulbs in the candelabra burst into life. In came a woman, silvery blonde and beautiful, with a light in her blue eyes. She dropped her medical case in the hall and dumped a bag of groceries on the worktop in the tiny kitchen area.

"Isobel, at last! Where on earth have you been?" Drax crossed the room towards her. "I'm starving." He grabbed the grocery bag and rummaged around inside it.

Isobel took off her raincoat and gave it a good shake.

"Well, my darling, that's not much of a greeting!" Her laugh was an icy tinkle. She reached up on tiptoe to kiss his cheek with cool lips. "The holy leaders sent me on a project, but I came home as soon as I could."

"I wish they'd stop giving you projects and just concentrate on their own work," muttered Drax, cramming a biscuit into his mouth. "The fools have lost track of the children."

"I know. I heard," said Isobel, as she calmly unpacked her shopping and put it away. "Don't stuff yourself! We're eating any minute." She moved smoothly back and forth among the starkly modern units. Stopping to stroke his cheek with manicured fingers, she murmured, "Don't worry, darling, they'll be found. It'll just delay things by a week or two."

"Delay! I just want to be rid of them now, this minute, and then get out of this shoebox." A look of triumph flashed across his face. "Actually, I did go out for a few hours today. There was a lunchtime piano recital."

"Well, that was foolish, darling." Her voice showed no trace of annoyance. "It's not only the police you have to worry about. If the holy leaders discover you've left this flat, they won't take the risk of getting you out of the country. They'll just dispose of you when you're least expecting it. On a bus, or in the park or somewhere."

She reached up and touched his hair. "If you feel you must go out, wear a disguise – a wig or a hat. Just be patient. As soon as we get rid of the children, you can move on."

18

He brushed her hand away petulantly, and paced back and forth. "I'd hate to wear a wig or a hat. I feel caged – incarcerated. What sort of life is this?"

The faintest breath of a sigh escaped Isobel's lips. "Don't be such a misery, darling. Just be thankful that at least one of your wives has a flat you can hide in – even if it's not up to your usual luxury standards." She pushed a frozen meal into the microwave and pressed the button.

Was that a note of sarcasm in her voice? Drax put his arm round her shoulder. "My beautiful Isobel, I don't know why I let you talk to me the way you do, especially when I think of all the wives I've sent for disposal over the years, just for uttering a couple of words against the Magnifico."

She laughed. "My offence is only against you, not the Magnifico, and it's for your own good. I don't think the holy leaders would think that a justification for disposing of me. I'm too useful to them. Good Doctors are in short supply at the moment, and I know I'm the best."

"You're always right." He hugged her close. "Best of Good Doctors, and best of all my wives. The others were just to please the holy leaders and produce a good supply of children to serve the Magnifico." He nuzzled her ear and whispered, "I took you to please me – and you, I hope."

"Of course it pleased me. Now lay the table, will you?"

He took cutlery and plates out of the sideboard, and stroked its pure-white, lacquered surface as he did so. The contrast of the white against the ice-blue walls never failed to invigorate him. A stab of energy ran through him, and he longed to be out and about, living his old life, bubbling with plans, furthering his accountancy career by fair means or foul, irritating his old enemy

Father Copse, and making money and more money. The memories filled him with optimism, and he laughed out loud. He opened a bottle of supermarket wine.

"This sort of stuff is not what I'm used to," he said waving it in the air, "but it's better than hiding under the railway arches and stalking my own children through the streets of London, which is what I was doing in September." He filled two glasses and took a sip. "It's a pity the police reached them before I did. I could have strangled them and dumped the bodies in the Thames. It would have saved all this hassle."

"You're so uncouth sometimes."

He laughed and took another sip and pulled a face. "This wine tastes like vinegar, but never mind. When I get to – let's think – Las Vegas, I'll be able to live well again."

"Mmm. That'll be wonderful!" purred Isobel. "And now that you've had a tiny drop of wine and eaten a biscuit, and should be in a better mood, let me give you the latest information I've had about the children."

He was instantly alert. "Aha!"

"They seem to have been sent out of London. It might mean a bit of a hold-up for you. We'll find them, of course. It's just a matter of time. The holy leaders are instructing infiltrators and agents to make enquiries all over the country at this very moment."

Drax snorted derisively. "Holy leaders! Those clowns! Well, I hope they do find them, because I can't wait to settle the score – especially with Dorothy. She's always been a rebel, just like her mother." He stopped short as he thought of Dorothy's mother. Her lovely face swam before him for a moment, and he felt a tiny pang of regret.

"It's a pity I had to have the mother disposed of, because she was very pretty, but that's what the rules say. As for David, I had hopes for him. After all, he's got good genes, so he should be clever." He shrugged. "Too late for all that now. He's mucked up all his chances. His own worst enemy."

"He'll have to go the same way as Dorothy," Isobel said. "There's no room for sentiment in the service of the Magnifico." Her face was expressionless. "If I get the chance, I'll administer the lethal injections myself, just to make sure the job's done properly. Some of the other Good Doctors can be a little careless and have to do it twice."

His jaw clenched. "You can be as careless as you like, as far as I'm concerned, so long as it's done."

"Now, now! Remember, Fathers must never be guided by their emotions – indeed, they shouldn't have any at all."

He relaxed and laughed. "Quite right! Just got carried away for a moment."

She placed a scented candle in the centre of the table and paused to breathe in the perfume.

"Lucy Copse will obviously have to go too, sometime before the trials," she said. "I'm not so sure about Paul. He's supposed to have special gifts or something. Their Aunt Sarah always said he had extraordinary powers of observation, so he'd probably make an outstanding infiltrator. Copse had great ambitions for him. He used to say he'd not be surprised if they made him the Holy Envoy one day, or at least deputy to the Holy Envoy."

"That fool Copse has delusions of grandeur. Why should he think himself capable of having fathered the Holy Envoy? The Magnifico's representative on earth! Copse's kid? Never!"

"Well, even so, I've heard that the holy leaders are keeping an eye on Paul. You never know, they might want to train him up to help revive the Holy Cause. So we'll have to treat him with some respect if we ever come across him, just in case."

The microwave gave a ping. Isobel took out their meal and arranged it elegantly on a square dish of cut glass. She garnished it prettily, and it suddenly looked delicious.

"You are as clever as you are beautiful!" exclaimed Drax in admiration.

He sat down, and leaned over to take her hand. They bowed their heads and thanked the Magnifico for the food before them, the clothes on their backs and the roof over their heads.

"And please help us to find the enemies of the Holy Cause, so that they may be brought to justice," Drax added before starting to serve them both.

Isobel murmured a response and unfolded her napkin.

"Well," said Drax, sitting back comfortably and twirling his wine glass, "as soon as we've got rid of the ungrateful pests, I'll be gone." He pointed towards the back of the sofa. "Once my visas arrive, I shall grab that briefcase and run."

They enjoyed their meal. Their pleasure was derived not only from the food and the wine, but also from the soft music that gently surrounded them, and the sweetly scented air. For Drax, the most delightful part of the evening was his own enthusiastic exposition on the possible merits of Australia as a haven for tall men. Isobel smiled and nodded as she mentally ran over the events of her day and planned her projects for tomorrow.

★

While Drax and Isobel were savouring their microwaved dish of coq au vin, peace reigned in the big brick house in Wales.

Lucy lay with her eyes open, staring at the dim grey of the sloping ceiling. She listened to Paul's gentle breathing. No way would she ever let that old Magnifico get at him! But how was she to know that Miss Clements wasn't one of the Mag's infiltrators? It was Mr Lovett who had checked her references and approved her. Lucy did believe he was genuinely trying to put Father Copse in prison, so she wanted to trust him, but anyone could make a mistake.

She couldn't sleep. As soon as she shut her eyes, ugly memories slithered into her mind and she could hear the Magnifico's voice churning out his threat of the fire of the melting flesh – *I can see you, I can hear you. I can watch your every action.* Of course, she was no longer so naïve as to really believe he existed, but he was always there – seeing, hearing, watching. *The fire awaits all sinners and their flesh will melt away.*

The old panic started to rise, and she slapped it down. Bad things had happened, but she must look for the good that arose out of them. It was one of the many philosophies that Aunt Sarah used to churn out, and it was true.

Just about the worst thing that had happened to Lucy the night Thomas burned the Copse house down, was his treachery towards her. The fact that he and his men had raided the house was nothing compared with the shock of discovering that he was not her one true friend and that all his kindness over the years had been a sham. The hurt of betrayal swept through her now, as powerfully as it had done when she realised the truth.

But good had come of that night. One good thing was that, with the utmost contempt for her stupidity, Thomas had told her that the Magnifico did not exist!

Another really good thing was that she'd found the file in which Father Copse recorded the births of all his children. It had shown that Paul was her real brother, not just a foster brother. Now she felt a pang of resentment. How mean they were not to have told her! It would have made all the difference to know she had someone of her own.

The file had also shown that she and Paul had a mother called Maria. That was the third good thing. They'd shared Maria with Dorothy and David when they visited her in hospital, but, of course, some things were too wonderful to last. The news that she had died was like a punch in the stomach for all of them, but even having known her briefly made Lucy feel more complete.

So, it was true that good could come out of bad.

The thought of giving evidence at Thomas's trial – and Father Copse's – made Lucy feel sick, but if it got them put away forever, then that would be a fourth good thing. It was amazing, when you thought about it, how much good could come out of evil.

Just as long as the Magnifico's men didn't find her and the others first!

★

Dorothy sat on the edge of David's bed, and they discussed the day's events in whispers.

24

"Mr Lovett said we'd be safe here," said Dorothy, "and I hope I'm not imagining it, but I think I do feel safer. That Miss Clements seems nice – though her sister's a bit weird. But, obviously, we can't really trust them."

David propped himself up on two pillows. "Wow! This bed's so comfy! Not only do I feel safer, but this is a taste of luxury – even if it is just until the trials. I wish I knew what Lucy was thinking. She still seems so remote sometimes."

"Well, she's got years of living with that horrible Father Copse to get over yet. At least you and I had the other kids in the commune. And we had Aunt Bertha. She was really kind – not like the other commune aunts!"

David laughed. "Yeah! Do you remember how she spent all that time trying to teach me how to behave like a gentleman? She reckoned it'd carry me through the most awkward of situations."

"Well, she should know. She told me once that, before she was converted to the Holy Cause, she came from a family where that sort of thing was really important."

"It didn't help us when we were in the disposal cells."

"No, but that was a bit extreme." Dorothy stood up. It had been a long day. "We're both shattered," she said. "You never know, we might actually be able to sleep tonight. Anyway, back to Lucy. I can't imagine what it must have been like living in Father Copse's house with just him and Aunt Sarah. She had no one till Paul came along, and she's certainly not remote with him. She absolutely adores him!"

"Well, I wish she adored me," muttered David.

"Of course she does. She loves you and me too – all of us. We're her family."

"I don't mean like that."

"I know, but she'll come round. You just have to be patient. It takes a while to get over never being allowed to show your feelings and always being threatened with the fire of the melting flesh. Maybe, if they're good to us here, she'll get a chance to unwind."

David snuggled down into his pillows and blew her a kiss. "Goodnight!" he whispered. "We'll sleep like logs in these beds."

Dorothy laughed softly and crept off to her own room, but she knew that as soon as their eyes were shut the walls of the disposal cells would close in on them.

Her bed was indeed comfy, just as David had said, but, as she tried to sleep, the nightly horror swept over her and took her breath away. She could feel the cold, black cloth as the commune aunts dropped the disposal gown over her head. Aunt Bertha was weeping quietly and she could hear Father Drax's voice in the corridor outside, "She won't feel a thing. So humane!"

The slimeball! If she ever got hold of him and a syringe, she'd make sure he felt more than a thing, and it certainly wouldn't be humane!

If only she could push the negative thoughts away, and replace them with something warm and kind. It was good that David had reminded her of Aunt Bertha. She had come to the Drax commune from somewhere in Kent. Dorothy must have been three or four years old then, because it wasn't long after the Magnifico's men had taken her away from her mother. The other aunts were always telling her she was a bad girl, but Aunt Bertha made her feel special. One evening, when most of the other aunts were at a prayer meeting, Aunt

Bertha had found Dorothy emptying the kitchen bin and throwing waste food all over the floor.

"I'm looking for my mamma's picture," Dorothy had explained.

Aunt Bertha had helped her to go through the rubbish, but there was no picture. After they'd put it all back in the bin and washed their hands, Aunt Bertha took her onto her lap. "I've got a very important job for you," she'd said. "There's a new little boy, who's just been brought in today. He's only two. I want you to look after him for me while I get on with the suppers. He's never had a mummy, because she gave him away as soon as he was born, so he needs someone special."

Dorothy had waited for David to finish his nap. When he woke, she took his hand. "I'm looking after you now," she said, "and you're looking after me."

Now, in her comfortable bed, Dorothy marvelled at how much she had to be grateful for. Aunt Bertha was living proof that not all the Magnifico's followers were evil. And she now had Lucy and Paul, as well as David. This was her family. Perhaps, for the time being at least, they could stop feeling afraid. They just needed time to beat the bad memories and move forward.

If she were to be of any use to the others, she had to be strong. She took a deep breath and pushed all thoughts of the disposal cells away. They had been saved, so why dwell on the ghastliness of it? Think of the good things. Over and over again, she forced herself to remember the most wonderful sound she had ever heard – Lucy whispering her name through the grille of the cell door.

★

No one was sleeping in the flat on the Cromwell Road. Drax and Isobel sat crouched over a computer screen searching out the Magnifico's agents. Their numbers had diminished drastically since the night Copse's house was burned down, when the Holy Cause had hit the news. Before September, all the big organisations – the police, public services, companies, and even schools and hospitals – had been riddled with agents, infiltrators and abductors. Now there was hardly anyone left to keep track of anything, including missing children.

"Either the agents we've got left have lost their touch or the other side has been very clever," grumbled Father Drax, closing down the computer. "Come on. We must get some sleep. You've got work in the morning."

"It's nearly morning now," said Isobel, straightening her back. "I don't need sleep. They want me at the Manchester disposal centre tomorrow, so I have to catch an early train. I'll be off as soon as I've had a shower. You go and lie down."

"You're my superwoman," he murmured, kissing the back of her neck, "but I'm not superman, so I'll do as I'm told. I'll have another go at the computer when I wake up. There might be some news by then."

He loped off and fell onto the king-sized bed. By the time Isobel was showered and dressed and ready to leave for work, he was asleep. She looked down at him. He was as beautiful as ever. Her upper lip curled with contempt.

Murmuring her early morning prayer to the Magnifico, she ran her hand over the top of the medicine cupboard in the bathroom and checked her stock of syringes. There were still some boxes left, but if the situation deteriorated further it might be difficult to get hold of supplies. She had a quick look through her medical bag. There was enough equipment for today's disposals. Everything was in order.

It was still pouring outside, and she took a fur-lined mackintosh out of the hall cupboard. It was sure to be cold as well as wet in Manchester. She popped a neat little rain hat on her head, wound a soft turquoise scarf round her neck, and looked in the mirror. It made one feel good to wear pretty colours.

She unlocked the front door. As she left, she mentally thanked the Magnifico for the freedom to pursue a career, unlike the aunts in the communes and the wives in the breeding rooms. She did sometimes wish she hadn't been lumbered with one of the Fathers. But there we are, we can't have everything, and she never failed to act the perfect wife to Drax. The Magnifico was her one true and passionate love, and she needed no one else. As she shut the front door softly behind her, there was joy in her heart and she smiled.

It was so annoying! Isobel tutted. There was mud on her designer shoes. Why did they always put disposal centres in abandoned farms? There must surely be suitably remote mud-less places in this world. She ploughed through the yard towards the processing rooms.

The files were on the desk waiting for her. They had to be checked before she could do anything. The criterion always was whether the patient would be useful in any way to the Magnifico and His Holy Cause. She was meticulous before administering a disposal. In the past, she had come across a few who had been wrongly assessed. She'd had to send them back to their various communes, of course, and the holy leaders had held inquiries.

The subject of the first file was a badly deformed baby. No problem there. She put the file straight into the out tray. The second was a four-year old boy with a neurological disorder. She sat down to think about that one. Was there a role he'd be able to fulfil when he reached adulthood – in the warehouse of one of the meat-processing plants perhaps? She read the file again. No. He'd be more of a nuisance than an asset. Definitely one for the out tray.

She helped herself from the coffee machine. It was time for a break. The train journey had been tedious. And all those awful people! She sipped her coffee slowly. There was a lot to be said for Drax's idea of a foreign country, just to get away for a bit – preferably without him, of course. But there would be awful people there too, and she did enjoy her work, except for having to travel out of London all the time. She checked her hair in her little hand mirror – immaculate, as always – and touched up her lips with a delicate shade of palest pink. Nothing garish! That vulgar woman opposite her in the carriage had been wearing such a vivid lipstick it was quite offensive to the eye.

At last, she sat down at the desk and opened the third file.

Well, well! This was interesting. Aunt Bertha of all people!

Isobel's mind flashed back to the Kent commune where she was born and to those gentle years when Aunt Bertha had brought her up until she left for medical school. As soft as butter and so tender-hearted, she had been the easiest person in the world to manipulate. In fact, now that Isobel thought of it, it was from copying Aunt Bertha that she had acquired her own sweetness of manner. Unlike Bertha's, hers was fake, of course, but very convincing.

She'd known for a long time that Aunt Bertha had been transferred to the Drax commune, but it never occurred to her to wonder what happened to her after the police raided the place last September. According to the file, she'd escaped to a commune in the North of England, and, now, here she was in the disposal centre, no longer useful to the Holy Cause. Arthritis in her hips and knees had made her slow.

Isobel tossed the file into the tray. A baby, a boy and Aunt Bertha, all outgoing and waiting for her in the next room. She checked her watch. Goodness! All that time dwelling on the past! She'd better get a move on or she'd miss her train back to London.

★

Late that evening, there was a little dissension in the flat on the Cromwell Road. Isobel had arrived home from Manchester carrying a large bag containing a wig, a hat and a false moustache.

"It's a hat or a wig, or both," she insisted, when her offerings had been rudely rejected.

"I'm not wearing a wig, and I'd feel a fool in a hat," said Drax. "It'll make me even taller."

"Well, you'll feel more of a fool if you're caught strolling through Harrods and one of your old buddies sees you being arrested. If you insist on leaving the flat, you'll have to wear a wig. I often have to wear one for hours on end for my work, and I don't complain. Lots of people wear wigs. It's a normal part of bald people's lives. And hats are trendy at the moment."

"I am neither bald nor trendy. Today, I cut my hair shorter than usual – as you can see – and that will have to do."

"Dye it, then."

"No."

"OK. Well, it's up to you. Don't grumble to me about being stuck indoors on your own all day".

He stood in front of the mirror and tried on the hat.

"It suits you."

"It doesn't."

They sat down to their meal in grumpy silence.

Eventually, he mumbled, "I wish I weren't so tall, and then no one would notice me."

Her face softened. "I'd notice you, my darling, if you were as tiny as Tom Thumb."

He smiled grudgingly. "You'd probably tread me underfoot and squash me flat."

Isobel giggled. "That's better," she said. "Now let's switch on the computer. Something new may have come through."

There was nothing.

"Whoever's hidden them has done a good job, but we'll find them yet," said Drax. "And, when we do, it'll be the chop for them and perhaps Barcelona for me."

"I'll visit you whenever I can get the holy leaders to give me a project over there."

"What's your Spanish like?"

"Still good, I hope, though a bit rusty. At least they taught languages really well at the Mag's school, in case we took up missionary work."

They snuggled together on the sofa, and she stroked the hair on his head. She smiled lovingly. "I'm getting used to the feel of these bristles. I think I'll dye them black while you're asleep."

"Don't you dare!" he laughed. "Come along. Let's go to bed. You've been up since yesterday morning."

"Ah, but I've done a lot in that time – three disposals by lethal injection, four fake death certificates, one fake birth certificate and two drug-induced comas, as well as our researches, of course."

"Then you need to rest. Let's go."

CHAPTER THREE

It was the Jones family's first full day in the big house. After breakfast, Miss Marilyn went off to the university – to do research, they were told. Miss Clements settled Donald in his basket and gave him a dried pig's ear as a treat. "We'll be back soon," she said lovingly. "You guard the house, there's a good boy."

Checking the money Beverley had given her, she shared some of it out equally into four separate envelopes, which she zipped up inside her bag. She put what remained into a cornflakes box labelled 'Children', and hid it in a safe place behind some tins in the larder – to foil burglars. The next time she went to the bank, she'd put it into her separate fostering account. As she was about to close the larder door, she remembered the scrap of paper with the three phone numbers. That might as well go in the box too. Best to keep everything together. Good. All sorted!

Putting on her coat, she called, "Right, my dears, we're off to the shops."

Lucy felt a flutter of excitement mixed with apprehension, as they stepped out through the wrought-iron gate. She held Paul's hand tightly and reminded herself that no one would ever find them here. They all followed Miss Clements down a steep road opposite the house. At the bottom, they turned left and then right.

"Now, stop here and take your bearings," said Miss Clements when they reached the crossroads in the middle of town. "Look to the right and you'll see the sea."

They stopped and stared. Down to their right, beyond the shops, the road seemed to end suddenly in nothing, and all they could see was a bright-blue sky.

"The world stops at the end of that street," said Paul.

"Now look to your left, and you'll see the station."

They looked.

"Now look neither to the right nor to the left, my dears. Look straight ahead up the street in front of you, and you will see lots of shops – nicer than the ones by the station, in my opinion. See on the left? That's the butcher where I buy my meat. Quality is so important when it comes to food. And now for the final direction. Look behind you. If you turn left and then right, you will see the hill that you came down, and at the top of that hill, you'll see our house."

"So we can't go wrong," said David. "Sea to the right, station to the left, shops straight ahead and the house behind us."

"Good. Well I'm glad you've mastered that, because I'll get my meat and go straight back in case Donald is fretting. You can have a look around. There's a town clock in a little square up at the top of this street – just beyond the shops, you can see it from here – so make sure you're back by one o'clock for lunch. Meal times are important."

She gave each of them an envelope with a generous supply of pocket money. "You can give yourselves a little treat today, my dears, but be careful because that money came from Mr Lovett and it has to last you a long time.

Try and note which shops sell what, so that tomorrow you can do a proper shop for what you really need, for school and daywear."

Lucy watched her as she crossed the road. Wasn't she supposed to keep an eye on them?

David turned towards the sea. "Let's explore!" he said.

They hurried straight down the street to the promenade and then onto a shingle beach. When they had tired of scrunching the fine pebbles under their feet and jumping away from the tiny ripples at the edge of the sea, they strolled along the prom, wandered onto a pier and roamed some backstreets. Then, to their delight, they discovered a castle.

They stood on a rampart and looked out over the sea. The sky was still a clear blue, and the air was sharp and cold. Seagulls swirled and screeched above them. The wind whipped up their hair and blew through their thin jackets, but it didn't trouble them. There was no place here for the Magnifico. They felt fresh and free.

"I like this place," said Paul.

Lucy's heart sang, and her soft, brown curls sprang up in the wind. She could feel Paul's happiness as well as her own.

"And me!" David pushed the thick, silver-blond hair out of his eyes. "I wish we could stay here forever."

"Well, I don't see why we shouldn't," said Dorothy. "Perhaps by the time the trials are over I'll be eighteen, and then I can get a job and save my wages. We'll find a little house and we'll all come back here to live."

They absorbed this picture of a dream life.

"I suppose you should finish your education first," said David, after a while. "Go to college or something."

"Some people do that even while they're working. It's called lifelong learning," explained Dorothy. "Once I've got some qualifications I'll get a better job and earn more money, so that you can all go to university. And when you've all finished in university and got good jobs, you can earn the money while I go to university and get a better job. Then we'll pool all our money and buy a bigger house and keep ourselves safe forever."

They savoured the idea, and it didn't seem impossible. In fact, it gave such hope that shivers ran down their spines.

"And we'll be going to a normal school and learning how to mix with people while we're staying with Miss Clements," said Lucy, "so that'll help with getting jobs. The school here is bound to be better than the Magnifico's school – no cruel punishments." She caught her breath as she pictured the guidance cane that used to hang on the headmaster's chair in the assembly hall.

There was a glum silence as the memories hit them. David flushed with shame as he remembered the time his fooling around had made Lucy giggle so much that she'd had the cane in front of the whole school assembly.

Lucy bore him no grudge about that. She was thinking of the trials. They all knew that Thomas, the gardener, was in one of them and Father Copse in another (unless he was too mad), but there was always the possibility that Father Drax would be caught and then there'd be a third one. The thought of one trial was bad enough, but it was horrible not knowing how many others there would be.

"I'm dreading the trials," she muttered.

"Mmm. And me," said Dorothy. "But, according to Mr Lovett, we'll be doing a public service when we give evidence. He said the sooner that lot are put away forever, the better."

Lucy blurted out a sickening thought that she had been trying to bury for weeks. "I just hope that Paul and I haven't got Father Copse's genes," she said.

Dorothy and David digested the possibility.

"Well, I suppose you must have some," said Dorothy at last, "the same as David and me with Father Drax's genes. After all, they are our fathers, even if we have disowned them. But that doesn't mean to say that we've got their bad genes. You only get fifty per cent from each parent. And anyway we might all take after our mothers. I can remember my mother and I feel warm when I think of her, so I know she was good."

David was thoughtful. "Do you know what?" he said, "It's never bothered me that I didn't have a mother. All I know is that she was some sort of saint who'd seen the light and presented me as a gift to the Magnifico when I was born. Goodness knows what her genes were like."

"Well, you're a good person, so we'll assume you inherited her good genes," said Dorothy briskly. "As for Paul and Lucy, you both look like Maria with that springy hair and creamy skin, so you obviously take after her."

No one spoke for a while, as all four of them thought sadly of what might have been had Maria recovered. They would have had a shared mother.

Dorothy tried not to think of her own mother. It was too painful, but she couldn't help it. Most of the memories were just a blur and a feeling of warmth, but the day she was taken from her was as clear as if it were yesterday.

★

The two of them had been sitting on the floor in a corner of the breeding rooms. It was almost too dark to see the right colours to put in her drawing book.

"Mamma, can we sit near the window?" she'd asked, scrabbling at the crayons scattered all around her.

"Not today," whispered her mother. "No one will notice us here. I want to show you a secret and you must keep it forever."

Dorothy had been excited.

"Pass me your drawing book," said her mother in her normal voice. "Let me see your pictures." She leafed through the book while Dorothy gathered up her crayons. "That's lovely, my darling," she said as she handed it back, still open.

There was something lying flat on the page. It was a snapshot of two beautiful women.

"That's me on the left," whispered her mother, "and that's my mamma, your *nonna*, on the right. I've written her name and address on the back for when you can read. Keep it safe."

Even now, after all these years, Dorothy could sense the bustling in the room as the door opened and Father Drax came in with two of the Magnifico's men. Other mothers held their toddlers close. Her own mother leaned over and shut the book hastily.

"Keep the picture in the book, and hide it," she'd whispered.

When the men carried Dorothy away, they took the drawing book from her. Although she searched and searched, she never saw the photograph or her mother again.

★

Now, Dorothy stood staring out to sea with her face turned away from the others, and was grateful for the pause while they gathered their own thoughts.

David broke the silence. "Look, it's clouding over and the sea has gone dark green," he said suddenly, "and we haven't done our pocket-money shopping yet."

They sheltered from the wind on some steps inside a ruined tower, and shared out their money. Some of it was in coins, and they examined the different pieces.

"I used to go shopping with Aunt Sarah sometimes," said Lucy, "so I know what they are. We can buy quite a lot of things with all this, so let's share out just a bit for each of us now, and then keep the rest to put towards our house for when Dorothy gets her job. It can be our housing fund."

They each put their allotted share in a pocket, and the remainder was returned to one of the envelopes and handed over to David.

"You've got the biggest pockets, so you'd better be in charge," said Dorothy.

"Our housing fund!" breathed Lucy.

They gazed at the envelope with reverence. Then they pulled themselves back to their immediate purpose – spending pocket money for the first time in their lives.

"Right!" said Dorothy. "Let's separate. Lucy, you take Paul with you, and David and I will each go on our own, and we'll all meet under that clock at half past twelve."

★

By the time they got back to the house, the blue sky had vanished completely, the wind had whipped up into a gale, and the sea was black. They arrived just as the rain started to come down in sheets. As they hung up their jackets, a delicious smell floated through the hall from the kitchen.

"Quick. Wash your hands, my dears, and come and lay the table. Gladys, the cleaner, isn't in today, so you'll have to do it. Your lunch is ready, and later you might like to show me what you bought – unless it's private of course."

"We've never had food like this before, Miss Clements," said Dorothy, gazing down at a plateful of succulent pork with crackling, apple sauce, roast potatoes and vegetables. "We had to learn cooking at our old school, but this is different."

"I'll teach you to cook, dear, once you've settled in. I've got some lovely recipes from when I was at cookery school in the South of France. It's a wonderful thing to enjoy cooking. It takes you quite out of yourself, and all your troubles disappear."

After lunch Miss Clements showed the children how to clean out and lay the fire in their sitting room, so that they could do it themselves on the days when Gladys wasn't in.

"I just don't have the time, you see," she said. "Gladys does the cleaning, but you'll have to do your own rooms, because she only comes in three days a week and she can't do everything. And this week she's up in London. She's going on a march to stop that Tony Blair going to war in Iraq. She says if there's a war now it'll be chaos in ten years' time, if not before. But I'm sure she's wrong. He seems such a nice man. Always smiling. And make sure the fireguard is fixed properly, because we don't want Paul or Donald to fall in, do we dears?"

When the fire had been lit and Miss Clements had left the room, they spread out their purchases on the coffee table. They had jointly bought a small pot plant for Miss Clements and a bar of scented soap for Miss Marilyn.

There had been some discussion about this when they were still in the castle grounds. "We can't give Miss Clements something and not Miss Marilyn, even if she is so cross-looking," Dorothy had said.

David had suggested that Miss Marilyn wasn't as cross as she looked. "I think that her mind is on something else far away," he said, "and she's only cross because we're distracting her from her thoughts."

"OK, Mr Perceptive," Dorothy had laughed. "Only joking. We wouldn't really be so mean as not to get her something."

Lucy felt uncomfortable about the whole thing, though she didn't say so. The Magnifico forbade the giving of presents. According to Aunt Sarah, it led to bribery and corruption, and was one of the many reasons why non-followers were rotten to the core. There were so many things that Lucy still found hard to accept, but she smiled now as she watched the other three, so excited about their gifts. What a mean old misery the Mag was, banning the pleasure of giving – not that he existed, of course.

They put their gifts to one side and examined what they had bought for themselves. Dorothy had bought a lipstick and mascara. Now she stood in front of the mirror over the mantelpiece and put the lipstick on. The others studied the effect.

"Make it more subtle," said Lucy.

David agreed. "Your lips are really red without lipstick, so you don't need it. I prefer you without it."

"Well, I like it," said Dorothy, rubbing it off and making her lips all the redder in the process. "Right, so what did you get, David?"

He had bought a mobile phone. "It was the cheapest one they had. Nine pounds ninety-nine. It's called 'pay as you go', but there was a special offer and they put ten pounds on my credit, so really I got it for nothing. The man in the shop showed me how to use it."

The others were impressed.

"Who are you going to ring?" asked Paul.

"Well, nobody yet, but we might make some friends at the school and we can ring them."

"Wow! It's 2003 and we've actually moved into the modern age!" said Dorothy. "Beverley was wrong when she said this was the back of beyond."

Lucy had bought a watch from a charity shop. "It seems to work," she said cautiously. "It says more or less the same time as the clock in the dining room."

"A watch!" exclaimed David. "How on earth have we managed without a watch all our lives? I'm going to buy one with our next pocket money – if we get any more, that is. Though, of course, we mustn't forget the housing fund. What did you get, Paul?"

Paul was already on the floor with a drawing book and crayons. Beside him lay a box with a bright picture of a farmyard on the lid.

"You can help me with the jigsaw puzzle if you like," he said, without looking up.

"I will later," said David "I've got to do something first."

"Where are you going?" asked Dorothy, as he was leaving the room.

"Upstairs. I won't be long."

When David reappeared, the others were sprawled in the chintz-covered armchairs, watching a television documentary on African elephants.

Dorothy glanced up as he entered. "Holy Magnifico! What have you done?"

"Please don't use that horrible expression. It still makes my stomach turn over even after all this time," said David crossly, shaking out his wet hair and rubbing it with a towel.

The others stared in horror.

"Holy Mag, sorry, Holy Bag!" cried Lucy. "Your beautiful, blond hair – it's pitch black!"

"Of course it's black. I know it's black. I dyed it black on purpose. I bought it in Boots,"

Miss Clements entered the room with cake and tea carefully arranged on a trolley. "Good gracious me! I'd never have recognised you. What happened?"

"I've dyed my hair."

"Oh, well, there we are then. That explains it," said Miss Clements. "Sometimes it's nice to have a change. Now, who wants a piece of Victoria sponge?"

As soon as she had left, Dorothy turned to David. "What on earth do you think you're doing? It's horrible."

"It's the genes," he mumbled. "I know I can't help looking like Father Drax, but least I can change my hair."

The two girls understood, and were silent.

"Father Drax's hair was different from yours," piped up Paul.

"You hardly ever met him," said Lucy.

"I know, but I saw him when we went to prayer meetings with Aunt Sarah, and once I had to sit next to him because there was nowhere else. He made my hum come. I looked hard at him and I saw his yellow hair."

Lucy remembered that occasion. Aunt Sarah had taken Paul out of the meeting because of the humming, and there had been no supper that night for either of them as a punishment.

Paul selected a green crayon and started to draw a tree. "And I looked at his hands," he said, "and there was a ginger freckle on his thumb, and his fingers were really long and thin. And there were little yellow hairs on the back of his hands, all silky." He sat upright to admire his work. "David's hair isn't yellow. It's silver."

The others absorbed this obvious piece of information. David's expression lifted a little, and Dorothy ruffled Paul's hair.

"Of course!" she said. "How could we be so stupid? You notice everything. Sometimes, I think you're the cleverest of us all."

She turned to David and smiled affectionately. "Well, you're stuck with the black for now, so we'd better get used to it. Your roots will show when it grows out, so we'll have to keep touching it up while we're at this school, or people will think you're odd."

"They might not," said Lucy. "I saw a boy with green hair in town today. Can you imagine such a thing in the Mag's school? He'd have been disposed of. Remember poor John? The Good Doctors took him, and all he'd done was twitch!"

★

"You three big ones will be starting at the school at the top of the hill on Monday," said Miss Clements at supper that night. "Tomorrow's Thursday, so you've got three days to get your uniforms. I've made a list for you.

45

And then, of course, you'll have to mark your names on everything."

"Do you think they'll let us come back here after the trials?" asked Lucy. "We like it here."

"I really don't know what happens next, dear," said Miss Clements as she started to collect the plates from the first course. "We'll have to wait and see. Now, David, would you be a kind boy, and take these to the kitchen and put them straight in the dishwasher for me? And, Lucy, would you please go with him and bring in the puddings? They're on the kitchen table."

As soon as Lucy and David were back in their seats, the conversation returned to the school.

"It seems a waste to spend money on a uniform if it's only for a few months," remarked Dorothy.

"That's true, dear. But wherever you go afterwards the uniform might be the same, so it could come in handy. A lot of schools have black, I believe."

"I'll be leaving school soon anyway, so I suppose it doesn't really matter. But I hate black. They put me in black when I was in the disposal cells."

There was a silence.

"Sorry!" said Dorothy, trying to think of something less harrowing to talk about. "But, what about Paul? Will he go to school?"

"Yes, I'll be taking him to the primary school down in the town. Now, pudding anyone? There's lemon meringue pie or banana cheesecake, or both."

★

46

Later that night, Miss Clements and her sister were in Miss Marilyn's sitting room, comfortably settled in two scratched, old leather armchairs and sipping a little drop of port before bed. The walls were lined with books, and the floor was completely obliterated by files and papers.

"I wish you'd make a bit more space on your floor, Marilyn, dear," said Miss Clements, putting her glass on a lop-sided stack of files, while she studied her knitting pattern. "I nearly fell over when I came in. They do say that a tidy room reflects a tidy mind."

"Huh! Who's they?"

"Well, I'm not quite sure, but I've heard that somewhere."

"Platitudes," snorted Miss Marilyn.

"Yes, dear. I expect so. Now tell me what you think of the children." Miss Clements made herself a little more comfortable and took another sip. "They've had a strange life so far, from what that Beverley told me – all that religion and frugality, and uncomfortable way of life. And to think of those poor women being abducted and kept prisoner, just for breeding! They seem like lovely children, but something must have rubbed off on them. They can't be normal – not like the disaffected youth the Social Services usually sends us. What do you think?"

Miss Marilyn's mouth pursed and twitched.

"I think the whole thing is quite revolting," she said, "especially that talk about breeding. It's disgusting! I'll be glad when they've gone. Plus it's unnatural how that Paul can draw so well. It gives me the creeps. His picture of Donald was almost like a photograph, but better." She sniffed and added indignantly, "And what's more, he did a picture of me and it's exactly like me – except it made me look really cross, which I'm not."

47

"He's probably got a special talent – one of those gifted children one reads about – and you do look so severe, my love. But they did bring you a present."

"Soap! Are they telling me something? And that bold girl, Dorothy. Who does she think she is? So tall and straight and full of herself. At least the younger one's quiet, though I don't like that watchful look she's got in her eyes, as though she can't trust anyone. And that David's eyes are too blue for my liking. They seem to pierce like icicles right through you, and now with that dyed-black hair there's something demonic about him. He's like an aging drug addict, not a fifteen-year-old boy."

If Jesus Christ himself walked in this minute, thought Miss Clements, Marilyn would find something nasty to say about him. She held up her knitting to the light and counted the rows.

"They're only children, dear," she said mildly. "Suffer the little children, and all that. And it's a nice change not to have foul language, and filth, and things being stolen or smashed up. We're getting good money. They're paying us double because of the security. We'll soon be in a position to retire to our little cottage in a nice warm climate, with groves of oranges or olives or vines, or some such thing to the rear, and the azure sea rippling away just outside our door. And we'll wear pretty red dresses – at least I will – and you will wear blue, because it suits you better. You'll look delightful in blue, to match your eyes and the colour of the sky."

Miss Marilyn was soothed. It was a dream worth fulfilling. She wondered if they would have broadband. Perhaps she would be able to finish her research over the internet.

CHAPTER FOUR

Down in the town, in a small terraced house near the station, Mrs Gwen Jones was sitting in her front room, watching her husband sleep. In moments like this his face was peaceful and the lines of sorrow softened. She sighed. If only she could sleep too! Maria's disappearance all those years ago had broken them both. Now, only weeks after they'd found her, they'd lost her again. What was worse? Years of not knowing where she was, or knowing now that she'd gone forever?

What did it matter? She and Evan were both dead inside too. She'd have to clear Maria's room some time. It was no use keeping it ready for her now, because she was never coming back. If they gave it a lick of emulsion, they might be able to take a lodger. They could do with the money, but she couldn't go back to work yet, not while Evan was so ill. She looked at him in his dreadful cardigan, and tried to remember when they last had new clothes. Even if she took up knitting again, wool was so expensive these days.

Her husband started snoring, and she leaned over to turn the gas fire down slightly. It made the air dry. She stood up quietly, so as not to disturb him, and tiptoed out to the kitchen, where she filled a bowl of water to put in front of the fire. In a way, his loss of mind was a blessing. At those times when his memory left him, he could be happy. She returned to the sitting room and put the bowl down gently. Picking up a photo that leaned against the clock on the mantelpiece, she studied the lovely, little face – a laughing Maria up on the castle, her hair blown into a thousand kiss-curls by the wind and the rain.

Evan shuffled a little. Gwen put the photo back and sat down again. She hoped he would sleep a little longer – or at least, if he did wake, that he'd not be in one of his remembering moods.

He opened his eyes and smiled.

"Hello, my darling," he murmured. Gwen smiled back. She could relax a little. He was back in the past. He'd be alright for a while now.

She hadn't dared tell him about the children. They must have arrived up at the big house by now. He had refused to meet them in the hospital in London, and she had been so focused on Maria that she hadn't really pressed it too hard. But, after all, they were Maria's children and they had saved her from the fire. It wasn't their fault that they had that evil Copse man for a father.

Unlike poor Evan, Gwen was still in her right mind and she couldn't just ignore the fact that, at this moment, two grandchildren whom she had never met were less than a quarter of a mile away. For Maria's sake, she and Evan should at least make the effort to meet them, and perhaps "help with their rehabilitation" as that Mr Lovett had put it.

Evan stirred again, and Gwen stood up. It was time for his supper and then bed. She made a decision. Tomorrow, after Evan had taken his morning walk along the avenue and back, and was dozing comfortably in his chair, she would pluck up her courage and go up to the big house – as long as he was in an amicable mood, of course.

50

★

"There's a visitor for you."

All four faces looked up with a mixture of curiosity and apprehension. Dorothy flicked shut her magazine, and David placed his new mobile back in its box. They both stood up.

"No, not you," said Miss Marilyn. "The other two."

Lucy put aside the book she'd been reading with Paul. Her heart pounded. Who on earth? They didn't know anyone here. She mustn't panic. Miss Marilyn would have checked. It must be someone quite harmless.

"If it's for Paul and me," she said, quietly but firmly, "it's for the others too. We do everything together."

"Well, you can't this time. Get a move on. I haven't got all day."

"We'll all come," said Dorothy, sailing through the wide-open door, followed by David. Lucy took Paul's hand, and they sidled past Miss Marilyn.

"In there," she said, pointing towards the dining room. Her mouth pursed and twitched furiously as she crossed the hall.

"All they do is have one visitor, and that's enough to make them think they're in charge," she spluttered angrily, as she entered the kitchen.

Miss Clements was stirring a pudding in a big earthenware bowl. "Do they, dear?" she said. "It's such a good thing for children to have a bit of confidence, don't you think? Did you check that the visitor was unlikely to abduct them?"

"It's that Gwen Evans or Williams or Jones or whatever, who's a nurse up at the hospital and lives near the station."

51

"Oh, I'm sure she's harmless if she's a nurse," said Miss Clements placidly, "though I don't really know her. Now the kettle's boiled, so shall we have a nice cup of tea with one of those caramel biscuits? They've just cooled down."

In a corner of the kitchen, a large man was poking around inside the boiler cupboard.

"Do put your tools down for a minute or two, Mr Nicholas, and sit with us," called Miss Clements. "Marilyn will make you a cup of tea, and you may help yourself to some of these biscuits."

★

In the hallway, the children stood outside the dining-room door.

"Do you think it's safe?" whispered Lucy. "They're supposed to check first before we see anyone."

"We'll never know if we don't find out," said Dorothy. "Come on, all of you. Stand up straight, and put your shoulders back. Paul and Lucy, you go first, as it's your visitor. David and I will follow right behind. I'll leave the door open for a quick getaway."

Calming her own nerves and straightening her back, she turned the knob and waved the others past her, then went in and left the door wide open.

Gwen rested her hand on the table to hide the trembling. Four youngsters stood in a row near the open door, backs straight and heads held high. She could tell at once which were Maria's children, but she couldn't speak. Her ears were ringing, and the room was going round and round.

Lucy had almost expected to see a stern representative of the Magnifico, come to whisk them away to the fire of the melting flesh. Instead, a tiny, fragile woman dressed in a shabby, beige mackintosh stood by the table. She was staring at Lucy. Her face flushed, then turned an ashen grey. For a moment, Lucy thought she was going to faint.

"How do you do," she said rather hastily. "I'm Lucy. We were told you wanted to see us. Would you like to sit down?"

The woman didn't move. "I can see straight away who you are." Her voice was barely above a whisper. She looked at Paul who had backed away behind Lucy. "And you too, little boy."

Dorothy was the first to gather her wits. It was obvious that the woman was too physically feeble to abduct even one of them, let alone all four.

"Do sit down," she said. "My name is Dorothy."

The woman sat down. She was trembling. She turned to Lucy. "I'm sorry, love, I must have frightened you."

"Not at all, madam," said Lucy, untruthfully.

"You rescued Maria from the fire?"

Lucy was taken aback. What did this woman know about them? She didn't want to talk about that terrifying night with a complete stranger, but she couldn't resist saying, "Yes. She was our mother, though we didn't know it then." It made her feel tremendously proud to say she'd had a mother.

"You're so like her," said Gwen, "that, for a second, I thought she was still here with me in this room."

Lucy was wondering how they could politely escape this crazy woman, when Gwen took a deep breath, and straightened herself up.

"My name is Gwen Jones, and Maria was my daughter." She paused. What was she letting herself into? There could be no going back. "I'm your grandmother," she said firmly. "You have a grandfather too, but I'm afraid he wasn't well enough to come with me."

As the words sank in, a mixture of incredulity and joy swept through Lucy. Then immediately alarm bells rang. A trap? A decoy? She knew Dorothy and David would be thinking the same thing, but, at the sound of the woman's voice, Paul had moved forward and was standing near her, looking up into her face and examining it intently.

"You've got the same ears as Maria," he remarked at last. "In the hospital, I noticed her ears, because they were little and so pretty." He drew a line with his finger down the side of the woman's ear. It was small and neat.

The woman relaxed a little and smiled at him. "That's true," she said gently. "Maria had my ears. Her father used to tease us both. He said our ears might be pretty, but his were more useful, because they were bigger." She ran her finger down her neck where Paul had touched it. "Apart from that, she was like him to look at. He used to be a good-looking man, and you're going to be just like him when you're grown up."

Lucy took in a deep breath, but said nothing. Mr Lovett would surely have told them if there was a grandmother.

Gwen stood up. "I can't stay because your grandfather isn't well, and he'll be wondering what's happened to me." She handed Lucy a bit of paper with an address and phone number, and a pencil-drawn map. "That's where we live. It's on the opposite side of the road from the station, but further up. I hope that one day, when your grandfather's a bit better, the people here will let you visit us. Are they kind to you?"

"Miss Clements is a really good cook," said Lucy.

The visitor gave a shaky laugh. "Well, that's wonderful. And where will you go to school?"

"Up the top of the hill. We'll walk there. Paul's going to a school down in the town."

As soon as she had spoken, she could have kicked herself. Now their routes and routines had been revealed to someone who might be a grandmother but who, on the other hand, might be a trap. She could feel David looking at her accusingly.

The woman was thoughtful for a moment. "I wonder if they'd let me come up every day and take Paul to school myself," she said slowly.

Oh no! The earth seemed to tremble – or was it Lucy's legs? Who was this woman?

"He'll be going to the primary school where Maria used to go, and I'd bring him back, of course. Your grandfather can be left for quite a while before he starts to get anxious, so it could work out. I must get back to him now, but I'll just have a quick word with Miss Clements about it before I go."

Her fragility seemed to have faded as they talked, and some of the dreadful despair in her face had lifted. She stood up straight and put her shoulders back in a manner wholly approved of by Dorothy.

Lucy pushed Paul firmly between Dorothy and David, whispering, "Hold their hands and don't let go," and ran to the kitchen. In the doorway, she stopped short. There was a man there, just in the process of putting the front onto the boiler. Lucy had a good look at him. He had a kind face, but you could never tell. Thomas the gardener had had a kind face.

Miss Clements was burrowing in a drawer near the sink and pulling out a wad of notes. Lucy hesitated. She'd already given away enough information for one day.

"Miss Clements, our visitor would like to speak to you, please, and she has to leave this minute."

Miss Clements was counting the money. "Just a moment, dear," she said. "I've got to pay Mr Nicholas for mending the boiler. Go and tell her I'll be there in a tick."

*

Miss Clements was more than a tick, and the woman was just saying she'd really have to go and would come some other time, when the front door closed behind Mr Nicholas and Miss Clements appeared in the dining room. The suggestion that Paul should be taken to school and brought home was nervously put and, to the children's horror, Miss Clements accepted at once without query. She was genuinely grateful, because the walk there and back twice a day would have disrupted her cooking programme.

At last, in a final hurried movement, the woman wound a bright multi-coloured scarf over the shoulders of her dreary mackintosh, and hastened away.

"We'll have to be really sure about this," said Lucy to the others, after they had settled themselves back in their sitting room with the door shut. She tried to quell the hope in her heart in case it was snatched away. "How can we tell she really is our grandmother, apart from the ears, of course? We can't possibly let Paul go to school with her unless we're certain he'll be safe."

"Let's have a look at that map," said David. "When we go down to buy our school stuff, we could find the house and wait outside, and we might see her husband going in or out. If Maria really did take after him, then he should look something like you and Paul, and we'll know it's true." He looked out of the window. "It's still bucketing, but it should have stopped by tomorrow, so we can go then. Let's go even if it hasn't stopped, because we've only got three more days before we start school."

★

"So you had a visitor! She said she was your grandmother," said Miss Clements at supper that night, as she carved tender slices of juicy lamb. "Dorothy, would you pass the plates up to everyone, please, dear? It's Mrs Gwen Jones. I've known her by sight for years, though I've never spoken to her. If she's really your grandmother, I've got her phone number, so I could check, but I can't remember where I put it."

Miss Marilyn rolled her eyes.

"I heard that the husband lost his mind," continued Miss Clements, "but one mustn't listen to gossip. Help yourselves to vegetables. Gravy, Marilyn? What a sad world it is."

★

By the following morning, the rain had stopped, and the sky was a clear blue. At breakfast, Lucy tried to suppress a peculiar combination of excitement and fear. She absolutely must not allow herself to be hopeful. Now that she'd been told she had a grandmother, the disappointment of not having one would be horrendous.

After they had cleared away the breakfast things and tidied their rooms, Miss Clements gave them their instructions. "I can't come with you, because I bake for the weekend on Fridays, so that Miss Marilyn and I can go to church on Sunday. Dorothy, dear, you're the eldest, so I suggest that you look after the money. That's the uniform list, and that's the list for the other things that you need, and that's the list of the shops to get it all from. And don't waste money on trendy rubbish. Make sure that what you get is warm and fits you a bit on the large side."

Dorothy smiled. As if they'd know what was trendy!

★

Half an hour later, they were in the hall, putting on their outdoor clothes.

"I can't believe this is happening to us," said Lucy. "Supposing it's not a trap? But that would be too good to be true. Do you think the Magnifico is going to spring a nasty shock on us?" She gave a nervous little giggle.

"No," said Dorothy firmly. "That's something I do not believe, and you mustn't allow yourself to think it, even if you're joking. The Magnifico does not exist. He's just a figment of the imagination of evil monsters, so they can control people in the name of religion."

Lucy was pulling Paul's arms into the sleeves of his coat. "I know," she said. "But it's hard not to think of the Mag when he's been dinned into us all those years. He's sort of like a habit that's hard to get rid of."

"A really nasty habit," agreed David. "The only way to get rid of it is to think good things. When the Mag comes into our minds, we must think of our housing plan."

Dorothy gathered herself up. She tossed back her black curls, and her beautiful, brown eyes were alight with determination. "We'll get there one day. It's up to us to make it happen. Now, let's go shopping!"

"Remember lunch is at one," Miss Clements called after them as they left the house. "Don't be late."

Dorothy clutched the communal purse, and the others felt in their pockets to make sure that what was left of their pocket money was safe.

"We need to be careful with our money," said Lucy, "in case we need it to escape."

"And to put in the housing fund," said David. He rubbed his black hair ruefully. "I wish I hadn't wasted it on that dye."

"And I wish I hadn't wasted it on that lipstick now," sighed Dorothy.

Lucy felt guilty too. She'd managed perfectly well without a watch up until now, and spending money on non-essentials was something Aunt Sarah would have deplored. Still, what was done was done.

"We've got quite a bit left between us all," she said. "I think it was supposed to last us until the trials. If we try not to spend it, it'll make a good start to the housing fund. We can ask Miss Clements if she's got a box we can keep it in."

They embellished their long-term plan as they sauntered down the hill to the shops.

"One thing I don't want to be when I grow up is a lawyer," said Lucy, "because Father Copse is a lawyer."

Dorothy agreed. "And David and I can't be accountants, because Father Drax is an accountant. Let's think what we can be, not what we can't be – positive thinking!"

"Perhaps I'll be a doctor, then," said David, "and help people. And, of course, Paul will be a great artist – or a spy or a detective, because he's so observant. And Lucy can be a dog groomer, because she likes Donald and he needs a haircut."

He and Dorothy started thinking up the weirdest professions they could possibly imagine, but Lucy couldn't join in. Her mind was too busy trying to balance the possibility of a trap against the possibility of a genuine grandmother.

"We'll get the shopping out of the way first," said Dorothy when they reached the bottom of the hill, "and then we can concentrate on detective work."

They bought the uniforms and then, studying Mrs Jones's map, they walked along the street on the opposite side to the station. The houses were terraced, and their doors opened straight onto the pavement.

"They all look the same," remarked David.

"No," said Paul, when they reached the right number. "It's got a blue door and a golden knocker. Nice colours."

"And it hasn't got net curtains," whispered Dorothy.

Lucy was almost afraid to look at the house. If the whole thing was a trap, she and the others would find a way out, as they always did. But if she allowed herself to hope, she didn't know how she could cope with the horrible disappointment of finding out that she didn't have a grandmother after all.

They strolled past as casually as they could and peered sideways into the front room. There was nobody there. The room was dark, but they could see a mantelpiece to the left, and the back of an armchair. They crossed the road and studied the house from the pavement opposite. It was a very ordinary house and told them nothing, except that the brass door knocker was highly polished and the door and window frames could do with a coat of paint.

"We need to think," said David. They turned into a long, wide avenue that ran parallel with the railway line. They threw their bags on the ground beside them and sat down on a bench to discuss the next move. It was decided that they would wait ten minutes by Lucy's watch, and then she and Paul would walk slowly past the house again and look through the window. Dorothy and David would stroll along a few yards behind, and do the same.

When the ten minutes had passed, Lucy took a deep breath and reached for Paul's hand. "Come on," she said. "Let's pretend we just happen to be passing."

They left the avenue and made their way down the street. Surely everyone was staring at them? But, no, the rest of the world was scurrying in all directions, uninterested in two children who might or might not have a grandmother. As they slowly passed the house with the blue door, Lucy glanced in, trying not to look as though she was staring through people's windows. Paul had no such inhibitions.

"There's a man in there," he whispered, "sitting in a chair with his back to the window. I can see the top of his head. He's got grey, curly hair with a little bald bit at the back."

Lucy pulled him along hastily, and they waited on the next corner.

"Did you see anything?" she asked eagerly, when the others caught up.

"A man got up out of a chair just as we went past," said David, "but I couldn't see what he looked like. Nor could Dorothy."

"What next?" Lucy asked.

Dorothy stood on the pavement holding three uniform bags. "Perhaps we should take these back to Miss Clements's house and plan things properly, and come back later."

"But we've got to do it now," David reminded her, "otherwise they might both be out by then, or gone away for the weekend."

Lucy's heart thumped. He was right. They had to do something now.

"You two stay here. Paul and I will go and knock. If the man comes to the door, we'll get a good look at him, and Paul is sure to notice something about him to give us a clue one way or the other. We'll say we've come to visit Mrs Jones and will come back later. And if she answers the door, we'll just ask politely when it would be convenient for us to visit them."

The pavement was narrow, and Dorothy stepped out of the way as a woman with a pushchair tried to pass. "Let's stand on the opposite side of the road," she said to David, "so we can watch without being noticed."

Lucy took Paul's hand. "Come on," she said. "Breathe deeply and put on your cap of courage, like that prince in the story I was reading you. They can't eat us, after all."

"The witch wanted to eat Hansel and Gretel."

"That was different – just a fairy story. This is real."

They stood in front of the door. There was no bell. Lucy lifted the golden knocker and gave a timorous tap.

CHAPTER FIVE

"There's nobody there," whispered Paul. "Let's go."

Lucy lifted the knocker again. Her chest tightened, and she could hardly breathe. "I'll just do it once more, a little louder."

They heard someone hurrying down the stairs, and a woman's voice called out, "Don't worry, Evan. I'll get it."

The door opened, and Gwen Jones gasped as she looked down at two upturned faces, both with olive skin and soft, brown hair that sprang up in curls as though it was alive. She clutched at her chest, and a look of joy passed over her face, only to be followed immediately by one of deep anxiety.

"Oh, how lovely to see you," she whispered. "You can't imagine how happy I am that you've come, but I'm worried about your grandfather. He might not be ready to cope with seeing you yet. Wait there a minute. Don't go away."

The children stood anxiously on the step. They heard the soft murmur of the woman's voice and then a bellow that made them jump. "Get rid of the scum! I'll not have that monster's spawn in my house – veins flowing with the devil's filthy blood!"

For a split second, Lucy froze. Then she grabbed Paul's hand and they ran. Dorothy and David watched aghast as they disappeared round the corner.

"Flaming flesh!" muttered Dorothy.

The woman came out onto the pavement, and looked up and down the road. She wrung her hands together and was obviously distressed. A tall man appeared in the doorway behind her.

"Where are they? Have they gone?" he shouted. "Good riddance to scum."

David thought rapidly. It was a risk, but it might work.

"Come on," he muttered tersely. "Let's go over. If they're not Maria's parents, we'll just apologise and say we've got the wrong house."

They waited for a car to pass and then crossed the road. The woman was in tears, and the man, scarlet with rage, stood waving his fist in both directions up and down the street.

David's insides twisted into a knot of apprehension. "Good morning, sir," he said in as confident a voice as he could muster. "Good morning, Mrs Jones."

The man stopped gesticulating and looked at him. "Who are you?"

"I'm David, sir." He clenched his fists to stop the shaking of his hands. "My sister here is called Dorothy. We were friends of your daughter's. We used to visit Maria in hospital. We've come to say how truly sorry we are for your loss."

Gwen held her breath. The man stared hard at David and then at Dorothy. His high colour subsided and his face softened. He put out his hand.

"Maria's friends? My dear boy, come in, and your sister, of course. Any friend of Maria's is welcome in this house. How did you come to know her? Come in and talk to me about her. She was our jewel, our joy. It's always good to talk to someone who knew her."

He put his hand on David's shoulder and steered him into the house.

Dorothy smiled uncertainly at Gwen. "We can't stay," she whispered. "We'll have to find Paul and Lucy."

"They'll be alright," said Gwen quietly. "It's difficult to get lost here. Just stay five minutes, so he can get used to you, and then we might be able to make progress from there."

The uniform bags brushed against the wall of the narrow hall. Dorothy put them down and followed Gwen into a small front room on the left. The floor was almost hidden by shelves full of books, a three-piece suite, two side tables and a piano. A black and white china spaniel sat on each side of the clock on the mantelpiece, and the spaces in between were cluttered with photographs. The artificial coals of a gas fire blazed away, and the man sat down in an armchair next to it, with his back to the window.

Dorothy observed him from the doorway. It was hard to tell if someone as old as he was looked like someone as young as Paul, but, now that the rage had gone from his face, she could see that he had the same olive skin, and that faded brownish-grey curls sprang around his head. Perhaps he wasn't really old, but his face was etched with lines of sorrow, and the skin hung down in unhappy folds. He reached up and took a photograph down from the mantelpiece.

"There's our Maria," he said. "Just a little girl she was then – twelve years old. She was always a little beauty with such a sweet temperament." He leaned back in his chair and closed his eyes.

Dorothy stepped forward and took the picture from his hand. The girl smiled up at her. A mass of springing brown curls surrounded a charming face. She was so like Lucy that Dorothy caught her breath. David took the photo, and she heard him gasp. The extent of this sad couple's loss engulfed them.

"She was still beautiful and had a sweet temperament when we knew her," said Dorothy gently.

Mr Jones seemed to be dozing. Just as Dorothy whispered, "We must go now," he opened his eyes.

"My great grandfather was a sea captain," he said, "and he brought back a bride from somewhere, no one was ever quite sure where. Maria took after her, according to my mother. That's where she got her looks and her pretty ways."

David handed back the photograph, and Mr Jones studied it fondly. "Will you come again?" he said. "We want to know all Maria's friends."

He fell asleep before they had time to answer, and his wife's face relaxed.

"He sleeps most of the time," she said softly. "It's a blessing. Come, I'll show you out."

Dorothy picked up the shopping bags and turned to kiss her cheek. "We'll come again," she whispered. She followed David out, and the door shut behind them. Shaky with relief, they stood on the pavement and looked at each other with a shared sense of terrible sorrow.

"I wonder how many more mothers and fathers have been made to suffer like that," said David quietly, "all in the name of the Magnifico."

Dorothy shifted her bags to one hand and took David's hand with the other, and they walked silently down the road and round the corner towards the sea. They found Paul and Lucy, ashen-faced and huddled together, on a bench near the bandstand. The sky that had been so blue earlier that morning was now grey and glowering. A sharp wind blew in great gusts, and all four children shivered.

"Let's get back," muttered David, and they made their way up to the house in silence. The table was already laid for lunch, and the food smelled delicious, but no one spoke. Lucy couldn't eat. She burned with the shame of rejection. Scum! That's what he'd called them!

"Are you ill, my dear?" asked Miss Clements.

"No," whispered Lucy. "It's just that my throat won't swallow."

"You must have a cold coming on. I should never have let you out on such a nasty day – though it was lovely first thing this morning, so how were we to know? Paul, dear, won't you just try some gravy and mashed potatoes?"

Paul shook his head. "My throat won't swallow either."

"Well, you'd better a have a quiet afternoon in front of the fire, and we'll see what you're like this evening. Dorothy, would you like to be in charge of getting everyone to mark their names on the uniforms? That'll be a good job done, and will save me a lot of trouble."

"Miss Clements," said Paul. "What's 'spawn'?"

She looked puzzled for a moment. Children were such strange creatures. Goodness knew what went on in their minds.

"It's something to do with frogs," she said. "Now come along, dear. You can lie on the sofa in the other room, and I'll cover you with a blanket and build up the fire."

There was no need. Paul's face had cleared. "It's alright, Lucy," he said. "That meat smells nice. He was talking about frogs. Monster frogs had hopped into the house."

Lucy managed to smile, but she was angry. How dare that horrible man call her little brother scum! She would never, ever go to that house again.

★

Gwen Jones was sitting sadly, opposite her sleeping husband, mentally going over the events of the morning. She should never have taken the risk of contacting the children so soon. It might be months or years before Evan could accept their existence, if ever. But already she longed to see them again, to get to know them and, perhaps, to love them. She wondered if they would ever be able to love her – or at least like her.

Evan opened his eyes. He was animated and his face was slightly flushed.

"I dreamed that Maria's friends from London turned up, just like that, out of the blue," he said. "What a wonderful thing it is to know that she had friends right up to the end – even it was only a dream." He seemed to have forgotten about the two earlier visitors.

Gwen smiled her agreement. "Wonderful! And it wasn't a dream. They did come, and we told them we hoped they'd come again."

It was a long time since she had seen him so happy, but her heart was heavy. Maria's children had been cruelly driven away from her home. She would take Paul to school on Monday as promised, and she would be a grandmother if the children would let her, but she would never be able to take back the hurt of Evan's words.

She gazed thoughtfully up at the photograph on the mantelpiece. It had been propped back against one of the china dogs. For Maria's sake she had to try to befriend those children, without setting off one of her husband's violent rages.

"I've taken a part-time job, Evan," she said after a while. "There's a Mary Ellis who needs someone to take her little boy to school and back every day while she's at work, and I said I'd do it. His name's Paul. I should be gone for about half an hour in the morning, while you're still in bed, and half an hour in the afternoon when you're having your nap."

Evan smiled. "Excellent, *cariad*! It'll make a change for you and get you out of the house." His eyes lit up as an idea struck him. "Perhaps she'd let you bring him here sometimes on the way back from school. It would be wonderful to have a child in the house again."

So, at least that went smoothly, thought Gwen, getting up and kissing the top of his head. "I'll make you a cup of tea, dear," she said.

It was a pity she'd had to lie, but it might bring him happiness in the end. She wondered if the authorities would let her bring Paul back to the house after school occasionally. Of course, she'd have to tell him not to say he'd been to the house before, and she wouldn't tell Evan who he was – and she'd have to hide the tablets and the tranquilising syringes away from curious little fingers.

*

That night, the occupants of the flat in the Cromwell Road were feeling a little more optimistic. Isobel had come home with a suggestion that they should look for the children in Wales.

"I discovered today that Wales hadn't occurred to any of the agents," she said. "Their excuse was that the Magnifico has hardly any followers there, apart from a few infiltrators in the councils." She rubbed the blond bristles at the top of Drax's head. "Mmm! Nice. These are growing fast. But how stupid can people be! I pointed out how that would be a very good reason for sending the children there. Anyway, they'll be getting some agents down there first thing in the morning. The only one I know is that Robin from the Kent commune. He's pretty competent. Let's hope the others are too and, you never know, we might strike lucky."

Drax was pleased. He switched off the television and uncurled himself from the sofa. "Good! But they should have had the sense to think of it without your help. I'll have to tell the holy leaders that their agents are not what they used to be."

Isobel went through her usual routine of putting away the shopping. Holy Mag! He could be pompous sometimes! She threw Drax a newspaper, and he caught it deftly.

"We just have to accept the fact that standards have dropped since Copse and Thomas were caught," she said. "Recruiting has virtually stopped, and a lot of the agents are slinking off. The Good Doctors are leaving too. Most of my colleagues have just slipped away. They're probably comfortably practising as family doctors in some nice, warm, foreign country."

"You could do the same and come with me to Mexico – or wherever."

"I'll never desert the Magnifico! When I married you, I married him."

"Of course you did, my darling. But he operates all over the world, remember, not just here. In fact, I might make a point of seeking an audience with the Holy Envoy when I'm abroad. There can be no harm in getting him to notice me, and he might well be glad to make use of my financial talents. The prospect of greater wealth is always attractive to wealthy people. Now, a change of subject! I went out to see a film today."

Isobel sighed. "I wish you wouldn't take risks. I can't understand why the holy leaders have been so tolerant. Why didn't they dispose of you as soon as they realised it was you who told Thomas to burn Drax's house?"

"They won't touch me because I'm brilliant at making money, and they need their share of it." Drax laughed with the confidence of self-satisfaction. "Anyway, life's no fun without risks. You'll be pleased to know, I wore the hat. I felt a complete fool, but I'll get used to it. How was your day?"

Isobel groaned. "I was sent on a computer project, teaching some of the less bright agents how to hack into secret networks." She rolled her eyes. "Flaming flesh, it was tedious! I wish the holy leaders wouldn't send me on rubbishy jobs."

She pouted prettily and Drax's cruel face melted into tenderness as he put his arm around her.

"I wish they wouldn't, too," he said, sniffing the back of her neck. "I'd much rather you could be with me always – even though you do swear like a quarryman!"

"It's not just the sending me away," she grumbled, ignoring his caresses. "It's the job satisfaction. I much prefer the medical projects. There's something very satisfying about euthanasia. It's all part of the purification process."

Her face lit up and her voice rose and trembled with emotion. "We'll rid the world of the tainted and the toxic. Bit by bit, we'll eliminate the weak, the rebellious and the comfort seekers."

She clasped her hands to her chest. "The world shall be united in purity of soul, and the Magnifico will reign in glory."

She rarely spoke of her inner feelings, and Drax gazed at her in admiration. "Wow! If anyone deserves to sit at the Magnifico's right-hand side, it's you."

CHAPTER SIX

Gwen Jones arrived in good time on the Monday morning to take Paul to school.

Lucy was too embarrassed to meet her eye when she opened the door to her, and no mention was made of the disastrous visit to the house. The photograph had confirmed to David and Dorothy that Mrs Jones was indeed her grandmother, and now she was mortified to think she'd suspected a trap. She was consumed with shame when she remembered her fleeting impression of a crazy lady. Mrs Jones wasn't a bit crazy. She had a really sweet face. But how did you speak to a grandmother when you hadn't known she existed, and when you'd thought she was a trap, and when you'd been shouted away from her door?

She wrapped Paul up warmly in his new clothes. "School will be fun," she said softly, trying to put the cruel memories of the Magnifico's school out of her own mind. "You'll have lots of other children to play with."

"Will you be here when I come back?" he whispered back.

"I think you might get back before I do because I'm going to school too, but I'll be with you in spirit all day." She fingered the gold circle that hung from the chain on her neck. "See this, with the tiny daffodils in the middle? That's you, remember, and the chain is me, so we're always together."

She bent to hug him tight and give him a kiss, and then handed him over to Gwen. In her head, she could hear Aunt Sarah's voice telling her to remember her manners – *if you're ever too embarrassed to look at someone in the eye, look at their chin.*

"Thank you for taking him," she said, looking at her grandmother's chin. "It'll be a great help to Miss Clements." She tried to smile, and held the door open for them.

Gwen could sense the chill in the courtesy, but a warm current of pleasure ran through her as Paul took hold of her hand. She tried to chat a little with him as they walked down the hill, but there was no response and she could feel his tension. His hand tightened as they reached the town, and he looked up at her.

"Will I see the monster frog?" he asked.

Gwen was puzzled. The boy must have seen something on television. "There's no monster frog," she said.

"What about the spawn? The spawn of the monster frog? That man didn't want them in your house."

"Aha!" she said with slow realisation. "That monster frog! No, it's gone now, and the spawn, so you won't see them. Frogs don't hurt you, so you needn't be afraid of them, but we certainly don't want them in the house or you might tread on them by mistake."

When they reached the school, he went into the playground without pulling back, and Gwen was relieved. She spoke to his teacher, gave him a kiss, and left him standing in a queue of little children waiting for the whistle.

★

74

"This is almost as terrifying as when we escaped from the disposal cells!" said Dorothy.

Finding the school had been no problem. They had just followed the stream of uniformed children uphill until they reached the building. Now they stood frozen with apprehension outside the main entrance, and looked at each other.

"We've never been with normal children before," whispered Lucy, "and there are so many of them!"

Even Dorothy was daunted.

"Well, we've been with each other, and we're normal," said David, eventually, making no attempt to go in.

Dorothy drew in a deep breath. "Right!" she said. "Head up, shoulders back."

★

When Lucy arrived back from school, Paul was waiting anxiously for her in the hall. He threw his arms round her, and she hugged him tight. There was Aunt Sarah's voice yet gain – *The Magnifico says no child shall receive comfort from the day he starts school.* So what? She took Paul's hand. They went upstairs and lay quietly on her bed until the tension seeped out of them. "Breathe deep breaths," she said, "very slowly, in and out."

★

"There are some really nice girls in my year," Dorothy said later that evening after supper. She was kneeling on the window seat, looking between parted curtains at the dark street outside. "A girl called Izzy lives in this same road, further up, and she invited me to a sleepover."

Lucy lay on her stomach on the rug in front of the fire, trying not to think about tomorrow and another day at school. She turned over a page of Paul's new reading book. "What's a sleepover?" she asked, without looking up.

"It means sleeping at her house with a whole lot of other girls."

Lucy sat bolt upright and stared at Dorothy.

"You can't do that!" exclaimed David, emerging from the depths of an armchair. "You have to be with us. They're strangers. You don't know who their parents are. It might be putting you in danger – and us."

"Yes, I know that, silly!" Dorothy tossed her head, a little crossly. "I told her I couldn't, but it was nice to be asked, and I do want to fit in." Her face brightened. "And there's a really good-looking boy called Jason in the year above. One of the girls said he was asking who I was." A pleased little smile crossed her face. "I might put on some of that mascara tomorrow before I go to school."

David laughed and relaxed back into his chair. He liked this school. Despite the cruelties at the Mag's school, he'd had a lot of fun there with his friends, but his best mate, Matthew, had turned out to be an infiltrator and he couldn't think of the place without revulsion. Holy Bag! It was no wonder they couldn't trust anyone. This new school felt different. People weren't afraid.

"What about you, Lucy?" he said.

"It'll be better tomorrow when I've got more used to it. There were two girls who were friendly, but it was awkward because they wanted to know why I'd moved down from London and why I'm with a foster mother, and obviously I couldn't tell them. And who on earth is Beyoncé? Is it a man or a woman? I felt a bit of a fool."

76

"I think Beyoncé's something to do with television," said David. "We can ask Miss Clements how to find programmes. If we watch the right ones, we can talk as though we know what people are on about. It's called being 'cool'."

"And," Dorothy reminded Lucy, "just remember, you've had experiences they've never had, so you know a lot more about some things than they do. I bet they've never rescued people from a fire, and from disposal cells, or captured someone evil like Father Copse and got him arrested, or slept under a railway arch in London."

"I know, but I think it's because of all those things that I feel I'll never fit in," replied Lucy

"Well, if I can fit in, you can. Don't shrink into yourself. Be proud." Dorothy jumped down from the window seat and straightened her back. "And another thing," she added, "at lunchtime I heard one of the boys say, 'Who's that exquisite little beauty with the pre-Raphaelite hair?' and he meant you. I didn't say anything, because the less people know about us the better, but one of my friends told them it was the new girl in year ten. So you've got your admirers already."

David scowled. "What a cheek!"

Lucy flushed. A tiny thrill of pleasure popped up inside her, but vanished immediately. They must have meant someone else. Aunt Sarah had often told her she was plain, and she could see that for herself when she looked in the mirror – though she couldn't help secretly thinking that she looked better these days, with her face slightly less pinched and her hair growing more thickly. It would probably be nice to be a beauty – and an exquisite one at that – but Aunt Sarah had warned her of the dangers. She said it was best to be as plain as you can, so you'll be allowed to keep house or learn a skill, instead of being cooped up in the breeding rooms for years.

"Well," she said eventually. "I like the teachers. That Mr Owen we had for the computer lesson was really nice. He was surprised I'd never done it before."

"Did you tell him that only the boys were allowed to do computers at our last school?" asked David.

"No. I didn't say anything, because he might have asked why, and then he'd think we must be very odd."

"Do we know why?" asked Dorothy, closing the curtains properly and throwing herself down on the sofa.

"Yes," replied Lucy. "Aunt Sarah told me. The holy leaders believe that only a very few specially chosen women are responsible enough to have that sort of skill, because it reaches out to the outside world. Most women should be concentrating on their duties in the communes."

David and Dorothy burst into fits of laughter.

"Pompous old fools!" spluttered Dorothy. "We'll concentrate on our duty to give evidence, and it'll put the lot of them in prison, with or without computers, and they'll have to shave off their revolting beards, and everyone will see their weak chins and droopy mouths."

Lucy smiled. It felt good to look at the holy leaders in a ridiculous light. "Anyway," she said, "Mr Owen showed me how to do a few things. He said I had an aptitude for computers and would soon catch up."

"I liked him too," said David. "I had a really good day. Some of the boys were friendly. And we did football, which was far more interesting than that pathetic old rounders we always used to play at the Mag's school. One boy gave me his mobile phone number, so I've actually got someone I can ring if I want to."

Paul wasn't listening. He had stood up and was singing a little song to himself. Suddenly, he barked, "*Bore da*, Miss Wyn Lloyd!"

The others looked at him in awe.

"He can speak Welsh!" exclaimed Dorothy in admiration. "If we learn some Welsh, it could make a really good code for us in an emergency. I bet the Mag's men don't speak Welsh."

"*Bore da*, Miss Wyn Lloyd!" chanted Paul again. "It means 'Good morning, Miss Wyn Lloyd.'"

The others chanted back at him, "*Bore da! Bore da! Bore da!*"

"I asked her why she had two names, and she said one was her mother's and the other was her father's, and they put them together to be fair and equal."

"*Bore da*, Miss Two Names," they sang.

★

The week passed pleasantly. They began to relax. Dorothy applied her mascara a little more thickly and thought a lot about Jason as the days went by. Some of the other girls in her class had boyfriends, and she did feel it would be exciting to have one of her own. Not a traitor like Tom, her so-called friend from last year in London, but one who could make her happy inside. She could tell that Jason liked her, but there were other girls who were prettier and far more sophisticated than she was, and she didn't dare hope that he would prefer her. She couldn't believe her luck when he asked if she'd meet him at the weekend.

When Saturday came, she asked Miss Clements at breakfast if they could go into town and take a stroll up the prom.

"Of course you may, dear. It's such a lovely, sunny day, so make the most of it while you can. There'll be plenty of nasty weather to get through before the spring. Remember to be back by one, in time for lunch."

It was nearly eleven when they left the house.

"We'll go this way," said Dorothy, hurrying them along. "Izzy said we have to turn right as we come out of the gate, go up to the end of the road and then down a hill."

They passed the entrance to a narrow path that led steeply up the hill immediately to the left of the house. Then, there was a row of big houses on their right and tennis courts below them on their left. At the end of the road, they turned left downhill, straight towards the sea and the promenade.

Dorothy sat down on the last bench, nearest the cliff.

"You can all go and investigate those rocks under the cliff, while I wait here," she said, "I'm meeting Jason on this bench at eleven o'clock. What's the time on your watch, Lucy?"

"Eleven o'clock on the dot, and – watch out everyone – here he comes!"

Dorothy watched as they dashed off to the beach, and then forgot all about them. She turned and her heart leaped. Jason was approaching with a huge grin on his handsome, good-natured face, and she felt happy. He sat down next to her and threw one arm around her shoulder. She reminded herself hastily that she must give nothing away about her background. The best technique would be to let him do most of the talking.

There was no awkward silence. He chatted about his sister, his dog and what he hoped to do for his A levels.

When he asked her about herself she told him she was living with a foster mother, and she was grateful for his sensitivity in not enquiring further. His great passion was rugby, and although Dorothy hardly knew one sport from another, she was amazed to find that she had a passion for rugby too.

Occasionally, she glanced over to check on the others, who were stepping gingerly over the rocks. It was not until they started to turn back that she thought of the time.

"What does it say on your watch?" she said.

"Nearly one o'clock."

"Flaming flesh!" she exclaimed.

Jason looked surprised.

"Sorry! It's just an expression. I have to be back by one. My foster mother is really strict about meal times."

★

Lucy held Paul's hand as he jumped down from the last rock, back onto the beach. He caught his balance and looked up. "I want to go on that train," he said, pointing at a little railway that ran up the side of the cliff.

They stood and watched as a carriage chugged steeply upwards and passed another one coming down.

"Wow! That's really neat!" exclaimed David, as the carriage reached its shelter at the top of the cliff, and people started climbing out. "One up and one down, both at the same time."

"We'd probably have to pay, so we can't go on it today," Lucy told Paul. "We'll have a treat after we've bought our house and feel safe. For the time being, we'll have to walk up there if we want to explore. Come on or we'll be late for lunch."

The beach was deep shingle, and it was difficult to move forward. To make their journey back more uncomfortable, Paul had fallen in a rock pool and was soaking wet. David held back and studied the cliff. There was no road up that way, so it could be an important escape route out of this town if the Mag's men ever caught up with them. He made mental notes. There was a path to the left of the railway. It twisted and disappeared round rock and gorse, then reappeared and disappeared again. They would have to try it out. Perhaps they'd go this afternoon.

He glanced towards the promenade. Dorothy and Jason were still on the bench, laughing uproariously at something. It was worrying. She was always warning them not to get too close to anyone, so why couldn't she see how risky this was? It was bad enough with her and that awful Izzy from up the road. And now there was Jason.

Lucy looked up. "What do you think of Jason?" she asked. "He's not as handsome as all that, is he?"

"He seems alright at school," said David, rather doubtfully, "but it's not his looks that matter. Supposing he's an infiltrator? After all, we had infiltrators in the Mag's school – like Matthew – so there could be some here too."

"I wonder if we'll ever stop being suspicious of people?" said Lucy.

Dorothy was already on her feet when they reached the promenade, and they ran ahead of her. When they were halfway up the hill they looked back. She was walking very slowly behind them, still chatting vigorously with Jason.

"She shouldn't let him walk back with her," grumbled David. "He'll see where we live. And just look at them!

They don't stop talking. She's bound to give something away."

"Well, they'd hardly have met up just to stay mute. I'm sure she's on her guard without showing it."

Secretly, Lucy was anxious about it too. Also, she was afraid Miss Clements would be angry when she saw that Paul was totally soaked. She speculated as to the sort of punishments that might be used at the big house if people fell in the water. Paul was grizzling that his bottom and his feet were cold, and that David had told him it was cruel to drop a stone on a shrimp.

"Stop whining," said Lucy sharply, "and get a move on."

"Your voice sounds just like Aunt Sarah's," he said.

★

Miss Clements noted Paul's wet clothes, but wasn't perturbed. As she told herself, there was no reason why she should be. It wasn't going to put her to any trouble. Lucy took Paul upstairs, rubbed him down, and helped him into dry clothes. When he was warm and comfortable, he put his arms round her and buried his face in her neck.

"You'll never leave me, will you?" His voice was muffled. "Not for some old boyfriend who's nothing to do with us."

"Of course not! If I ever have a boyfriend, which is unlikely, he'll be everything to do with us, and you'll come with me."

"You can marry David, and we'll be together."

Lucy thought for a moment. "No. I don't think I could do that. We all took that vow to be blood brothers and sisters. It might not seem right."

Downstairs in the kitchen she followed Miss Clements's instructions and bundled the salty, wet clothes into the washing machine. How easy life was with machinery! No wonder poor Aunt Sarah had always been so cross if they came in wet. She'd had to wash everything by hand, and then there was nowhere to dry it unless the sun was shining and a good wind blowing.

★

David was on his own in the children's sitting room when Paul and Lucy came in. The fire was blazing, and he was sprawled across an armchair, staring thoughtfully at the ceiling. He wished he hadn't reminded himself of the infiltrators at the Mag's school. Matthew's treachery was a horrible thing to remember.

He was disgusted with himself as he recalled his own reaction when he saw Matthew's body, crushed by the wheels of Thomas's car. "Serves him right!" He'd actually said that! It wasn't poor old Matthew's fault. He'd simply been doing what he'd been brought up to do. But Dorothy had to be careful. You shouldn't even trust your best mates.

Dorothy turned up just in time for lunch. She was looking pink and happy. Her short black curls had blown wild about her head, and her brown eyes were full of laughter. David was silent, and Lucy asked her politely if she'd had a nice chat.

"Yes. He's lovely." Dorothy flung herself down on the sofa. "Hey, you lot! What's the matter with you? I've got a nice, new friend, and you go all frosty. He's cheerful and makes me laugh, and it's fun."

"It's so risky," muttered David.

"Lucy says she'll never leave me," said Paul.

"Well, I'll never leave you either, but that doesn't mean I can't have friends."

"Just think of Matthew at the Mag's school," said David crossly. "He was always cheerful and made everyone laugh. He was my best mate, and all that time he was an infiltrator and ended up betraying us."

No one replied. Dorothy, her pleasure dampened, went upstairs to take off her mascara and comb her hair. Surely David knew she'd never betray them. After all, she wasn't as naïve as she'd been last year when she'd run away from the commune and Tom had found her wandering aimlessly round the streets. Now she squirmed with embarrassment as she remembered how she had trusted him. She'd certainly learned her lesson about overly-charming men. It wasn't the fact that he'd disappeared with her money and her mobile phone. What was sickening was that he and his friend had nearly tricked her into a job in that sleazy dump which, just in time, she'd guessed was not really a hotel.

She'd learned a lot from that experience. David should realise by now that she'd never be taken in by a charming man again. Still, Tom had taught her some useful things. He'd shown her the best places to find food in the alleyways behind the West End restaurants, and the safest railway arches to sleep under. It wasn't all bad.

She straightened herself up and shook off her annoyance. After all, David was right. There was no such thing as being too cautious after what they'd been through. She was sorry now that she'd made him worry.

David was staring glumly at the television when she went back downstairs. She dropped a kiss on the top of his head. He grunted, and she laughed. Then she popped her head round the kitchen door and asked if she could help with the lunch.

"Come on in, dear," said Miss Clements, "and I'll show you how to make good gravy."

CHAPTER SEVEN

Sunday dawned bright and fine. At breakfast Miss Clements asked if anyone would like to come to church with her and Miss Marilyn.

"No, thank you, Miss Clements. I'm meeting Jason," said Dorothy, putting home-made, black cherry jam on her croissant, and trying to appear nonchalant.

Miss Clements looked a bit uncertain. "Remember that Beverley said you were to keep together if you went out."

"I'll go with Dorothy," said Lucy. "We'll all go with her."

Paul objected. "I want to see what a church looks like."

In the end it was agreed that Paul would go with Miss Clements and Miss Marilyn, and the other two would go with Dorothy.

"I don't want you hanging around too close," she whispered, as they left the dining room.

David was annoyed. "We don't want to listen in on your silly conversations," he snapped. "We just want to make sure you're safe – because if you're not safe, none of us are."

They tidied their bedrooms and Lucy brushed Paul's hair. It wouldn't lie down, so she fluffed it with her hands and stood back to admire him. "You look very nice," she said, giving him a kiss. "Just what people in a church are supposed to look like, I think."

At quarter to ten, she took him down to the hall, where Miss Clements and her sister were waiting in grey hats and grey coats, with grey handbags dangling from their arms. Their clothes didn't tell you anything about them, thought Lucy, as she handed over an excited Paul.

She found the others in the sitting room, silent and grumpy, staring at the remains of last night's fire. Lucy fetched a brush and pan, and knelt down to clear the ashes from the grate. Dorothy wasn't due to meet Jason until eleven thirty, so they had time to fill. She stood up, saying she was going upstairs to finish off some homework.

"Huh!" muttered David under his breath. "To plaster yourself with make-up, more likely."

"I heard that!" snapped Dorothy as she left the room.

Upstairs, she washed her face and put the lipstick and mascara away in a drawer, and sat sadly on the bed. The thought of having a boyfriend was such fun, but she knew David was right. If she got too close to anyone, even if he wasn't an infiltrator like Matthew, there would always be a risk of giving information away accidentally. She'd been really careful with Jason, but she'd still slipped up with that 'Flaming flesh!'

She sighed. It was just that all her life she'd been told she'd have to marry one of the Fathers when she reached sixteen, and the prospect of being free to choose a boyfriend, or whether to marry at all, was so exhilarating! But she wasn't stupid. She could see the dangers. For the time being, she would have to go around with a crowd, not just Jason. It would be safer and wouldn't be for forever.

She'd meet him at half past eleven as arranged, but would tell him she couldn't go out with him anymore because she was so behind with her school work. And that was true. She'd tell him she wanted to stay friends, and would see him whenever they went out with the gang. She slid off the bed and stood up straight and held her head high. Just wait till the trials were over, and then she'd really let her hair down!

★

David was lolling on the sofa next to Lucy. The television was on, but he saw none of it. All thoughts of Jason had vanished, and he was mentally going over the details of yesterday's exploration of the cliff. They had followed the path that ran next to the railway until it forked into two possible escape routes. One was difficult, up a sheer stretch of rock. It would be much too awkward to abduct anyone from there, so they'd be safe going that way. The other route was easy, over the cliff railway via a little wooden bridge. They had stood on the bridge for quite a while, watching the trains chug up and down. It had been fun.

By the time Dorothy came downstairs, any crossness between her and David had vanished. She squeezed in between him and Lucy on the sofa, and the three of them stared at a documentary about Greece and the International Monetary Fund until, to joint astonishment, they heard the front door opening and shutting with slightly more of a bang than usual. The three of them emerged from their sitting room, and Donald came from his bed in the kitchen. Miss Clements had lost her normally bland expression, and Miss Marilyn's mouth was twitching furiously.

"You said you'd be gone for an hour and a half!" exclaimed Dorothy. "What happened?"

Miss Marilyn made a snorting noise and took off her coat.

"We couldn't stay," said Miss Clements. She seemed agitated. "As soon as we got into the church Paul started humming and he wouldn't stop, and it got louder and louder and we just had to leave. So embarrassing!"

"I dread to think what our parents would have done to us if we'd behaved badly in church," snorted Miss Marilyn angrily, "or anywhere else for that matter."

Miss Clements caught her breath and put her hand up to her heart.

Paul ran over to Lucy and put his arms round her waist.

"It was the dead man," he said. "Hanging in the air."

Lucy's stomach lurched.

Miss Clements stared at Paul. What on earth was he talking about?

Miss Marilyn's jaw clamped so tightly she couldn't have twitched her mouth if she'd tried, and she marched upstairs without a word.

Aha! thought Miss Clements as realisation struck. Through a child's eyes! We do all see things differently in this old world.

Lucy gathered her wits. She gave Paul a hug. "It's alright, darling. I'm sure there wasn't a dead man. It was probably someone resting on a balcony, or a statue or something. You don't have to go again."

She looked up at Miss Clements. "I'm so sorry," she said. "He always hums if he's anxious. It's really bad that he embarrassed you, but he senses things and then it makes him hum. There must have been something that frightened him."

Miss Clements had recovered her composure and her benign expression. "Well, there we are then," she said placidly. "It takes all sorts. It's a shame though, because there was a new young man there – so handsome – and I was going to invite him here for tea. Robert, or Robin, or something. One should always try to welcome strangers to the congregation."

She took off her coat, and went straight to the kitchen to soothe her nerves with a nice cup of coffee with cream. Trust Marilyn to remind her of bad times. But she was not displeased with the way things had turned out. It gave her a little more time to try out a new recipe for a chocolate pudding. Perhaps she'd stay at home next Sunday.

★

"Mr Lovett rang today." Miss Clements briefly looked up from her whisking bowl as the children came into the kitchen after school. "That Thomas's trial is towards the end of this month, though they can't give us the exact date yet. They won't need Dorothy this time, just Lucy and David. You'd better pack a bag each, so you're ready if Beverley comes for you at short notice."

The shock that ran through Lucy took her breath away. She looked at David. The colour had drained from his face. Dorothy was standing stock still, her school bag dangling from her hand. Of course they had known this day would come, but there had always been the secret hope that something might happen to stop it.

"Mr Lovett told me you'll give your evidence from behind a screen, so no one will see you," said Miss Clements, as she poured pudding mixture into patty tins. "Beverley will see to your accommodation and everything, so you're not to worry about a thing. You're going to stay in a hotel. I expect Mr Lovett will give you your instructions." She looked up and saw the stricken faces, and tried to think of something encouraging. "In a way, my dears, it'll be a helpful experience for you, because you're all going to have to give evidence in Father Copse's trial later on. And then again, if they catch Father Drax. At least by then you'll have some idea of what happens."

It was a helpful experience they would rather have done without.

"Now put the kettle on," she said, and make yourselves a cup of tea, and there's cake in that tin. You may take it to your sitting room or eat it here, whichever you prefer. Paul's having tea at Mrs Jones's house. Her husband seems to have taken quite a shine to him."

Lucy dumped her school bag in a corner of the kitchen and sat down at the table. How could she possibly eat cake!

"Aunt Sarah died that night, just before Thomas and Father Drax's men came to burn the house down," she said sadly, "and I know it was for the best because she was spared the fright of it all, but I can't help wishing she was still alive. She was really strict and always going on about saving our souls, but I know that inside her she loved Paul and me."

David and Dorothy said nothing. They filled the kettle, and set out some mugs and plates.

"I used to envy the children in the commune, like Dorothy and David, because they had company," said Lucy, "but now I realise how lucky Paul and I were to have Aunt Sarah, because she did really care about us as well as our souls."

Miss Clements was genuinely interested, but she didn't want to hear the sad details, oh dear, no. It would be too upsetting. Lucy must have been a very lonely little girl, she thought. No wonder she was so quiet, and always with her nose in a book. Escapism, that's what that was.

"Well, well," she said soothingly. "I'm sure Aunt Sarah was a very good woman, and it's nice to think she's at peace. Now dears, what would you like for supper tonight – escalope of veal or moussaka?"

★

The days passed somehow. Lucy's throat tightened and it was difficult to eat. Sometimes she found it hard to breathe.

Miss Clements discovered an old Ventolin inhaler left in a cupboard by one of her previous foster children. "You never know, it might work," she said. "I'll make an appointment for you to see the doctor when you come back from London."

It did work and Lucy could breathe, but she still had no appetite, and grew thinner and thinner, until she was almost the puny little girl she used to be. Each night she lay awake, and dark circles formed under her eyes. She remembered every detail of the night of the fire. Thomas had found her hiding behind the curtain, and his look of contempt had shrivelled her very soul. This was the Thomas who had given her sweeties and made her feel special. She had loved his kind face and gentle manner. Now of course, she knew it was a sham. He was an infiltrator and had just been using her to spy on Father Copse – and training her up to be an infiltrator herself. Never would she completely trust anyone again, apart from her family.

She fleetingly wondered if she would ever be able to trust people just enough to make friends easily like Dorothy, always with a crowd of chattering boys and girls around her. It really didn't matter, because the only future she could visualise was the trial, and then more trials.

CHAPTER EIGHT

The Magnifico's agents were sniffing around Wales. Thomas had taken a photo of a trusting Lucy on his mobile phone, shortly before the house was burned down, and it had now been retrieved from the holy leaders' archives and distributed to the agents. It showed the pinched little face of an undernourished child, her hair scraped back flat into a pigtail, squinting into the camera with an air of mixed surprise and pleasure.

Photos were rarely taken of the Magnifico's children, so this was the only one the agents had to go on, but written descriptions had been sent out with it. They were looking for a fifteen-year-old girl and her five-year-old brother, both of whom had brown hair and olive skin. The other two were a wiry boy, also fifteen, tall and strikingly handsome with silver-blond hair – and a sixteen-year-old girl called Dorothy, slim with black curls, rosy cheeks and full, red lips.

★

Robin was standing outside the school at the top of the hill. He had covered most of the secondary schools across mid-Wales, attended church services and scout meetings, and lurked around playgrounds, but all without success.

Maybe he should forget about the Magnifico and look for a job in the outside world, because if he didn't find the kids, he wouldn't get paid. There wasn't much of a future in working for the holy leaders these days. His ambition had been to train as a Father, but they'd told him that to be a Father he had to be both handsome and brilliantly clever, and he just didn't have the brains. That had been quite hurtful, because he knew some of them were thicker than he was, silly old goats. Still, this job was important. Most of the other agents had already gone, so at the moment he was a valuable asset. If he could just pull it off they might pay him enough to buy a nice little *finca* in Spain with a swimming pool, and then he could disappear.

He felt in his pocket for credentials and checked that he had the right ones. Criminal Investigation Department, they said – CID. OK, time to go in. He stepped into the school foyer.

Ten minutes later, he stepped out again. No, they were sorry, but couldn't help. There was no one called Copse or Drax on their list of pupils. The sense of failure was becoming too familiar. He slouched off, wondering if he might as well throw in the towel and disappear to Spain right now. At least his Spanish was pretty good, thanks to the Mag's school, and he could always set himself up as a private investigator, or work for some con man.

As he turned out of the school grounds, a bell rang inside the building and seconds later, children began to pour out of the main entrance. What a bunch of scruffs! He stood near the gates and focused on the heads of hair. There were plenty of fair-haired kids, but not a single silver blond. He'd give it a go for three nights, and then move on down the coast.

★

It was Izzy who first noticed the young man standing nonchalantly just outside the school grounds.

"Wow!" she exclaimed nudging Dorothy with her elbow. "Look at that gorgeous guy!"

Dorothy took a sideways peep as she hurried through the gates.

"Don't stare!" hissed Izzy, while staring brazenly herself.

Dorothy took another peep. He certainly was very handsome – almost too good-looking. "I wonder who he's waiting for," she said. "It must be a teacher. He's a bit old, even for the sixth-formers."

"Never mind his age," breathed Izzy. "He's certainly not too old for me."

Dorothy laughed. Izzy had no shame! There was no time to talk about handsome men. David and Lucy would be waiting for her at the main road.

"I've got to catch the others up," she said, and hurried off.

She didn't think she'd ever want a boyfriend that good-looking. People like Izzy would always be pursuing him and she'd never feel secure. Tom, last year in London, had been handsome – or so she'd thought at the time – but this one was like a film star. Well, good luck to Izzy! No harm in reaching for the skies! Jason was handsome and a good laugh, and that would have suited Dorothy perfectly – if only she hadn't had to finish with him.

★

Robin was luckier the next night.

The chattering crowd had thinned out. There was still no sign of an ash-blond boy, and Robin was about to turn away when someone shouted, "See ya, Dorothy!" He looked over quickly and spotted a tall, slim girl with black bobbing curls. She was laughing and waving to a friend.

His heart lifted. It could be the one. There weren't many Dorothies around these days. Old-fashioned name — not one he'd choose himself. He took a good look as she walked towards the gate with two other kids. Holy Magnifico! She was a stunner! The description was perfect – tall and slim with dark-brown curls and rosy cheeks. And just look at those luscious lips! She was absolutely ripe for abduction. He could just see her in a cave house attached to his little Spanish *finca*. Locked in, of course.

There was still no sign of the ash-blond boy or the scrawny kid from the photo, but he could certainly move in on this one.

He followed the girl and her two friends from a distance. Halfway down the hill they stopped and waited for a gap in the fast-moving traffic, and then crossed over and turned right up a side street. By the time Robin had managed to cross without being killed, they had disappeared. No problem. This was exciting. He'd have another go tomorrow.

The following day, he was luckier. Keeping a good distance behind, he saw which house they went into, noted the address and casually walked on past. The holy leaders would have to change their tune about his brains once this job was over. If they still refused to make him a Father, he'd just take his money and go. It'd be their loss.

A bit of land around the *finca* would be ideal, with no neighbours to poke their noses into his business. But he mustn't get carried away. There were three other kids to track down first. One quick and pleasant chat with this Dorothy and he'd probably get all the information he needed. Girls were like that. Give them a bit of charm and flattery and you could get anything you liked out of them – especially when you were a real good-looker like him.

He'd watch the house on Saturday morning. She was bound to go out into town at some stage, and there would be an accidental meeting – in a bookshop, perhaps, or a café. His heart raced with the thrill of it all. This was surely the best job in the world! He'd show those holy leaders. They wouldn't be able to deny that his tactics called for intelligence worthy of any Father. There'd be money, promotion and a beautiful wife at the end of it all – if they let him have her.

★

"I'm meeting Izzy and some friends on the pier at eleven," announced Dorothy, at breakfast the following Saturday.

Miss Clements reminded her, somewhat absentmindedly, that she was not to go out alone, and went off to the kitchen to start on a lemon surprise pudding.

"Keep far back, as though you don't belong to me, but near enough in case," said Dorothy, shortly before eleven o'clock. She put on her mascara and stepped out of the house. Dare she hope that Jason might be there? He'd taken it really well when she explained why she couldn't commit herself to any one person with exams looming. At first, he'd looked terribly hurt, so she'd explained that she did like him, but the exams were really important because she was going to have to provide for her family. The hurt went from his face. He'd asked no questions, but said she was right, and he needed to swot too. Now she was worried that he hadn't really been that interested in her. She sighed as she crossed the road. Having boyfriends made life complicated, even after you'd finished with them. It would be much simpler not to bother. The trouble was, it was all so interesting.

She turned to check that the others were there. Paul and David were crossing the road, and Lucy was just behind them with Donald on his lead.

Miss Clements was standing anxiously at the gate. "Don't rush him, dear," she called. "He's not used to exercise. And don't let him near other dogs. He can be quite aggressive."

Dorothy smiled to herself. Life was pleasant even without a boyfriend. She was so lucky.

★

Robin moved behind the parked cars and watched. He kept well behind as Dorothy hurried down the hill with those other three trailing after her.

Wow! Despite her haste, she walked like an angel – sort of skimmed the ground. It took a bit of skill to keep up with them all while trying not to look like a stalker, but he was nothing if not subtle. Holy fire! She was the most beautiful girl he had ever seen. He'd not seen her out of school uniform before. No one could say that her weekend clothes were trendy and, in fact, they were decidedly old-fashioned, but she wore them with such elegance it was enough to make a fellow lick his lips.

But first things first! He must focus on the job in hand – track down the blond boy and the titchy kid in the photo, and report to the holy leaders. Then watch the money roll in. After that, who knew? With money in the bank all things were possible.

★

There was no one on the pier when Dorothy arrived. David sauntered over to a bench on the promenade, and Lucy and Paul leaned over the railings to watch the waves as they dashed onto the rocks below. Dorothy was wondering whether to join them or wait on the pier, when a soft, husky voice said, "Hello, Dorothy."

She turned and looked into the eyes of a remarkably handsome young man, and recognised him straight away. Her heart missed a beat. How did he know her name?

"Do I know you?" she asked coldly.

Robin was taken aback, but quickly recovered his aplomb. "I'm Robin," he said with his most charming smile. "I work in the admin office up at the school and I see you around. This is your first term, isn't it? How are you getting on?"

Dorothy froze. His voice was pleasant and his eyes crinkled attractively as he smiled, but his teeth were too white – fake white, fake smile. There was something wrong. And why would someone who worked in the admin office have been waiting at the school gate the other day?

David stood up and started walking over towards her. Lucy, Paul and Donald joined him. Before they could reach her, Izzy came hurtling onto the pier shouting that the meeting place had been changed. The young man melted away.

Dorothy looked at Izzy's skinny jeans and cropped top, and for the first time in her life was horribly conscious of feeling drab. How on earth could she face the rest of the gang dressed like this?

"Wow! I just love your funky London outfit!" exclaimed Izzy, looking her up and down. "You'll make us all feel so non-cool! And that seriously hot male creature you were talking to, we saw him up at the school. Who is he?"

"No idea," said Dorothy. "He said his name's Robin and he works in the admin office."

"No way! And I never noticed him till the other day! Either I'm slipping, or he's only just started there. I'll have to make enquiries! Come on. Let's go and find the others. They're up on the castle."

"He gave me the creeps," said Dorothy.

"Each to our own taste! Let's run. Everyone's there except Jason. He said he's swotting but might join us later."

So Jason had been genuine when he said he needed to swot. There was nothing fake about him! Dorothy's spirits soared.

The two girls ran. Lucy and David waited to give them a head start, and then walked hurriedly after them.

Paul turned and watched Robin disappearing down the promenade. "Funny walk, that man," he commented as he caught up with Lucy.

"Looks normal to me," she said, glancing back over her shoulder.

"No. His left foot swings out. See?"

"Anyway, he's gone now. Let's get a move on."

★

That same Saturday evening, the residents of the flat on the Cromwell Road were curled up comfortably on the blue-velvet sofa, sipping their brandies, when Isobel's phone made a purring noise. She stretched her arm languidly towards the coffee table and picked up the receiver. Suddenly, she uncurled herself and sat up straight and listened intently.

"OK, right," she said, "Thank you. Goodbye." She put the phone down and laughed excitedly. "They've found Dorothy!"

Drax was pleased of course, but puzzled. It was common knowledge that the children had refused to be separated. "Why only her? Surely they're all in the same place?"

"Apparently Robin watched the comings and goings from where Dorothy's living, and there are other children, but not the ones we want. There's a girl of about twelve and a teenage boy with black hair. There's also a small boy, but he's not been seen close-up."

"Thanks be to the Magnifico! One Drax kid down and one to go. Never mind about Copse's kids. With a bit of luck I'll soon be free." Drax's excitement was mixed with frustration. "But I can't disappear without identities and visas, and just look at me! I'd be spotted straight away. Perhaps I'd better have plastic surgery. Change my nose or lips or something."

"Well, I can't do it here in this flat, or you'd get blood poisoning." Isobel tried to hide her irritation. All he ever thought about was himself! "I keep telling you, grow a moustache or something. And tell the holy leaders to get a move on with those documents."

She stood up. "Come on. I'll make us some coffee and we'll open that box of chocolates to celebrate." She poured the chocolates into a silver dish, and put out tiny cups and saucers, and silver coffee spoons. "Won't it be lovely to go out to good restaurants again, and sip the most expensive wine on the list," she sighed. She sat down at the table and poured the coffee.

Drax chuckled and dropped himself gracefully into his chair. Isobel never ceased to marvel at the elegance of his movements – and how could such a tall man take up so little room? Her hand lay on the table, and he put his over it and stroked it gently with his thumb.

"Somehow I don't think our expensive tastes quite fit the Magnifico's frugality requirements," he said with a little laugh. "But there you are. Nobody's perfect."

As they sipped their coffees, a second message came through for Isobel. It confirmed that Dorothy had been traced to a school in Wales. The computer teacher, a Mr Owen, had been removed, and his body would be washed up on a beach somewhere along the coast. Isobel was to go down the following day, ready to work as a supply teacher on Monday. If the other children were at the same school, she would be ideally placed to identify them.

Their celebratory mood was destroyed.

"Holy fire!" Isobel swore quietly as she filled her suitcase. "May their flesh melt in eternity!" She waved a couple of wigs in the air. "I suppose I'll have to put these horrible things in, just in case. It's not pleasant to have to make myself deliberately hideous – and they itch." She packed her medical equipment carefully and placed a dowdy old mac on top of it. "I hope I don't have to wear that. Ugh!"

"You'll still look lovely underneath it all."

"Creep!" laughed Isobel, and then groaned again. "I'll be in the back of beyond, bored stiff, teaching revolting children to send each other emails." She took another chocolate. "Ah well! It won't be forever. The end is in sight."

CHAPTER NINE

"There's a new computer teacher," said Lucy after they'd arrived back from school a few days before the trial.

All four children were in David's bedroom. He was sitting on a straight-backed chair, with a large towel over his shoulders. Dorothy had a paint brush in her hand, and was touching up his silver roots with black hair dye.

"I know," she said, "I've seen her. And she's not like a normal computer teacher. She's stunningly beautiful with wonderful auburn hair, and so charming the boys in my class were falling over to please her. I'm dying to see David's reaction."

She didn't grudge the new teacher her ravishing looks, but there was something icy cold beneath that charm, and it made her shiver. "I'm so tired of being suspicious of everyone," she sighed.

Dorothy was feeling down. She was worrying about the meeting with Robin. Was she being paranoid? Perhaps he'd genuinely meant to be friendly. She didn't want to hurt people who were just being kind. Supposing she bumped into him again? Should she be polite or ignore him? Izzy had thought he looked like a genuinely nice guy, but Dorothy was not so sure.

"Well, we can't be rude to people we don't know just because they say, 'Hello, Dorothy'," said Lucy, "but we do have to be cautious."

David snorted. "We're already so cautious," he muttered bitterly, "I'll be suspecting myself soon."

★

Robin had left for London. He would collect his reward for finding Dorothy, and then scoot off to Spain. In a few hours he would be on his way to the airport with enough euros in his wallet to put down the deposit on the *finca* with a cave house at the back. He'd seen it the last time he was over there, and now he'd have the money. It would be just perfect.

He would make the cave house nice and secure and, if Dr Isobel Drax managed to track down David and Lucy at the school, the holy leaders would pay him more and then send for him to get Paul. They might be too stupid to see that he had brains, but life had its compensations, and the final pay-off would follow. He'd be rich. His only problem would be to make sure that they didn't dispose of Dorothy straight away before he had a chance to keep her for himself. But he'd think of something. Maybe they'd let him have her in part payment for Paul.

★

David was in a different stream from Lucy and didn't see the new teacher until the following day. He had a shock when she swept into the classroom. He'd been told she was stunning, but he was not prepared for such an icy beauty. When her blue eyes glanced in his direction they seemed to pierce right through him. She moved around the class, looking at the screens one by one. Despite the coldness of her eyes, her voice was warm – like the soft, red-gold colour of her hair – and almost tender. The other boys blushed and melted before her, but when she came over to look at David's screen, the hair rose on the back of his neck.

"Jesus! Could you feel it?" said one boy when the class was over. "There was warmth just oozing out of her, as though you were the only person in the world that mattered."

"It's her aura," said another. "It's charisma, or charm, or something."

"You should never trust charm," said David.

The other boys jeered. "Just because she didn't spend much time with you!"

★

"You were right about the new teacher," David told Dorothy that night, as they sat in front of the sitting-room fire. She put down her cookery magazine and looked at him with interest.

"The other boys were swooning over her," he said, "but she gave me goose pimples. It's a real shame Mr Owen left. I'm never going to be able to learn from that woman".

Lucy and Paul were sitting close together on the sofa with a large tray full of jigsaw puzzle across their laps.

"She's only temporary," said Lucy, slotting a piece into place. "Perhaps Mr Owen will come back soon. He showed me how to create an email address, so if you give me yours, I can send you messages in class."

★

All thoughts of the new teacher vanished at supper time.

"Somebody rang today to say that Beverley's fetching David and Lucy tomorrow," said Miss Clements, as they sat round the mahogany dining table. "So go up as soon as you've finished your meal, and double-check your bags. You might be away a few days, and I suppose you're expected to look tidy if you go to court even if you are behind a screen."

Lucy shuddered. "I'll be sick if I see Thomas again."

"Now, now, we don't use words like that at the table, do we dear?"

"Sorry," muttered Lucy. "Perhaps I'll just faint, and then they won't be able to get a word out of me."

"I'll faint if I have to see that Beverley again," said Dorothy. "She treats us like half-wits."

"Well, I expect she went to college or got a qualification or something," said Miss Clements kindly, "so that makes her feel important. We must try and be tolerant of other people's little weaknesses, mustn't we?"

Her sister sniffed and twitched her nose. "I don't see why we should," she snapped.

"Have another slice of apple pie with cream, Marilyn dear."

★

David and Lucy were ready with their bags before breakfast. When Gwen Jones arrived to take Paul to school, Lucy took off the gold chain with the daffodil circle and put it round his neck.

"Keep it hidden under your shirt," she whispered, "so no one will see it. But when you're wondering where I am, just feel it with your fingers and you'll

109

know I'm with you in spirit. I'll be thinking of you all the time."

Fifteen minutes later Dorothy appeared in the hall with her school bag. She threw her arms round David and Lucy. "Good luck!" she mumbled into their necks.

"Dorothy! Wait for me to put on my coat," said Miss Clements. "You mustn't go out on your own, remember. Donald and I will come with you as far as the main road. You'll have plenty of company from there on."

"Thank you, but it's alright," said Dorothy. "There's no need. Izzy from down the road says I can walk with her while the others are away. She's waiting at the gate for me."

"Are you sure, dear?" Miss Clements was relieved. It did upset things when her routine had to be changed. "Well, there we are then. That's settled."

Beverley arrived at nine o'clock. "Come along, kiddos, Pete's waiting, and we've got a meeting with Mr Lovett this afternoon." She almost pushed them out of the front door. "I expect you made arrangements for Dorothy to be escorted to school and back," she called to Miss Clements as she hurried down the path.

"Don't worry. It's all sorted."

*

Lucy and David had their meeting with Mr Lovett and a barrister in the afternoon, and went over their statements. Mr Lovett told them to ring him if they thought of anything else he needed to know, and David entered the office number onto his mobile phone. By the end of the meeting they were even more terrified at the thought of cross-examination than they had been at the beginning, and they left the office hardly able speak.

"Don't worry, kiddywinkies," said Beverley cheerfully. "The sooner it happens, the sooner it's over."

She hustled them along, and by six o'clock they were settled into two single rooms in a hotel in Bloomsbury. Lucy was worried that people would come through to use the bathroom, but Beverley explained with great amusement that it was for her own private use. "It's called an *on sweet*," she said. "That's French."

★

Thomas's trial lasted several days. The night before she was due to give evidence, Lucy lay awake in her hotel bed, going over the same old memories. She remembered how kind Thomas had been when she was little, and had fallen and cut her knee, and how patient he was when he'd taught her how to use his tools. Irrational doubts and hopes popped up in her mind. Perhaps it was all a terrible mistake. Was it possible that the Thomas of the fire was a different Thomas?

She could still picture the little garden he had helped Paul to create, with its flowers and carrots and prettily laid-out stones. It was he who had soothed Paul's screams that time when Aunt Sarah stopped him sprinkling rat poison over his pansies. She felt a powerful surge of indignation when she remembered that, at school the next day, one of the Drax girls had the cheek to accuse her of giving Paul the poison!

Suddenly she sat up in bed. Of course! How could she not have realised? Drax must have paid Thomas to plant the poison, so that Lucy would be blamed and bring dishonour on Copse's house. This was exactly what David had warned her about at the time, and she hadn't believed him. She felt hot with shame as she remembered how she'd told him that she couldn't trust him – David, her truest friend in the whole world.

Now she was consumed by anger, and a flash of red swept before her eyes. Thomas had been prepared to risk her innocent little brother's life, just for the sake of pleasing Drax! Plus, no doubt, for a hefty fee! She could hardly wait to give her evidence. Thomas would cringe.

That night she slept better than she had for weeks.

★

Lucy stood her ground. The horrible man who cross-examined her suggested she was lying and had made things up just to get attention to herself. He even suggested that she and David had planned the fire together in revenge for punishments. She was undaunted. Never in her life had she felt so strong.

David's evidence didn't take as long as hers did, and after it was all over Beverley hurried them out through the side of the court building. Pete was waiting for them and she bundled them into the back of his car. Lucy tried to relax. For once she found Beverley's ceaseless chatter quite soothing. She gazed out of the window and focused on the world outside. As they turned into the main road, she gasped and clutched David's sleeve.

"Bernie!" she whispered.

David peered across her. A heavily built individual was hurrying out of the main entrance of the court building. At the bottom of the steps he stood to one side and scrutinised the emerging public.

"I recognise him," said David quietly. "Who is he? Is he looking for us?"

"It's Bernie, the caretaker at the Copse commune."

The car moved on.

"Now, both of you go and have a lie-down to calm your nerves," said Beverley, when they arrived back at their hotel.

David gripped her arm. "We saw Bernie from the Copse commune. He was looking for us outside the court."

Beverley was taken aback. She stopped to think. "No," she said at last. "There's no way he could have found out where you're staying. We've been super-duper, extra careful. He couldn't have seen you in court, because of the screen – nor in the car, because of those black windows – like royalty."

She relaxed. "Phew! You gave me a fright there. He's probably gone off to poke his nose in someone else's business by now. I'll report it to Mr Lovett, but I know he'll say you're safe. Now, off you go for that lie-down. I'll be back later. We'll be eating in the hotel restaurant at seven, so don't you go down for one of their luxury afternoon teas."

*

Back in her room, Lucy couldn't lie down. She sat on her bed and shivered. Her throat was tight and something gripped her chest. Thank goodness she'd brought Miss Clements's inhaler. On the third puff her breathing eased. Her hands felt shaky, and she was wondering if that was the Ventolin or just nerves when David's head appeared round the door.

"Hi there!" he said and stopped short. He was shocked.

Lucy seemed to have shrunk. She was trembling and stared at him with haunted eyes. He wanted to put his arms round her and hold her close, to comfort himself as well as her, but he was afraid she would rebuff him.

"Come on," he said, as cheerfully as he could. "Let's go down and order one of their luxury afternoon teas."

★

David dropped his bag on the floor of the hotel foyer. Pete was coming for him any minute, but he had to say goodbye properly to Lucy. He'd asked Mr Lovett if he could stay but he'd said no, he mustn't miss any more school, and Lucy would be sent back double-quick, as soon as Mr Lovett was sure he wouldn't need her any more.

While Beverley was hovering in the hotel entrance looking out for Pete, he took Lucy's hand.

"If anything goes wrong, get a bus to Victoria coach station," he said quietly. "The receptionist told me. Then you can get a coach all the way home."

Lucy nodded. Home! Only a temporary home perhaps, but what a comfortable word!

Pete drove up and honked the horn. He leaned over and flung open the passenger door. "Get slippy!" he called. "I can't stop here."

David gave Lucy a big hug. "I wish you could come back with me. Or at least that I could stay with you."

Lucy was grateful, but she was too tense to hug him back, and he was disappointed.

She smiled and said, "With you in spirit! Tell Paul I'll be back soon."

★

Even after Thomas had been found guilty, there was more to come.

"You've got a couple more days in London, I'm afraid," said Beverley, as they made their way to the tube station. "That's Thomas out of the way. They'll probably send him down for life, and good riddance. But the lawyers want to see you about the case against Father Copse – and Father Drax if they can find him. You've got an appointment with Mr Lovett at ten o'clock on Wednesday."

Lucy's heart sank. Paul must be fretting for her, and it just seemed to go on forever. She'd ask Beverley if she could use her mobile phone to ring him tonight. "I wish something would happen to Father Copse's case so I never have to go to court again," she said.

"Well, there's no point in wishing," said Beverley, pushing her into a crowded carriage. "You'll be a major witness if it happens. But, you never know. There's still a chance they'll say he's too crazy to stand trial."

"If only the others could be up here with me, so I wouldn't be on my own."

"You're not on your own," said Beverley indignantly. "I've been with you the whole time."

CHAPTER TEN

It was Tuesday. When Dorothy and David arrived back from school, Paul was in the kitchen drinking milky tea and eating angel cake. "Very delicious!" he announced.

"Take the tray to your room," said Miss Clements. "It'll be nice and cosy for you there after walking back in that horrid wind."

In the sitting room the fire was roaring and the flames lit up the colours in the carpet. David turned on the television and threw himself back in an armchair. Dorothy put down the tea tray, and they each took a piece of the angel cake.

"The easy life," remarked David. "I wonder what Lucy's doing."

The doorbell rang through to the kitchen. Miss Clements sighed and wished she hadn't told the children never to open the door unless they knew who it was. All this coming and going was so inconvenient, was it not? She put down her wooden spoon, took off her apron and crossed the hall to the front door. The visitor introduced herself. Miss Clements ushered her into the dining room, and then poked her head round the sitting room door.

"Dorothy," she said, "There's a Miss Morris from the school to see you."

All three children stood up and went into the hall.

"She only wants you, dear," said Miss Clements to Dorothy. "Well, I'm sure there's no reason why you shouldn't all go in if you want to," she added, as they stepped into the dining room together.

Miss Morris came forward smiling and gracious. "Hello, Dorothy – oh, and your friends as well! I didn't realise David lived in the same house as you. Or is he just visiting? Hello, David. And who's this little fellow?"

David felt his skin prickling. He mumbled "Hello," but avoided her piercing gaze. Paul started humming, and Dorothy gave him a little push. The sound diminished, but didn't quite stop.

"It's nice of you to call, Miss Morris," said Dorothy. "Is there a problem with my work?"

"Not at all! You're doing very well for a beginner, but I did wonder if you'd like a little private tuition, say once or twice a week?"

Dorothy was taken aback.

"I wouldn't expect you to pay me," continued Miss Morris, "because it would give me pleasure to help you." Her smile was warm and kind. "I can see that you'd benefit enormously. It would only take a month or so for you to master all the basics."

"Oh," said Dorothy, trying to think quickly. "That's very generous of you. I'd have to ask Miss Clements. She's my foster mother, you know."

"Of course. I'll have a word with her. You could come to my flat after school, just for an hour twice a week, and we'll see how we get on."

The humming increased in volume.

"Thank you so much for coming," said Dorothy hastily. "I'll speak to Miss Clements myself and let you know in class tomorrow."

117

She hustled Paul out of the room. "Take him, David. I'll just see Miss Morris out."

Miss Clements appeared just as Miss Morris was leaving, and she explained the purpose of her visit once more. Miss Marilyn's face peeped over the landing banister rail. Her face twitched.

"What a good idea, Dorothy, my love," said Miss Clements. "You were only saying yesterday it would be really useful to be expert on the computer."

"I've told Miss Morris that I'll think about it and discuss it with you. I'm not sure how I could do it, what with all my homework and revision. I'll let her know tomorrow. Thank you, Miss Morris."

Dorothy didn't quite push Miss Morris, but she did close the door rather quickly after her.

"Well, it's your choice, dear, but so very kind of her," said Miss Clements as she went back to her kitchen.

"Holy fire! What was all that about?" said Dorothy, shutting the sitting-room door. "I'd love to have extra tuition and be really expert, but no way am I going to her flat!"

"Thank the Bag, she's gone!" exclaimed David. "She makes my hair stand on end. You can't possibly have private lessons with her!"

"She makes my hum come," said Paul.

The topic of conversation for the rest of the afternoon was Miss Morris's visit, and it continued at supper.

"Why don't you ask her if she'd like to give the lessons here, in the dining room?" asked Miss Clements. "Then she won't have to tidy her sitting room for you, and I could bring her a cup of tea and a piece of cake, just to check everything's alright. You could give me a signal if something was wrong."

"Phew! Brilliant!" exclaimed Dorothy with relief. "It's just that she's so weird. I don't want to be with her in a strange place."

She decided she'd take up the offer on that basis. "It can't do any harm," she said, "and I'd be learning something really useful for when I get a job."

"Don't trust her!" snapped Miss Marilyn. They all stared at her, but she gave no explanation.

"Do you know her, dear?" asked Miss Clements.

"No," replied Miss Marilyn abruptly, "but I've got eyes in my head. I'd put my faith in Lucifer himself before I'd trust that woman!"

"I thought she seemed very pleasant," murmured Miss Clements. "You really should try and look for the good in people Marilyn dear. Pre-judgment is such a horrid thing, is it not?"

Miss Marilyn snorted, and Dorothy changed the subject.

"I'm going to do my swotting over the holiday," she said. "If I can just pass maths and English this summer I'll be able to get a job when the trials are over. I'll be seventeen in September."

Miss Clements's normally bland expression gave a flicker of surprise.

"Why should you want to get a job so soon, dear? You must think of your education and go to college if you want a really good job, a clever girl like you."

"I'll catch up on it while I'm working," said Dorothy. "Lots of people do. If I get a job, I can support the others while they get an education, and when they have good jobs I'll get on with my own education and get a better job. Then, we'll be able to save enough for our house. It's our three-step housing plan. Step one, job; step two, education; step three, house. And then we'll be safe."

As soon as she finished speaking she remembered she was supposed to be careful what she said in front of Miss Clements – and anyone else for that matter. The trouble was that they had become so used to her they were beginning to trust her. Though, as David had once pointed out, it wasn't so much that she couldn't be trusted, but that she was unreliable, unless, of course, it was something to do with food.

"That's a very long-term plan," murmured Miss Clements. "So that's what you children intend to do! Well, I'm full of admiration, though I'm sorry that you don't feel safe in this house. Dear me, we don't know the half of what's going on in people's minds."

"Just as well," snapped Miss Marilyn.

Miss Clements pushed back her chair and stood up. "Now, I've got to rush, dears. The Women's Institute is meeting tonight, and after that I'm going to my friend Mary's house for a bit of a chat, so I'll be late back. She's the registrar for all the weddings, and it's so interesting to hear about the strange ceremonies people ask for. Would you be kind and clear up for me, and put the dishes in the machine and lay for breakfast. Not you Marilyn, of course. The children can manage. It would be such a help."

Having to rush did not mean the same thing to Miss Clements as it did for other people. She puffed upstairs. The dishes had been cleared and the breakfast things laid before she reappeared. She put on her coat, and then popped into the kitchen to check that she'd remembered to take a steak and kidney pie out of the freezer.

"Right, I'm off," she said at last. "And I'll probably have a lie-in in the morning, because late nights don't suit me, so you may have to make your own breakfasts."

★

In her flat on the sea front, Isobel sat thinking and staring out at the sea. What an interesting visit that had been. She had no doubt that the girl was the Dorothy they were looking for, but there were only three children not four. If the missing one was Copse's daughter, she should be back from Thomas's trial by now. The little boy could well be Paul, but he was of no interest to her until she'd found the right David. And, although the older boy had the right name and blue eyes, he had the wrong hair. He certainly didn't fit the description of handsome either. His skin had a grey unhealthy pallor to it, and although she never liked to be unkind, she really would have described him as ugly.

It was time to report her day's activities to the holy leaders. Typing into her laptop in code, she told them of her plan to persuade Dorothy to come to her flat, and asked them to send down two abduction agents, to be available when needed. When she had finished her report and closed the laptop down, she picked up her mobile phone and rang Drax. There was no response. She left a message for him to contact her and went downstairs to the restaurant below. It was busy and noisy, despite this being a weeknight and dreadful weather.

There was a small table near the window, looking out across the promenade to the sea. A nice spot if one liked that sort of thing. She grimaced inwardly at the menu and ordered an omelette with salad. While she was waiting, her mind wandered to the tempting thought of joining Drax abroad. Not that she was keen on having to put up with him, but she would if she had to, and she liked the idea of living in a warm country. They both had enough funds stashed away to keep them in luxury forever. But she would miss London and she would miss her work. There was so much she could still do to help the Holy Cause through this difficult time, and she would be ready for high recognition once it was back on its feet.

Like Drax, she had no difficulty in reconciling her love of good things with the Magnifico's strict ban on comfort. Of course it was a sin to indulge, but Isobel was confident that her soul would be saved because of her unflagging devotion to her duties. There were few Good Doctors in the Magnifico's service who could perform a disposal as painlessly as she could – and with such a kindly and gentle manner about her – or who could deliver a new-born baby and assess its worth reliably, and take the responsible decision as to whether it should live or die.

She knew she had all the right qualities to serve the Magnifico, but prided herself on one above all others. She had no compassion. That was her secret to success. Drax was her equal in that respect – though not in other ways, of course.

The sea was pounding over the wall of the promenade, hurling spray against the window. What a ghastly place to live! One would have to wear hideous windproof clothes like anoraks and woolly hats. She looked around her. All these locals chattering and laughing grated on her nerves. A thought struck her. This would be the ideal place to set up a mission base. Virtually the entire population would be ripe for either conversion or disposal. What an opportunity! She would discuss it with the holy leaders when she got back to civilisation. If it weren't for the sea and the gulls, and so on, she wouldn't mind being one of the missionaries herself for a while. Her spirits lifted.

She finished her meal and, leaving a tip, crossed over to the counter to pay the bill.

"That was delicious!" she purred with her charming smile. "Thank you so much."

The man at the till felt warm all over. What a lovely woman!

★

As soon as Isobel was back in the flat, Drax rang. Her first words were sharp. "Where on earth have you been?"

"I couldn't stand it any longer," he said, "so I went to the cinema."

"Flaming flesh! Not again?" She threw her bag down on the sofa and kicked off her shoes. "You couldn't have gone more public! Are you asking to be caught or what?"

"I don't like to hear you swear," said Drax reprovingly. "It was OK. I wore the hat. I put some of your eye shadow under my eyes and concealer on my mouth, so I looked really ill." He was gazing into a small hand mirror as he spoke. "I looked almost ugly, not like me at all."

She laughed at his vanity, and then was immediately struck by the obvious.

"Holy Magnifico! How could I have missed what was staring me in the face," she exclaimed. "There's an ugly boy here called David!"

"Well, then, it can't be the real David. He's not ugly. In fact, he's remarkably handsome. He's very like me except his hair's lighter."

"It's the hair that could have fooled me." Isobel spoke slowly. She was trying to picture what the gaunt, pallid schoolboy would look like with ash-blond hair.

Drax studied his own hair in the mirror and smoothed it back – his crowning glory, if one could apply that to a man. Did he spot a streak of grey? No. What a relief! Even Copse's lustrous black locks couldn't compare to these golden waves.

"Are you listening?" called Isobel.

"Of course, my darling. I've been longing to hear your voice all day."

"He's about the right age," continued Isobel, "and lives with the same foster mother as Dorothy, but he's got black hair, and looks ill and sinister. He's certainly not the blond young Adonis we're supposed to be looking out for. I don't know why I didn't think of it sooner, but he could have dyed his hair."

Drax was only half-listening. He was savouring the thought that the son and daughter who had betrayed him might soon be brought to justice. It made him extraordinarily happy. He placed the mirror on the coffee table and threw himself comfortably down in an armchair.

"Do you love me?" he whispered down the phone.

"Oh, for the Mag's sake!" she snapped. "I've got other things to think of at this moment." She stepped over to the window and closed the curtains. The booming of the waves was unsettling. It made her irritable.

Drax studied his long, tapering fingers and blew on his nails to buff them up a little. He wished he could have brought his piano here. It would have been soothing to see those elegant fingers dancing gracefully over the keys. So therapeutic!

"You sound as though things might not be going too well for you," he said eventually.

"Sorry," she said, shifting her bag off the sofa and lying down. "It'll be alright. I've got a plan, and if it works, we'll be fine. If it doesn't, I'll think of something else."

She had never liked the sea. It was ominous and uncontrollable. The constant pounding and frothing of the waves and the screeching of the seagulls had given her a headache. The traffic noise of the Cromwell Road rumbled down through the phone and she could almost smell the exhaust fumes. Delicious! She longed for London. Traffic could be controlled and the sea could not. This place gave her bad vibes.

"Tomorrow, I'm going to try and arrange to have Dorothy in my flat for coaching in computers," she said wearily. "I can tell she's not keen, but I'm hoping a powerful onslaught of charm will put her mind to rest. If she agrees to come, the abductors will have an easy job. Otherwise I'll have to get her some other way. I've briefly met the foster mother, and there's something about her that makes me suspect a weakness. I'm not sure what it might be."

"The most usual one is money."

"I was thinking the same, but I'd have to assess her a bit more before I could risk that one. As for the boy, I'll be looking at the top of his head in class tomorrow to see if there are any ash-blond roots showing through, and maybe all will be revealed."

She blew a kiss down the phone, rang off and closed her eyes. What a prize if she could get David as well as Dorothy!

*

On the Wednesday morning, Gwen Jones arrived late and out of breath. Dorothy and David had already left for

125

school, and Paul was on his own in the sitting room with his drawing book. Miss Clements answered the front door in her dressing gown, and Gwen was full of apologies.

"I'm so sorry!" she gasped. "Evan had one of his night terrors and it's put everything late. I had to use one of his tranquilising syringes, which I never do if I can avoid it."

"Don't worry dear," said Miss Clements soothingly. "I've only just got up myself. A late night, you know. The children got their own breakfast."

"I'll apologise to his teacher." Gwen bent down to push Paul's arms through his coat sleeves. "Did you see? That computer teacher from the school? It was on the news. They found his body just down the coast from here."

"Oh, my goodness!" Miss Clements was truly shocked. "Was it that nice Mr Owen? He's been missing since Monday."

"Yes, I think that was the name. Terrible! They're suggesting it was suicide – threw himself off a cliff!"

Gwen reminded herself she was in too much of a rush to get caught up in conversation.

"I wanted to ask you, though I'm short of time now, but would it be alright if I were to take Paul home with me after school to stay the night on Friday, just for the weekend, until Lucy comes back?" She hardly dared hope for a positive answer. "My husband thinks I'm looking after him for a neighbour and he's taken quite a fancy to him," she said hurriedly. "Just for two nights, that is if the authorities will allow it. And of course I'd make sure that Evan took his bed-time sedation."

Miss Clements was only too glad to push any talk of suicide out of the way.

126

"Well, I know Lucy's got some more meetings with the lawyers, so she might not be back till Monday or Tuesday. I don't see that a couple of nights' visit with his own grandparents over the weekend would be forbidden, Mrs Jones. He has been very anxious about Lucy, humming a lot you know, and fiddling with that gold chain round his neck. David or Dorothy can get his overnight bag ready for you to take when you pick him up for school on Friday morning."

Gwen's voice cracked. "Thank you," she said. Her eyes filled tears. "You can't imagine how wonderful it is to have something of Maria back in the house again."

Miss Clements took her two hands in hers, hoping fervently that the moment wouldn't develop into anything too distressing. "May he bring joy to your hearts. Bless you, my dear," she murmured.

CHAPTER ELEVEN

Lucy and Beverley attended Mr Lovett's office at ten o'clock on the Wednesday, as arranged. Mr Lovett ushered them into his room. He introduced them to another man who was already seated in one of the leather armchairs, and whose name Lucy immediately forgot. Beverley sat down in a corner and hoped this wouldn't take too long. Thank God it was an early appointment. She was feeling quite peaky.

"This is the young lady the judge praised for her extraordinary courage," Mr Lovett told the other man, waving his hand towards Lucy.

He spoke to Lucy in his kindly but rather pompous manner. She gave him a weak smile, but wished it could all be over. The room had become familiar to her after many meetings with Mr Lovett, but she still glanced warily around as she sat down. The walls were lined with books. Everything was brown – the carpet, the curtains and the leather chairs. Even the backs of the books were brown. *The colour of security dear*, Miss Clements would have said, thought Lucy.

Mr Lovett sat facing her from behind his massive desk. He shuffled through a pile of papers, took out a cardboard sheet of photographs, and set it to one side. Lucy briefly wondered if he had a photo of her and David. He shuffled a bit more, found what he was looking for, and handed it over to the other man. Then, they both started putting questions about Father Copse. It was tedious. Lucy had been through all this many times before.

She answered patiently, gave explanations, and reiterated what she had already told them over and over again. What a waste of time! The police had taken statements months ago, and she had described in detail her life in Father Copse's house. Now she just wanted to get back to Paul. Then they started questioning her about Father Drax but, although she had often visited his commune for prayer meetings, there was little she could tell them about him as a person. They would have to ask David and Dorothy.

At last, they seemed to have all the information she was able to give them, and they stood up to leave the room.

"Stay where you are, there's a good little lady," said Mr Lovett. "We've just got to sort out some documentation." Lucy wondered if it would have sounded less patronising if he'd said, "good young woman," and decided that it wouldn't. It didn't really matter. He was trying to be nice.

Beverly got to her feet, looking very pale. "I'll just get a breath of fresh air," she said.

As soon as the door had closed, Lucy stood up from the squishy leather armchair and stretched her legs. She looked at the backs of the books. They didn't mean anything to her, and nor did the papers on the desk. There was nothing interesting as far as she could see, apart from the sheet of photographs lying to the right of where Mr Lovett had been sitting.

She studied the photos. A quick glance told her that David and she weren't on it, but she recognised Father

Drax straight away, with his yellow hair and handsome, cruel face. There were two women she recognised as aunts from the Drax commune and some others whom she didn't know. When she reached the bottom picture – the last on the page – something twisted inside her, just below her ribs. She knew that face! No, she didn't. She frowned. There was something about it, but she didn't know what. She stared down at piercing blue eyes and a porcelain complexion framed by smooth, shining, silver-blonde hair. Underneath was written, "Isobel Drax, wife No. 8."

By the time Mr Lovett returned, she was back in the leather chair, and he already had his mind on other things. "Good girl. I hope we didn't take too long. You may go now," he said, picking up another file from his desk and flicking through it. "Back tomorrow at two, please. I've told Beverley." His phone rang and he waved her out of the room.

★

"Who is wife number eight?" asked Lucy, as they stepped out into the rain.

"Don't speak to me," groaned Beverley, clutching her stomach. They swerved past a group of black-clad barristers and almost tripped over a homeless man in a wet sleeping bag. Lucy hardly noticed any of them. Who on earth was wife number eight? She'd seen most of Drax's wives at one time or another, when the communes met up for prayer meetings, and she would surely have noticed that silver hair.

By the time they reached the hotel, Beverley was almost bent double. "I must lie down," she moaned. "It's the breakfast – that black pudding."

Lucy's heart sank. They would never get back to Wales if Beverley was ill. She pulled herself together. How selfish could she be!

"Can I do anything for you? Shall I get reception to send a doctor?" she asked.

"No, but thanks." Beverley pressed the lift button. "It'll pass." She groaned again. "Just don't you go anywhere. Don't leave your room." She fished a plastic carrier bag out of her pocket. "My God! I thought I'd throw up in Lovett's office."

They reached their floor and Beverley staggered along the corridor, holding the plastic bag open in front of her face. "You'll have to order room service," she gasped, as she unlocked her door with shaking hands. "There's a menu and a phone number. I'll ring old Lovett."

Lucy went back to her room. She dragged the armchair from its corner and pushed it up against the door. The face of the eighth wife swam before her eyes. It was no one she knew, so why was it familiar?

She sat on the bed and picked up the menu. It was too early for lunch, but there was no harm in choosing what to have. Such sophistication! She couldn't wait to tell the others about it. They'd all be at school now, but perhaps she could ring them later on the room phone. It was stupid that she didn't know David's mobile number. There had been no point before, because they were always together. Suddenly, she longed to speak to him, not only about the photo and the room service, but just to hear his voice. She felt terribly homesick – if that was the right word when you didn't really have a home.

The phone rang and she jumped. It was Mr Lovett.

"Everything alright there?" he boomed heartily. "It looks as though Beverley's going to be out of action for at least one more day, so I'm afraid you'll have to stay in your room for your own safety. Have you got a good book to read?" He didn't wait for an answer. "I'm sending someone round to escort you for tomorrow's appointment. Her name's Margaret. I've used her as a temporary escort on many occasions, and she's absolutely reliable." He laughed. "If anyone will keep abductors away, it's Margaret."

"OK," said Lucy rather doubtfully. "Where shall I meet her?"

"She'll knock on your door at 10 o'clock tomorrow morning – make sure you order breakfast in your room – and she'll show you her identification. Your appointment is at two, and she'll escort you here and back. Don't discuss our business with her. She'll stay with you for the rest of the day, take you shopping or to a film or something and then, if Beverley's still not well enough on Friday, she'll escort you back to Wales."

Friday? Day after tomorrow! Lucy's heart leaped. She'd been told she'd be here till next week.

"Next week's appointment has been cancelled. I've had an urgent call up to the North of England. Something about a Father Arthur, so I might ask you about that tomorrow."

Lucy didn't know anything about a Father Arthur, but she didn't care. She was too elated. How many hours before she saw the others? Forty-eight, no, forty-nine.

"I've just rung Miss Clements," continued Mr Lovett, "and told her you'll be back about lunchtime on Friday. See you tomorrow. And, remember, don't leave your room till Margaret arrives."

A soon as he'd rung off, Lucy checked the time on the alarm radio next to the bed. It was twelve o'clock. Paul would be in playtime at this very moment. Just picturing him brought a smile to her face. David would be in double maths, and Dorothy would be about to go to her computer class. Mr Owen might be back by now, instead of that creepy woman.

What on earth was it that made her creepy? She tried to picture Miss Morris's face.

Lucy had only met her once and hadn't looked at her properly after the first polite good morning. In fact, she had made a conscious effort to avoid that piercing gaze. But one thing was certain – Miss Morris had wavy, auburn hair, rosy cheeks and a soft voice, and if it hadn't been for the icicle eyes she would have seemed warm and cosy. She wasn't remotely like the woman in the photograph with her shining, silver bob and not a hint of roses in her cheeks.

So why this feeling? Lucy tried to visualise the actual features of the face in the photo. If she had a chance, she'd look at it again tomorrow. In fact, she'd ask Mr Lovett if she could see the photo sheet. She picked up a book and tried to read. A minute later she jumped up and pulled the armchair away from the door.

Down in the foyer she approached the reception desk, and asked the way to a cyber café.

"I don't think there is cyber café around here," said the receptionist. "But there's a computer for guests in that little room over there. You have to pay a pound and I give you a code for security."

Lucy sat down in a booth and stared at the screen and tried to think. Whether it was Mr Owen or Miss Morris, there was always a risk that the teacher would read any email that arrived during class time. It had to be in code. She tapped in Dorothy's address and stopped. First, she had to alert her, to show this wasn't just a fun thing.

At last, she typed rapidly: "Two things: A. *Bore da!* B. Wear new T-shir." Dorothy would surely query why the "t" was missing. She pressed 'send'. David's lesson was at three o'clock. Lucy typed in his email address and sent the same message all over again.

CHAPTER TWELVE

"What on earth's that supposed to mean?" Miss Morris laughed softly as she leaned over Dorothy's shoulder.

Dorothy thought quickly. She had recognised the alert code straight away. "The *'bore da'* means 'good morning'. I think it must be from my friend Izzy because of the T-shirt bit."

"Is that Izzy's email address?"

"I don't know. We've never messaged each other before."

Miss Morris's voice was like honey. "Well, I suggest you delete it. If there's ever anything odd about an email or you're not sure where it's come from, get rid of it. If it was Izzy, then we have her to thank for an important lesson."

Dorothy pressed 'delete'. She'd bring the message back as soon as Miss Morris moved away. Unfortunately, Miss Morris didn't move away. She hovered between Dorothy and the people on each side of her throughout most of the lesson. Never mind. Dorothy knew the "*bore da"* bit was a warning, and she would remember the bit about wearing a new T-shirt. She and David would work it out later. The important thing was that, for now, she had to be super vigilant of everyone and everything.

When the lesson ended, she waited till most of the other pupils had erupted into the corridor, free at last to exclaim and speculate about Mr Owen's death. She had been horrified to find the school buzzing with the news that morning, and had an uncomfortable feeling that there was more to it than just jumping off a cliff. After all, how had the school managed to get hold of a supply teacher so soon after he disappeared? He had been here only last Friday, and Miss Morris had turned up on Monday. Was she being over-suspicious?

She breathed deeply as she approached Miss Morris, and tried to appear calm and collected. It was important to keep a clear head. This was going to be a test.

"Miss Clements suggested that I might have my extra tuition in her house," she said, "so as not to intrude on your private arrangements." She studied Miss Morris's face carefully. It was impassive.

"That's so considerate of her. I must remember to thank her. However, I have some very good equipment at the flat, and I would be able to explain so much more to you than if I were simply to bring a laptop to the house."

"Very well, then. Thank you for your offer." Dorothy's heart was thumping. "Perhaps we could arrange something for after my exams. I've got so much revision, I don't see how I can fit it in at the moment."

"I may not be here after the exams," said Isobel. "Remember, I'm only a supply teacher."

"I'll have to leave it in that case," said Dorothy as firmly as she could, "but thank you so much. Excuse me, but I must rush." She grabbed her bag and left.

Isobel was now pretty certain that the girl suspected something, and that made things difficult. It might be best to hold back for a couple of days or to think of an alternative plan. She checked her watch. It was time for the lunch break, and she didn't have a class till three o'clock. The email message could wait till later. She'd call it up and check the sender's address as soon as she came back. She put on her coat, closed the classroom door and made her way down the hill to the big house. If she was lucky Miss Clements would be at home alone. There would be no point talking to that lemon-faced half-wit who'd been lurking on the landing last night.

Miss Clements was at home and Miss Marilyn was out. Good, thought Isobel, as she was ushered into the dining room.

"I'll have to get back to school by quarter to three," she said. "I do hope I'm not disturbing you in your lunch break, but there's so little time during the day to talk quietly and sensibly with you about the children."

"You're not disturbing me at all, dear. My sister's gone to the library, and I rarely eat in the middle of the day, except at weekends when the children are here. It makes one so sleepy, don't you think? Do sit down. This room's not very comfortable, but the children didn't clear up their sitting room very well last night, so it's a bit messy in there. They'll have to see to it when they get back, because I do try to encourage them to be unselfish and not rely on others to do everything for them."

Having been brought up in one of the communes herself, Isobel was well aware that if these were the children she was looking for, they would never have relied on others to do anything for them. The aunts would have brought them up to follow a strict regime of chores, and they would have had little opportunity to be selfish. Weakness number one, she thought: takes money for looking after these children, but won't put herself out for them.

She sat down in a straight-backed chair next to the table. "As you know, I've suggested to Dorothy that I give her free tuition, but she has declined."

"Ah, foolish girl! If only these young people could appreciate the value of education," said Miss Clements, forgetting for a moment her admiration of the three-step housing plan. "I was never clever enough to take advantage of schooling, but fortunately I had a talent for cooking and that's given me a livelihood."

"And a very worthwhile livelihood it is, Miss Clements, "taking the place of a mother for children in need of a good home."

Miss Clements wondered if she seemed rude, standing while her visitor was sitting, but she really did want to get back to her kitchen before the pastry cooked hard.

"Yes," she said, "and these children are no trouble. They're well behaved and polite, and appreciate my cooking, but it's not always like that, I can assure you. Some of the children I foster are extremely uncomfortable to have around, and all they want is chips."

"I know from my teaching experience how difficult some children can be," murmured Miss Morris soothingly, "but to have them in your home and give them the love and attention that they need – you must have some very special qualities."

"It's not easy, but it won't be forever, I hope." Miss Clements sniffed the air and wondered if she could smell burning. "My sister and I intend to live abroad when we're in a financial position to do so. That's the beauty of cooking, you know. You can do it anywhere in the world."

Weakness number two, thought Isobel: they had a plan, and needed money to carry it out.

"I had been thinking of helping out the boy, David, as well as Dorothy," she said. "He's got quite a good knowledge of computing skills, but something seems to be holding him back a little. I wondered if you could tell me anything about David's background that would help me to help him."

Miss Marilyn's Lucifer comment suddenly popped into Miss Clements's mind, and alarm bells began to compete with the call of the pastry.

"I'm sorry, Miss Morris," she said rather coldly, "but the background details of children in my care, including Dorothy and her half-brother, always have to be totally confidential. The school is aware that they have had a different education from the sort our more fortunate children in Wales are used to, and, of course, they may need encouragement in some subjects, but I can't say more than that."

Isobel smiled to herself. So David was Dorothy's half-brother! She mentally thanked Miss Clements for that information. That was really all she needed for the next step.

"Of course. You are quite right to respect their confidentiality. Would it help you if I were to tell you that they have a very rich father who loves them dearly and is longing to have them back?"

"All I know is that their father may be living abroad, and that there's been a court case about a gardener who burned a house down," said Miss Clements. "It's been in all the papers. As to what's happened to their mother or mothers, I've no idea. I never pry, you know."

"Their father would be in a position to pay handsomely for the return of his children."

"Is that so, Miss Morris?" Miss Clements nodded her head slightly towards the door. "Now, if you'll excuse me, I'll have to get back to the kitchen. I've got some tarts in the oven and I have to stuff six chicken Kievs for tonight's meal."

Miss Morris stayed put. "The children were caught up somehow in that dreadful court case. It has nothing to do with their father, and his heart is breaking for them," she said sadly. "He would reward you well if you could help him see them again."

"I would be in severe trouble with the authorities if I were to lose sight of those children. Responsibility for children like that is my livelihood. I'd never get work again."

"I wonder if a hundred thousand pounds per child would help?"

"Certainly not!" Miss Clements was outraged, and it was a most uncomfortable feeling. "I am a woman of integrity!" She paused for a moment wondering what she should do or say next. "I'll have to report your visit to the police, and to the school, and to the authorities. And I'll have to send the children back to London."

Isobel rose. "Well, before you do, think about half a million – a quarter for Dorothy and a quarter for David."

"Never!" said Miss Clements, but her heart missed a beat. Something flickered in her face, which did not go unnoticed. She held the door open with affronted dignity, and Isobel left.

"I'll come back tomorrow at the same time," she said.

Miss Clements shut the front door and leaned against it. Her face was burning hot. She must ring the school straight away to send the children home. She wished she'd asked where the woman was staying. The police would need to know, so they could trap her when she came back tomorrow. Supposing the father stole the children in the meantime? Or supposing the police didn't come and the woman came back tomorrow, and somehow or other her offer was accepted?

She nearly swooned with the shock of such a thought, but, as she reached out for the phone, it was enough to make her withdraw her hand. She'd have to ring that Mr Lovett. Beverley had told her she mustn't ring the local police. There was a reason. Had she said they were full of spies? Miss Clements couldn't remember. Where on earth had she put Mr Lovett's phone number? It was in a safe place. He'd rung her this very morning about something, but whatever it was it had gone completely out of her mind. If only he'd waited till after this woman had been! She could have told him all about it, and taken his number. She'd have a cup of tea now, and when the shock in her head had died down, she might remember where it was.

Marilyn wouldn't be back until the library closed. A vision of the little cottage on the Greek island was trying to dance across Miss Clements's mind. She pushed it away, almost breathless, as the enormity of the thought hit her – trading children to a man whom she knew to be sought by police.

She cut herself a piece of last night's pudding – lemon meringue pie – to help calm her nerves. No wonder Marilyn was so thin. She couldn't appreciate a piece of fine baking. The cottage on the Greek island did its little dance again. There would be a lovely kitchen, with glowing copper pots on the walls, and rustic shelves full of herbs and spices. Maybe she'd have to adjust to foreign stoves, but she'd always been a quick learner where cooking was concerned.

141

The doorbell rang. It was Mr Nicholas, the boiler man. She let him in and tried to put off thinking until after he'd gone. And what with offering him another piece of cherry cake to go with his second cup of tea, and preparing supper, and listening to Paul's chatter when he came in from school, there was no time to sit quietly and put her mind in order.

When Dorothy and David burst in through the back door, Paul was sitting at the kitchen table eating cherry cake and putting the final touches to a portrait of Miss Wyn Lloyd.

"Miss Morris didn't turn up for my class this afternoon," said David helping himself to cake. "We had to practise on the computers on our own, and guess what? There was an email from Lucy. It didn't make sense. I printed it out." He fished a piece of paper out of his pocket.

Miss Clements was moving around the kitchen, opening and shutting cupboards, and rummaging through drawers. She didn't seem to be listening. Even so, Dorothy gave David a warning look, and he hastily stuffed the paper into his school bag.

"I don't want you two to go to school tomorrow," announced Miss Clements suddenly. "Just Paul." She lifted the lid of the bread bin and looked inside, and then turned to pop a tray of chicken Kievs in the oven.

The children stared at her in surprise. They had never heard her speak firmly before, except about punctuality at mealtimes.

"You're both to stay indoors – upstairs, in fact. You're not to come downstairs without my permission. Paul, you'll be going back to Mrs Jones's house on Friday when she picks you up from school. She's invited you to stay there till Lucy comes back from London."

Dorothy and David both felt a stab of fear, but Paul looked pleased.

"I like going there," he said. "Mrs Jones loves me she said, and there's man called Mr Jones who's very nice but he hates frogs." His face suddenly fell. He fingered the gold circle on his neck. "But I want my Lucy back."

"She'll be back soon, dear," said Miss Clements soothingly. "You'll be surprised how quickly the time will pass when you're with Mrs Jones."

"Has something happened?" asked David.

"It's that Miss Morris. She makes me nervous," said Miss Clements. "She came here today, and was much too pushy. I'd feel more comfortable if you were to stay out of sight for a few days. You can use the front room upstairs with the balcony, and I'll serve your meals up there. There are plenty of books to read and the TV, and Dorothy can get on with her revision. If she comes again, I'll tell her you're in London."

As soon as they had closed the upstairs sitting room door behind them, Dorothy and David looked at each other.

"Lucy's email!" said David. He scrabbled around in his school bag and found the printout.

Paul tried to take it from him. "It's from Lucy. Let me see, let me see."

"Don't snatch!" said David. "You won't understand it anyway, because I don't. I'll read it out. This is what it says." He read slowly. "'Two things: A. *Bore da!* B. Wear new T-shir.'"

They digested it in silence. He read it again.

Dorothy nodded. "I had exactly the same message. The *"bore da"* is obviously an alert. It's the rest of it. We haven't got any new T-shirts. What on earth's she on about?"

Paul was humming. He put the lid on his drawing materials. The pencils and crayons had all been counted and everything was neat and tidy. The hum turned into a song.

"'B. Wear new T-shir' – beware new teacher," he sang. "Beware of the dog. Beware the wicked witch. Beware the Prince of Darkness." He stopped for a moment and looked anxious, then started again. "I want my Lucy," he sang, fingering the gold circle on his neck. "Beware, beware, beware."

Dorothy and David stared at him.

"Of course!" exclaimed David.

The phone rang twice that evening, but they couldn't hear it from upstairs, and Miss Clements was afraid to answer it in case it was that woman.

★

Margaret turned up at ten o'clock sharp on the Thursday morning. She flashed her identification so fast that Lucy had to ask her to show it again. There was her photograph sure enough, iron-grey hair in a hard perm and an expression so sharp it could have cut Lucy in half.

The two of them spent a tedious morning in the hotel lounge. Lucy would never have expected to long for Beverley's chatter, but she did. "Do you know how Beverley is?" she ventured.

"No idea," said Margaret.

She sat in stony silence and her hawk-like eyes flashed in all directions. No wonder Mr Lovett had said abductors wouldn't stand a chance, thought Lucy. Margaret would see them coming before they knew it

144

themselves. If it was Beverley she'd be so busy talking she'd miss an army of abductors.

Lucy had a book, but she was too worried to concentrate. No one had answered the phone when she rang last night. She'd tried twice. Maybe they were upstairs, in which case, they wouldn't have heard it. But Miss Clements should have heard it from the kitchen, unless she was too focused on her cooking. Supposing they hadn't deciphered her email? She knew they'd work it out in due course, because their minds operated as hers did, but what if it took them too long? They could have been abducted by now, and she hadn't been there to help them.

They had an uncomfortable bar lunch, and then set off for their two o'clock appointment with Mr Lovett. It didn't take long. He asked her whether she knew anything about a disposal centre outside Manchester, which she didn't, and did she know that the Father Arthur in the North of England had, in fact, been her own father – Father Copse – under an assumed name. She hadn't known that either, so at least it was something new. At last, the meeting seemed to be drawing to an end, and she asked if she could look at the sheet of photographs.

She stared at the picture of wife number eight. If only Paul were here, he'd be able to spot differences or likenesses straight away. Lucy put her hand over the hair and tried to imagine it as reddish, and thick and wavy, but that didn't help. The skin looked much finer than Miss Morris's. Make-up on such fine skin would look almost clown-like, which Miss Morris's rosy cheeks were certainly not.

So her suspicions had been wrong. And, looking at the picture now, she didn't even have the same feeling about it. Well, never mind, it was an enormous relief. She'd been worrying about the others for nothing, and just hoped her email hadn't frightened them.

The meeting ended in a rush, as Mr Lovett remembered he had a train to catch, and Lucy and Margaret set off for the hotel. As they emerged from the tube station, Lucy stopped and looked around. There were so many people it was impossible to imagine how London could sustain them all. It would be easy to disappear among them, especially in this rain with hoods and umbrellas adding to the confusion. She stood for moment and studied the buses. At least two of them were going to Victoria.

Margaret grabbed her arm. "Don't even think it!" she snapped.

There was no need. She'd be going home tomorrow.

CHAPTER THIRTEEN

"I notice I haven't been arrested yet," said Miss Morris, as she walked straight into the dining room, "so you obviously had the good sense not to call the police – though, of course, I did have to leave my flat rather hurriedly, and my work at the school, just in case." She removed her sunglasses and a charming, little red cloche hat, and shook out her red-gold hair. "I felt a bit silly in these sunglasses in this weather. Is it always like this in Wales?"

"According to the weatherman, it's raining in London at this moment," said Miss Clements coldly.

Miss Morris put the briefcase on the table and opened the lid. It was packed with notes. "Half a million," she said. "I've got a driver outside. Would you please go and tell Dorothy and David they're to go to London immediately on urgent business with the lawyers?"

"I can't. They're not here. They had to go back to London." Miss Clements strained to catch any sound from upstairs – footsteps, a book falling or a door opening? All was quiet.

"I'm afraid I don't believe you. We've been watching the house. Their father won't be pleased if he doesn't get them back. He can get quite fierce when he's angry." Miss Morris looked around the pleasantly furnished dining room. "It'd be such a shame if all this were destroyed, when you could so easily have made things comfortable for yourself and your sister. Just think of what all that money could do for you."

Miss Clements was shaking. She tried not to look at the money, but her eyes seemed to have a mind of their own.

"I tell you what," said Miss Morris. "You have them here tomorrow morning by ten o'clock sharp. Father Drax doesn't want the little boy, only his own children – and Lucy Copse if she's here. Tell them they're needed in London to make statements. Your livelihood won't be at risk, if that's what worries you, because you'll say somebody rang from London and gave you instructions, and you thought they were official."

With a delicate gesture, she placed one hand lightly on top of the stack of bank notes. "Even if you were to lose the work, you needn't worry, because you'd have half a million staring you in the face. I shall leave this briefcase here, so you can look at it now and then, and think about what all that money could do for you."

Miss Clements's eyes shifted involuntarily to the briefcase. "Don't talk such rubbish. I'll do no such thing. Take it away."

"Then why haven't you called the police? Why haven't I been arrested? Of course you'll take the money, and I'll take the children."

Miss Morris studied the round, anxious face carefully. She could see the flush, and noticed the difficulty in breathing.

"Come now," she said gently. "You've worked hard all your life. You don't really like children very much. I can see behind that benign expression of yours. You've been stuck with looking after kids because it was the only thing you could do, and for years you've been putting on a kindly face to hide the tedium you really feel about the whole thing. Once these exceptionally nice children have moved on, you'll be back to making chips with tomato sauce for future criminals." She gave a little laugh. "I must say, I may be a lot cleverer than you, but you've beaten me on that. I could never look after children. I can't stand them."

Miss Clements grabbed the edge of the table. She thought she would pass out. How did this woman, whom she had only met twice, know how she felt? Did those piercing, blue eyes penetrate her very mind and soul? She longed for peace and freedom, and middle age was almost upon her. There was so little time to live a life for herself. Suddenly, she felt powerless under this woman's gaze. Was this what hypnotism felt like? No, it couldn't be that. Not if she was wide awake and a woman of principle. She straightened her back, and the colour drained from her face.

"I'll do it," she whispered.

Miss Morris closed the briefcase, and pushed it towards her.

"Happy retirement," she said. "Ten o'clock sharp. Don't keep us waiting. There are double yellow lines outside." She put the little red hat back on her head. "I won't need the sunglasses. It's getting dark already, with all these black clouds. Such a dismal place. It's a shame to have to leave this lovely, comfortable room. Oh, and as we have a deal now, I must warn you. I'm sure you're an honourable woman and take pride in keeping your word, but if you do let us down, you and your sister will be in the gravest possible danger."

She held out her hand, but it was ignored. Picking up her bag, she gave the hat a little tweak and made for the front door.

"By the way," she said, "our agents have infiltrated your local police, so it's just as well you didn't ring them."

She smiled to herself. Miss Clements was not to know that was untrue. There simply weren't enough agents to go round these days.

As Miss Morris let herself out, the blood rushed to Miss Clements's head, and there was a searing pain across her forehead. A band of black swept over her eyes and blinded her. She felt her way over to the nearest chair and sat down to wait for it to pass. Ten minutes or more went by before her vision cleared. She stood up shakily and looked at the briefcase.

The deal was done now, and, if those threats were real, there was no going back. She had no experience of what people like this might do if they were double-crossed, but she guessed it would be something pretty horrible. Her peaceful life was in fragments, and she felt ill, not just for herself but for Marilyn – and those poor children! With the briefcase in one hand and the other clutching at the wall, then a chair and then the newel post of the stairs, she tottered across the hall to the kitchen.

*

When Marilyn arrived back from the library, she took one look at her sister and stopped dead in the middle of one of her grumbles.

"What on earth is the matter? You look dreadful. Did you forget your blood pressure pills?"

Miss Clements shook her head, unable to speak.

"Come and sit down quickly," said Miss Marilyn.

"I'll put a pack of frozen peas on your head."

She dashed to the freezer, and slapped a bag of peas on the top of her sister's head and spinach at the back of her neck.

Miss Clements slowly recovered her power of speech. She pointed to the briefcase that lay on the kitchen table. "Look in there," she said hoarsely.

Miss Marilyn opened the bag, and gasped. "What is it? Is it forged?"

"I've done a deal," wailed Miss Clements. "With that horrible woman with the ginger hair. That money is for us. The children will be picked up tomorrow at ten o'clock and taken to their father."

She put her head in her hands and howled. Donald looked up in surprise from his bed in the corner, turned himself round and went back to sleep.

"I don't know what came over me. She's got some dreadful hypnotic power. It was as if she could see right inside my mind. And, now, if I call the police or don't hand over the children, you and I are going to be murdered or tortured or buried in concrete – or whatever criminals do."

Miss Marilyn was now the one to feel faint. She plonked herself down on a chair and gaped open-mouthed at her sister. "You can't have said what I just thought you said."

"I did say it," groaned Miss Clements.

"You've sold the children back to those crazy religious lunatics? What on earth came over you? We don't need the money."

"It was the cottage. She somehow knew about the Greek cottage, and I've never told a soul – except you, of course."

"You could buy half a dozen cottages if you sold this house – or more. We don't want the money. It's filth." She stood up. "I'm going to call the police."

Miss Clements grabbed her arm. "Don't! They've been infiltrated. You don't know who you'll be talking to. It could be one of their spies. It'll be the end of us."

"I'd rather that than take money for delivering up those children." Miss Marilyn's voice was raised firmly above its usual whine. "Even if I can't bear them," she added.

"What is to become of us?" moaned Miss Clements, turning the peas and the spinach over onto to their cooler sides.

"What has already become of you, I'd like to know," snorted Miss Marilyn. "My ever-calm, ever-compassionate sister, to sacrifice children to the devil!"

At this point Miss Clements really did swoon. The spinach and peas slipped off with two wet thumps as she slid from her chair to the floor. Miss Marilyn made a valiant effort to lift her with her skinny arms, but couldn't. Her sister was fat and heavy. She slapped her face and tried to shake her, and eventually covered her up with a couple of kitchen towels and a dishcloth.

Her mind was racing in meaningless directions. She went to the cupboard and took out a loaf. There was cheese in the fridge and sliced ham. Huh! Processed. So much for home cooking! She buttered the bread and made four thick sandwiches, two ham and two cheese.

"What a fool!" she muttered to herself. "What a fool!" She put the sandwiches into two plastic boxes and filled two Tupperware mugs with milk. "That'll have to do," she said aloud.

Miss Clements stirred, but didn't open her eyes.

"Idiot!" snorted Miss Marilyn, as she stepped over her body to the drawer where they kept their passports. "Fool!"

She went upstairs, and packed two wheelie suitcases and put them by the front door. When supper time came at seven o'clock, she took up a tray to the children in the first-floor sitting room. They were staring at the television, fed up with their incarceration.

"It's last night's supper, cold," said Miss Marilyn, banging the tray down on a coffee table. "Miss Clements is ill, so you'll have to put up with it."

"Oh, dear!" said Dorothy. "Can we help? Is she very bad?"

"She brought it on herself. Cast your bread upon the waters and it'll come back to you," was the abrupt reply, and Miss Marilyn disappeared down the stairs.

★

When Miss Clements eventually started coming to, Miss Marilyn was sitting at the table checking the contents of the briefcase. She counted out two separate bundles of five hundred pounds, and put them into envelopes, which she attached to the sandwich boxes with elastic bands. Then she changed her mind.

"No, that's not right," she muttered. "I'd be tainting innocent children with the devil's filthy lucre."

She put it back in the briefcase and closed the lid and then burrowed around for cash in the housekeeping drawer. Her sister had paid Mr Nicholas for doing something to the boiler, and there was only ten pounds left. That man had double his wages in the cakes he ate.

"If this is all there is in the house, it'll have to do," she said aloud and put five pounds into each envelope. "It's better than nothing."

Miss Clements opened her eyes and rubbed her head. "What am I doing here?" she croaked. Then she remembered. "Oh, my God! What's to be done?" She grabbed hold of the table leg and pulled herself up to a sitting position.

"You fainted, that's all," said Miss Marilyn. "You deserve to drop dead in shame after what you've done, but you only fainted. I don't know why the Lord didn't strike you down." She put the kettle on. "You have a cup of tea now and something sweet to give you strength, and then get up to bed. I'll see to the children. We'll all be leaving first thing in the morning."

Miss Clements felt too unwell to protest. She had a cup of tea and one of her fruit buttermilk scones. They had come out really well, she thought. She must use that recipe again. Then she lumbered to her feet and, with her sister pushing her from behind, made her way up to her room on the first floor.

Miss Marilyn hurried back to the kitchen. She put the sandwich boxes, milk and money envelopes into two plastic carrier bags, and deposited them by the front door.

Paul was asleep when she went upstairs. His overnight bag had been packed ready for tomorrow. She took it downstairs and propped it against the wall next to the other bags, rang Gwen Jones, and then went back up to the upstairs sitting room. The scene was peaceful. Dorothy was curled up in an armchair, looking at the pictures in a recipe book Miss Clements had lent her. Her revision notes lay unopened on the coffee table. David sat cross-legged on the floor, poking a tiny screwdriver into the back of a broken clock.

Both youngsters looked up and smiled as Miss Marilyn entered. For a split second, she thought how nice it was when children smiled.

"How's Miss Clements?" asked Dorothy. "Is she any better?"

"Yes. She's recovered a little and she's gone to bed. Be very quiet when you go up to your rooms. You'd better go up soon and get some sleep, because you're going to have to leave very early, before it gets light."

The children stared at her. Their skin prickled.

"What's happened?" whispered Dorothy.

"It's that woman – that ginger Jezebel. You were right about her. She's laid a trap and she's coming for you at ten tomorrow to take you to your father."

There was a horrified silence and then they both jumped to their feet.

"We must go now, straight away," said David. "It'll be the abductors – the disposal agents. They won't wait till ten o'clock. They'll be watching the house all night. How do we get out of here?"

"We can't leave Paul!"

"He'll be alright," said Miss Marilyn. "I've rung Mrs Jones and told her to pick him up tonight because my sister's not well. His bag's ready in the hall. She should be here any minute."

As she spoke, the doorbell rang, and Dorothy dashed downstairs.

"I'm so sorry to hear about Miss Clements," said Gwen, as she came hurriedly into the hall. "I do hope it's nothing serious."

She followed Dorothy up to the top floor, where Paul lay fast asleep on his little bed under the window in Lucy's room. Dorothy shook him gently.

"Paul, wake up." He rubbed his eyes and asked if it was morning. "Not yet," said Dorothy, "but you're going to visit Mrs Jones tonight instead of tomorrow night. You'll be able to go back to sleep again when you get to her house. It's because Miss Clements isn't very well. She'll get better soon, so it's nothing serious."

"Will Lucy know where I am?" he asked, anxiously, as he clambered out of bed.

CHAPTER FOURTEEN

As soon as Paul had left, sleepily clutching Mrs Jones's hand, Dorothy and David sprang into action.

"Hurry!" said Dorothy. "We mustn't panic! For Bag's sake, David, what are you doing with that clock? You don't want to take that with you."

He threw the clock down and shoved the screwdriver into his pocket.

"How can we get out without being seen?" he said. "They'll be watching."

"You'll have to go over the side wall at the back," snapped Miss Marilyn. "You'll get onto that path that runs up the hill alongside the house. They might not have noticed it." She paused and twitched. "On the other hand, they might have, so don't raise your hopes."

She disappeared down the stairs, but reappeared shortly. Her hair was wet and her cheeks were flushed. She looked even crosser than ever.

"I need your help. I can't get the ladder out on my own," she said. "Anyway, you can't go now. It's pouring with rain. You can go in the morning, very early."

They followed her down the stairs, through the kitchen and out into the yard. A sheet of rain drenched them immediately, but they hardly noticed. The storage shed was built into an extension to the left of the back door. Miss Marilyn reached inside and switched on a light. They could see the bottom rungs of a ladder sticking out from under a bucket and a pile of garden tools.

"Be very quiet," she said sharply. "The slightest noise will carry."

Dorothy and David slipped inside. They moved the tools and bucket out into the yard. Silently, they lifted out the ladder and laid it flat on the ground.

"It won't be long enough," whispered Dorothy.

"It is." Miss Marilyn was abrupt. "It unfolds."

The rain ran down her face, and dripped off her nose and her chin. David straightened the ladder out to twice its original length and they quietly propped it up against the side wall of the yard, to the left of the backdoor. It almost reached the top.

"We'll just have to pull ourselves up that final bit when we get there," whispered Dorothy. "But it's a bit wobbly."

David wedged a piece of wood underneath one foot of the ladder and gripped it firmly. "It seems OK," he said.

They hurried inside, dripping all over the kitchen floor.

"Go and change into something dry. Have you packed yet? Get some sleep, and I'll wake you at four. And put on layers of your warmest clothes. There are sandwiches in two plastic carrier bags by the door, and a little money. Very little, but it was all I could find. Put them in your backpacks."

★

When Miss Marilyn knocked on their doors at four o'clock on the Friday morning, Dorothy and David were already up and dressed.

"Eat something first," said Miss Marilyn.

They gobbled down some toast and coffee, pulled their anoraks over their uniform jumpers, and grabbed their backpacks. Miss Marilyn pushed them out through the back door into the yard. The hill rose almost vertically behind the house. The ladder looked miserably short up against the side wall.

"There's a steep path going up the hill on the other side of that wall." Miss Marilyn gabbled so fast they could hardly understand her. "Get onto that and just keep walking. You'll go through a golf course and then along the top of the cliff, and once you get to the other side you'll be in among caravans and no one will have seen you get there, because they'll be watching the roads that go out of town."

David was steadying the ladder. "It's still a bit wobbly."

Miss Marilyn held it firmly at the bottom as he climbed up. He heaved himself over the last two feet, looked down the path towards the road and gave a silent thumbs-up.

"I don't know how much it costs to go to London," said Miss Marilyn as Dorothy started up the ladder, "but try and get there if you can, even if you have to hitch-hike."

Dorothy stopped. "Thank you for everything, Miss Marilyn," she whispered. "We're truly grateful." She turned. "Oh, but we haven't said goodbye to Miss Clements."

"No time. I'll say it for you. Just go!"

As soon as Dorothy and David had disappeared over the wall, Miss Marilyn ran back into the house and up the

159

stairs. She found Miss Clements slowly putting on her shoes.

"For heaven's sake, Primrose, do you have no sense of urgency?"

Miss Clements smiled placidly. "More haste makes less speed, does it not, Marilyn, dear?"

"So, you're back to normal!" was the exasperated response.

They left the house before dawn. Miss Marilyn locked the front door behind them. She laid the briefcase flat on the floor of the porch. The money was intact, and she placed a large sheet of paper on top of the case, saying 'NO DEAL' in clear capital letters.

Their modest little car was parked in a side road running up the hill to the right of the house. Miss Clements puffed her way up the pavement with difficulty. Miss Marilyn strode ahead of her and kept looking back.

"For God's sake, Primrose, do you have to be so slow?" she whispered crossly.

★

"There they go," said the gentleman in the passenger seat of the car on the double yellow lines. He and the driver watched as two almost-middle-aged ladies, draped in transparent plastic macs, pulled their wheelie suitcases up the slope.

"Where's the briefcase?" said the driver. "They must have put it in one of the bags."

The passenger got out of the car.

"I'll check the house." He grabbed a bunch of keys out of the glovebox, pulled his collar up against the rain, and disappeared up the path.

After several minutes he returned, carrying the briefcase and a bit of paper. "I've been through the house. There's no one there." He threw the briefcase into the boot and climbed into the passenger seat, waving the bit of paper. "This was left in the porch on top of the briefcase. It says 'NO DEAL'. The holy leaders aren't going to like that."

"I don't like it either," called Isobel from the back of the car, "Nor does the Magnifico."

"Look! They've loaded their stuff into the boot," said the driver. He switched on the engine. "OK, they're in. Here we go!"

★

"Thank God, at last!" said Miss Marilyn, as she drove past the harbour, over the mouth of the river and out of town. "If only this rain would stop, we could be on the motorway in just over an hour." They both relaxed and had time to think.

"I've changed my mind!" Miss Clements announced suddenly.

"Don't make me jump like that! You made me swerve. I nearly hit that lamp post!"

"We must phone the police! She said they were infiltrated, but, even so, I should have done it straight away. And I couldn't remember where I'd put that Mr Lovett's phone number. I don't know what's the matter with me. I just can't think straight. My mind's gone to pieces."

Miss Marilyn groaned. If she had known any swear words she would have used them at this moment.

"Keep your eyes open for a public phone box," said Miss Clements. "You look that side, and I'll look this side."

They cruised through one village after another, their eyes darting left and right, looking for a tall, red booth.

"There must be one somewhere," said Miss Clements.

"This is why people have mobile phones," said Miss Marilyn bitterly. "When I wanted us to get one, you said we didn't need one of those new-fangled things." Her mouth, which had forgotten its pursing and twitching since last night's shock, now started working away furiously.

"I wish you wouldn't do that, dear," said Miss Clements. "It's so unbecoming."

"Do what?"

Miss Clements didn't reply.

"There must be one in the next village," said Miss Marilyn, "and, now I remember, I'm sure someone told me they're not red any more. They're glass, like bus stops. It's deliberate, so you don't notice them."

The road wound and curved, and rose up steep hills and down others. It was now almost light. The car behind them switched off its headlamps, but they didn't notice. They swooped up the next hill and round a bend at the top.

"The sea looks rough," said Miss Clements looking across her sister and down to their right. "The land is so flat down there it's a miracle those farms have not been inundated. I wonder how high up we are."

Miss Marilyn wasn't listening. "That car behind us is much too close," she said indignantly.

It was speeding up to overtake them.

"Stop! Turn back!" screeched Miss Clements. "I forgot Donald!"

Miss Marilyn swerved across the road. The car behind caught up and, with a twist and a shove into their side, it sent them hurtling over the cliff towards the flat farmland below. The little car turned over and over, and landed on its left side in a crumpled heap halfway down the cliff in the middle of a cluster of gorse bushes. Miss Marilyn's right arm was free enough to enable her to turn off the engine. She just had time to marvel at her own presence of mind before her mouth opened wide of its own accord and let out a piercing scream. Then everything went blank.

When she opened her eyes again it was broad daylight, and she could see the waves dancing down below. With her right hand, she prodded her leg to check that she was still alive. Apart from turning her head to look at her sister, that was the only movement she could make.

"Primrose?" she called, but there was no reply. All she could see was a large mound of grey cloth. Angry tears rolled down her cheeks.

"Serves you right, you silly, old bat!" snorted Miss Marilyn.

CHAPTER FIFTEEN

The rain had stopped. David looked behind him. It was still too dark to see anything, but Dorothy was there somewhere. He could hear the soft swish as her legs brushed against the bracken.

"There's a light back there," she whispered as she loomed out of the darkness. "It's moving."

He pulled her away from the path and down into the gorse. The prickles tore at their hands and clothes, but they didn't move. They waited and listened to the approaching sound of heavy breathing. A torch flickered back and forth along the path, and a figure lumbered past them up the hill.

As soon as the light had disappeared, David stood up and pulled himself away from the thorns.

"Inland," he whispered.

★

David could kick himself. What an idiot he was! Weeks ago, he'd dragged them all up that cliff and worked out alternative escape routes, but it had never occurred to him to explore the hill above the house. And now they were lost.

Dorothy was just a moving blur in front of him. It should be almost daylight, but the clouds were so full and heavy that it was still as dark as night. They had crossed rough ground, a golf course, and stiles and paths, and neither of them had a clue where they were. Supposing Lucy rang the house and no one answered? She would be frantic with worry. What if she came home next week and they weren't there? They had vowed never to be separated, and this was exactly the sort of thing that could happen if they were.

He stood still and tried to find some sort of bearing. It started to rain again. He was almost blinded as it swept into his face in horizontal gusts, but he thanked his lucky stars as at least it told him something. The wind here usually blew inland. He was facing the sea. They'd been going round in a circle and had come back on themselves.

Dorothy disappeared down a slope and then reappeared. "It's the railway shed!" she spluttered, wiping the rain from her face. "Let's get under cover till this stops!"

They scrambled down the embankment and over to the further railway track, where the train stood under its shelter, waiting for its next descent.

"I'm getting into the carriage before I drown," said Dorothy. "Holy Bag!" she muttered to herself as the rain swept through the open front. "It's as bad in here as out there."

David tried the door in the back of the railway shed. It was padlocked, but seemed pretty flimsy. He fished the little screwdriver out of his pocket and jiggled it about in the lock and then gave the door a good shove. There was a loud cracking sound and it flew open. In the dark, he felt along the far wall and found a switch, but didn't turn it on. They couldn't risk lighting themselves up for all the abductors in the world to see. As his eyes became more used to the dark, he could just about make out another switch and a pedal.

"Hey!" he called out softly. "We could go down in the train." Through the beating of the rain on the shed roof, he could hear Dorothy laughing. "Don't you dare!"

A moment later there was a scrambling sound and she came hurtling through the door. "I saw a face! On the bridge! It was looking directly at me."

They clutched each other and listened. All they could hear was the wind and the driving rain. Together they peered out through the doorway.

"Perhaps I imagined it."

As she spoke, a man's shape loomed against the skyline to their left. It slithered awkwardly down the bank, crossed over the empty track to the waiting train and, with difficulty, pulled itself up into the front carriage.

There was a grunting noise, and then a growl – "I know you're there," The torch flashed over the carriage floor and under the seat, and then up towards the back of the shed. "Gotcha! Here I come!"

David moved quickly. He darted back to the switch and pressed it. If there was supposed to be a light it didn't work. Never mind that now. He threw his weight onto the pedal. The train lurched, trundled steeply downwards and picked up speed.

"Stop!" cried Dorothy. "He's jumping off the wrong side. He'll crash into the wall!"

The train clattered on for a few more yards and then stopped. It left behind the crumpled figure of a man squeezed up against the concrete wall.

"Perhaps he's dead," whispered Dorothy. The man moved and uncurled himself. He struggled to push himself up, but collapsed. "He's done something to his foot."

"Look, he's trying to use his mobile," said David, "and it's not working."

Suddenly, the phone went hurtling down the track.

"Wow! He's in a real temper," said Dorothy. "Thank goodness he can't get up."

"We can't just leave him there."

"Don't be daft. Of course we can. Let's go!"

"Did you see who it was?" whispered David as they scrambled up the cliff.

"It looked like Bernie, the caretaker from the Copse commune."

★

Down on the coast road, a car cruised along at a sensible pace, attracting no attention and without even a mark on its bodywork.

"Fancy turning down that money!" said the driver. "They must 'ave a screw loose."

"Yeah, well. It was fake, anyway," replied the passenger.

Isobel sat in the back seat, talking to head office on her mobile phone. She turned it off and leaned forward. "Change of instructions," she said. "I've got to go back."

Both men groaned.

"They've lost contact with Bernie. He's supposed to be trailing the kids, but his phone's gone dead. No reception, I suppose. You're both to go on to London, but I have to switch cars down a lane further on. I'll tell you when we get there. It's just past a pub called the Red Lion."

They drove on through a small seaside town of prettily coloured houses, up yet another hill.

"That's it," called out Isobel from the back of the car. "Turn next right, just past the garage."

A car was waiting for her at the end of a quiet lane, facing out to sea. They pulled up behind it and stopped.

Isobel thanked the driver as she climbed out, giving him and his passenger her warmest smile. It was important to treat inferiors with appreciation and respect. You never knew when you might need some extra little favour. She pulled her suitcase out of the boot, and stepped over to the other car.

"Hello there!" she said. "Get out and have a cigarette, or stretch your legs or something, while I just sort myself out."

She threw her case onto the back seat and opened it up. Her medical equipment lay on top, and she laid it to one side.

"I think I'll wear the mousy one," she said aloud to herself, as she rummaged in the case. "It'll suit the location."

A dull, brown wig and a small make-up bag transformed her. Five minutes later, the car drove off. In the front passenger seat sat a drab-looking woman with permed hair, thin lips and round glasses with pinkish-rimmed frames. She wore a khaki-coloured mackintosh with a hood, and its place in the suitcase had been taken up by a smart, black jacket.

★

It was broad daylight. Dorothy and David stood on the cliff top and looked down at the caravan site.

168

"We'll stand out like a sore thumb if we go there," said Dorothy. "It's the sort of place where people stare at strangers."

The howling wind whipped at their faces, and they clutched at their hoods. A great gust nearly blew them both over, and they sat down for a while in the meagre shelter of a deformed gorse bush, bent permanently against the force of the wind.

"Let's go back," said David eventually. "We can go down by the difficult route. Even if they are still around they won't know about it. They'll only know the obvious route, over the railway bridge."

They peered round the edge of the bush. All they could see was sky and sea and the wind-battered green of the cliff top. The town was back there somewhere behind them.

"But what do we do when we get there?" said Dorothy. "We can't knock on Mrs Jones's door. We might be seen. It'd be risky for her and Paul."

"Her number's on my mobile, but she'll be scared stiff if she hears the abductors are here. It'll bring it all back to her – about Maria, I mean."

"Let's try Miss Clements first. She might be better by now."

"Unless, of course, she's in cahoots with the Mag's men. There was something fishy about all that 'being ill' business."

They were silent for a while. The wind screamed, piercing the shelter of the gorse bush and spitting spiteful shards of icy rain into the backs of their heads.

"We're going to die of exposure if we're not careful," shouted Dorothy over the roar of the gale. "Let's go back. At least there are shelters on the prom. After all,

'Life is full of risks, dear, is it not', as Miss Clements would say."

David laughed and stood up, pulling Dorothy up after him.

"I doubt she's ever done anything as exciting as taking a risk in her life," he said, "unless, of course, she is really an infiltrator. Let's go before we freeze to death."

★

The rain had stopped and the wind had died down. As David and Dorothy came over the cliff towards the town, they stopped for a moment to take in the mid-morning scene that lay before them. The promenade was busy with people walking dogs, pushing prams, jogging, or just leaning on the railings and looking at the sea.

"I'm not going to let them drive me out of this place," muttered David, forgetting the misery of his wet clothes and sodden shoes for a moment. "Look how alive it is! It makes me feel alive too."

"Me too," shivered Dorothy, "but I feel pretty dead at this moment."

When they reached the prom, David fished in his anorak pocket for his phone.

"Let's try the house," he said. "If Miss Clements answers, I'll cut off, just in case. If Miss Marilyn answers, I'll ask if it's safe to come back."

There was no answer.

"Perhaps they scarpered," he said. "If Miss Clements is genuine, it must have been really scary for them. Worse than for us, because we're used to people like that, and they're not."

They sat in a shelter to eat Miss Marilyn's sandwiches. It was impossible to relax. Dorothy finished her sandwich and stood up. "They might not be looking for us here," she said, brushing crumbs off her legs. "If Bernie managed to get away, he'll have told them he last saw us going up the cliff."

"Yeah. They'll look for us over the other side. We could risk going up to the castle and perhaps sleep in that tower tonight. We'll just have to sit in a café or something in the meantime, to get our clothes dry."

★

By six o'clock, all sense of caution had vanished. The evening wind was gathering strength. Their clothes had still not dried out despite a visit to the public library, a stroll inside various shops, and sitting in a café. They went past the castle to the south end of the promenade, and down some steps to the harbour.

"We'll go back to the castle if we don't find anything here," said Dorothy.

Boats with cabins were all locked up, but they found a rowing boat covered in a sheet of tarpaulin that flapped in the wind.

David pointed. "Look, the cover's loose. We could get under it, and spend the night in there. It'd be out of the wind at least, which the castle won't be."

"No. If the tide goes out, the boat will go down with the water and we won't be able to climb back up."

They wandered around to see if there was anything more promising. It was difficult to appear nonchalant while they were both shivering with cold and half-expecting to see the Magnifico's men pop out from every corner, but they did their best to stroll along as though they didn't have a care in the world. They tried the doors that were set into the harbour walls, but they were all padlocked. A tramp was already settling down for the night against one doorway, spreading out his bits of cardboard and sacking.

"It'll have to be the castle," said Dorothy. "The shelters on the prom would be too obvious."

They went back along the promenade, and wandered through the streets until they found a fish and chip shop, and settled themselves down in the furthest corner, away from the door. At last, they felt warm.

"It's so good," sighed David. "I nearly thanked the Mag for fish and chips."

"We'll stay as long as we can," whispered Dorothy. "I wonder what time they shut." They ordered cups of tea and drew out the drinking process, until a group of Friday night revellers burst in. The place suddenly became crowded and there weren't enough tables.

"Let's go before we're joined by those drunks," said David. "I can't drink any more tea, and we need to hang on to what's left of our change. If we'd been thinking straight we'd have brought the housing fund."

They pushed the door open against the wind and made their way towards the castle.

"We've got more money somewhere," said Dorothy, "but Miss Clements can't remember where she put it. She said it's in a safe place, and it's all ours when she finds it." She was still wondering if Miss Clements had really been ill last night, but it seemed shameful to think that someone who had always seemed so kind might have betrayed them.

The tide was high, and huge waves thumped against the promenade. Spray flew up and caught them both, soaking their partially dried-out clothes. They found their tower and checked that there was no one around to see them. Pulling their hoods close to their heads, they lay on the stone floor, out of the wind, and snuggled as close together as they could.

"I wonder what Lucy's doing at this minute," muttered David.

"Settling comfortably into a nice, warm hotel bed, I expect,"

They were quiet for a while, but they couldn't sleep. The cold seeped through their clothes and into their bones.

There must be a better place than this, thought Dorothy. Perhaps they should risk using one of the shelters on the prom. She dismissed the idea. That Bernie, or anyone else lurking around in doorways, would spot them straight away if they ventured into the streets at this time of night.

What would Aunt Bertha think of her now?

"I have a very important job for you," she had said. Well, that important job was to look after David, and she had failed. She had let Aunt Bertha down as well as David. If she'd not gone on and on about running away all her life, he'd be safe now – still in the commune, probably, if it hadn't been closed down.

She wondered what had happened to Aunt Bertha after the night of the fire. Tears trickled silently down her cold cheeks as she remembered how kind she had been to them both while they, with the carelessness of children, had never thanked her. When they had their own house, they would track her down and look after her, and treat her like a queen.

"Do you think Lucy's alright?" whispered David after a while.

Oh, for Bag's sake, thought Dorothy. "Of course she is!"

"I should have given her my mobile number. It didn't occur to me, because we're always together. I haven't given it to you either, come to think of it."

"Well, we can't do anything about it now," Dorothy snapped. She immediately felt ashamed, and her voice softened. "There's no reason why she shouldn't be alright. She's got a hotel room and hotel food and, ugh! Beverley. So she's fine. Go to sleep."

David tried to picture the sweetness of Lucy's smile, but all he could see was the tension in her face when he'd left her in London. If only he'd hugged her harder, she might have hugged him back. He smiled to himself. If he'd hugged her any harder he'd have squeezed the life out of her, she was so fragile. Dorothy was right. Lucy would be OK. She might look frail, but she was tough.

CHAPTER SIXTEEN

Lucy lay in bed unable to sleep. Only a few more hours till tomorrow, yet it seemed a thousand years away. At least Beverley had emerged from her sickbed, so she wouldn't have to travel down with that po-faced Margaret.

Beverley had appeared while Lucy was having her room-service supper of salmon and salad.

"I must be better," she'd said, plonking herself down on the bed, "because what you've got there looks very nice."

Lucy had offered her some.

"No, thanks. I'll ring down for something when I get back to my room." She'd been feeling quite pleased with herself because her trousers were less tight when she put them on this evening. She'd probably lost a couple of pounds, so every cloud had a silver lining.

"Off tomorrow at crack of dawn. Straight down, drop you off, and straight back again. Pete has to be back with the car for a late afternoon job."

★

Lucy fell asleep eventually, and was woken after two hours to the sound of Beverley banging on the door and telling her to get her skates on.

The journey back seemed interminable.

"Timbuktu at last," said Beverley with an elaborate sigh of relief. "Why does everything have to be so far away? And tractors holding us up on those bendy roads. It shouldn't be allowed."

Pete put Lucy's bag on the pavement in front of the big house, and Beverley climbed out to stretch her legs.

"We're running late, so I won't come in. Miss Clements is expecting you. Old Lovett rang her on Wednesday, and I left a message on her answerphone before we left. I must say you've been a good, brave girl, just like the judge said. Let's hope you won't be stuck here for much longer." She gave Lucy a peck on the cheek.

"We're not stuck," said Lucy. "We like it here. For us, it's the hub of the universe."

"OK, that's good. Each to their own. Ta-ta then. God bless. Don't do anything I wouldn't do."

Pete leaned over and opened the passenger window. "Buck up there, Sugarlips. We ain't got time to kill."

"Just coming." She climbed back in, waggled her fingers at Lucy, and the car drove off.

Lucy picked up her bag and hurried through the wrought-iron gate. Miss Clements would have prepared a nice little lunch especially for her, and the others would be excited to see her when they got back from school. Her heart soared. She brushed past yellow forsythia and evergreens that still bore their scarlet berries. Little leaf buds sprouted on the shrubs, and primroses peeped through the grass on the tiny front lawn. Spring meant happiness, and tears came to her eyes at the thought of seeing Paul again.

For some reason, the side gate was locked. That was odd. It was never locked because it saved Miss Clements having to open the front door to them when they came back from school.

Lucy stepped into the porch and pulled the front doorbell. She could hear it clanging away in the hall. There was no answer, so she knocked and flapped the letter box. Donald started barking at the back of the house, but nobody came. This wasn't right. There was usually somebody in, even if it was only Miss Marilyn. Donald stopped barking, as though he was listening, and she called his name through the letter box. The barks began again, and turned into yelps and howls.

Perhaps there was someone outside in the back yard. Leaving her bag in the porch, Lucy hurried round to the public footpath that ran uphill to the left of the house, and leaned perilously over the wall. She peeped down into the yard. There was no sign of Miss Clements or anyone else, and the back door was shut.

Her heart missed a beat and then fell into a dive as she noticed the top rung of a ladder leaning against the wall. Just like London, she thought grimly. There was no need to wonder what it was doing there, because she knew immediately. A ladder meant escape. Something had happened to her family. She swung her leg over the wall. The ladder tipped slightly sideways. She shifted her weight and descended cautiously.

As she landed Donald shot out of his dog flap, beside himself with excitement. He ran round and round in circles, and jumped up to lick her face. She pulled him to her.

"Why are you so pleased to see me, Donald?" she asked. "What's happened? Speak to me."

The back door was locked. Lucy bent down and peeped through the keyhole. It was empty, as she knew it

177

would be. The key was always kept on the draining board when the door was locked, so that burglars couldn't reach it. No problem. She knew where the spare key was kept. The door to the storage shed was wide open. That too was odd. Miss Clements always kept it shut. Lucy peeped inside. There was no window, and it was dark and spidery. She tried not to breathe in the smell of damp as she reached up and lifted the key off its hook.

It was rusty and difficult to turn, but to her relief the door opened, and she and Donald stepped into the kitchen. As she stood at the sink and washed the rust off her hands, he waddled straight over to his water bowl. It was empty. So was his food bowl. It was obvious he'd been on his own for some time. Lucy gave him water and he drank loudly. She found some cooked chicken in the fridge, and hoped it wasn't too old. It would be awful if she gave him food poisoning. He gobbled it up and then settled down in his bed, keeping one eye open and fixed on Lucy.

The house felt eerily deserted. Lucy couldn't even hope that Gladys might turn up to do the cleaning, because she never came on a Friday. Moving silently, she looked into the downstairs rooms and then crept up the stairs to the top floor. Donald followed her. As soon as she saw that Paul's bed was unmade her stomach started churning. Dorothy and David hadn't made their beds either, and drawers had been left open, with clothes spilling out onto the floor. The housing-fund box was on top of the chest. Lucy checked inside and counted the money. It was all there. Wherever they had gone, David and Dorothy would have had little, or nothing, in their pockets.

It was clear that something was terribly wrong. None of them, even Paul, ever failed to make their beds and tidy up. It was ingrained in them. Such a lapse would have been unheard of in Father Copse's house, and in the communes. Orderliness reflected purity of soul.

If only she'd caught one of those buses to Victoria! She could have outrun that Margaret easily, and been home by the evening.

She sat down on the edge of David's bed to calm the pounding of her heart. A discarded shirt lay on the floor, and she could see that his bag had gone. Had he been abducted? That couldn't be right, because he wouldn't have had time to take his bag. Also, Miss Clements and Miss Marilyn seemed to have gone as well. Even the Magnifico's agents, with every abducting skill in the world, would have difficulty in taking three youngsters and two women in their forties, all at the same time.

Nor could they have run away, reasoned Lucy, because Miss Clements would never have left Donald on his own. They were bound to come back soon, she told herself, because of Donald. They must have just popped out, telling him they'd be back in a minute, and then got held up. But that didn't explain why the children's rooms were in a mess and why their bags had gone.

The house felt big and lonely. Lucy went down to the first floor. The corridor to the back bedrooms was forbidden to the children, but she tiptoed along, consumed by a sense of guilt and fear of being caught. She put her ear to the first door on the right and listened. There wasn't a sound. She peeped cautiously into a sitting room, cosy with a sofa and armchairs, and immaculately tidy. Knitting books, and recipe books, and travel books on Greece were propped up neatly in descending size between two elephant bookends on a side table, and the pot plant they had given Miss Clements was on the mantelpiece. But it wasn't just one room. Towards the rear, there was a bedroom. Its floor and an adjoining bathroom were strewn with shoes and woolly cardigans that she recognised, and nightdresses and slippers. This obviously belonged to Miss Clements, and she must have left in a hurry.

Down the left-hand side of the corridor was another sitting room. Here, the floor was completely obliterated. Recognisable contents of open drawers spilled out to mingle with scattered papers and files, precarious stacks of books, computer equipment, and tangled wires. There wasn't even a tiny space for Lucy to put her feet. A door at the far end of the room stood wide open, and she could see through it to a mess of clothes and shoes, more books and papers, and the tumbled sheets and pillows of an unmade bed.

Her heart was thumping and her throat was tight as she went back down to the kitchen. She felt oddly alert. There could be no doubt that everyone had left, and had done so in a hurry. She tried to tell herself she needn't feel afraid for herself as long as she was in this house. It was a safe house. But she was terribly afraid for the others, especially Paul.

She thought fleetingly about ringing the police, but knew she could never do that. It was a police infiltrator who had returned Dorothy to the commune when she ran away last year. As for Social Services, she couldn't ring them. One of their infiltrators had grabbed David from the police station after the fire. Both he and Dorothy had ended up in the disposal cells, and would be dead by now if Lucy and Paul hadn't reached them just in time. Suppose there were police infiltrators here, or social workers, just waiting for her phone call? She couldn't take the risk.

Mr Lovett had given David his phone number, and she realised now that she too should have made a note of it, even though she didn't have a phone. What a fool she was! She crossed the hall to the dining room and checked in the note book that Miss Clements kept next to the phone on the mantelpiece. The butcher's number was there, and Mr Nicholas's and there was someone called Mary. In fact, the little book was full of names in a haphazard non-alphabetical muddle, but there was no mention of Mr Lovett, or Beverley, or even Gwen Jones. Maybe they were supposed to be confidential or something. Lucy felt a prick of irritation. Miss Clements seemed to have a fuzzy view of life, except where it related to food. Aunt Sarah would have had everyone's numbers set out efficiently in an accessible place. If they were confidential she would simply have told Lucy not to look, and that the Magnifico would be watching if she disobeyed.

She searched in the kitchen drawers and even went back up to Miss Clements's room to have a guilty peek through her spare handbag, but Mr Lovett's number was nowhere to be found. She mustn't panic. There was always an explanation for everything. If only David were here he'd know what to do. He was the practical one.

By the time darkness fell, she had given up hoping that anyone would come back that night. Anyway, they wouldn't have packed their bags if they'd meant to come back. She closed the curtains in the downstairs sitting room before she put on the lights – not that she was nervous, oh no, just cautious. And it helped make the place feel cosy. She cleaned out the open hearth, and carefully laid a fire with kindling and logs. It blazed up quickly. Together she and Donald sat on the sofa and watched the flames flicker.

Looking at the fire reminded her of the night Copse's house had burned down. It had been a night of horror, but looking back at it now, it was the best thing that had ever happened to her. It had freed her from the Magnifico and had led to the creation of her family.

The trouble with having a family was that she was always worried about them. They must have left so quickly that there wasn't even time for them to tell Beverley or Mr Lovett. Mrs Jones, her grandmother, might have news of them, but no way could Lucy go to that house. Never in her life had she faced such sickening hatred. The thought of the man and the scum and the devil's spawn, brought a pain to her stomach.

That night, she lay on the bed, fully dressed and ready for flight. If only the silence wouldn't swish around her so loudly! It deafened her as she strained for the sound of soft footsteps on the stairs. The slightest of draughts blew in from somewhere – was that the whiff of cigarettes from a smoker's strangling fingers? Or was it the hot breath of the fire of the melting flesh? She fell asleep as dawn was breaking.

*

It was Saturday, and still there was no sign of the others. Lucy's fears of the night seemed less oppressive. Once again the house felt safe. She drank a cup of tea but couldn't eat and, after she had given Donald some breakfast, she found his lead and took him for a walk up the footpath at the side of the house. At the top of the hill they stopped, and she gazed out over the town and the bay beyond. The grey of the sky had lifted, and the sea had turned to a deep navy blue. Ireland must be over there somewhere, and beyond that was America.

Over to the left she could see the castle, and the spire of the church next to it. To the right, she could see the cliff and the train carriage at the top of the little railway. And in between, out of view behind the hotel roofs, she could picture the promenade with its shelters and benches and bandstand and pier, and the empty paddling pool awaiting the arrival of summer.

They had been privileged to have found this place, and now something had gone terribly wrong. If only she knew where Paul was! He'd be frightened without her. They would all have been here or at school on Wednesday, because that's when Mr Lovett spoke to Miss Clements. They must have gone that night, or on Thursday – not yesterday, or there would still have been water in Donald's bowl.

*

Paul, in fact, was enjoying himself immensely. Every night and every morning he checked that the gold chain was still round his neck, to make sure that Lucy was with him in spirit. He had a kind grandmother called Mrs Jones, and there was a jolly old gentleman called Mr Jones who sat him on his lap and told him jokes and sometimes talked to him in that language that Paul spoke at school. "*Bore da!*" Paul would say, and Mr Jones would smile with pleasure and call him a clever fellow.

When Lucy was up on the hill on the Saturday, looking out over the town, Paul was in the playground up by the castle. Gwen Jones was pushing him on a swing, while her husband sat on a bench and wondered where he was.

"Where's the graveyard?" he asked an old woman sitting on the bench next to him.

"They dug that up years ago," she said. "Look." She pointed behind him. "See? They propped all the gravestones up against the wall to make a little park."

"Well, I'm blowed!" said Evan. "What will they think of next? Mind you, a playground's a cheerful thing to have and a graveyard's sad, so it's probably for the best."

She smiled. "Yes, you're right. It's good to look at it like that."

When the woman left, Gwen gave up pushing, and Paul disappeared with another child into a wooden tower. She sat down next to Evan, and he took her hand.

"Ah, it's lovely to have you close," he said. "Who's that little boy you were playing with?"

"Don't you remember? He's Mary Ellis's little boy, Paul. I take him to school every day and he's staying with us over the weekend while she's away."

"He reminds me of Maria at that age. When does she finish in college? She should be home soon, shouldn't she?"

"Yes, she should," said Mrs Jones.

He looked around him.

"I'm not sure where we are," he said. "Shouldn't there be a graveyard here?"

"They made it into a little park and put in this playground," said Mrs Jones. "It's a happy use for it. Shall we go home now and have a nice cup of tea?"

"That would be lovely, my darling," he said, putting his arm through hers.

How blessed were these moments when he forgot, thought Gwen. If only he could always be sleeping or forgetting! She called to Paul.

"Who is that little boy?" asked Evan. "He reminds me of Maria."

"Yes. He reminds me of her too," said Gwen.

★

"When's Lucy coming back?" asked Paul, as they sat down at the kitchen table with their cups of tea. "She'll want some of this nice cake."

"Who's Lucy?" asked Evan. "That's such a pretty name. It means 'light'."

"She is my light, and she'll never leave me."

CHAPTER SEVENTEEN

After two nights in the tower, Dorothy and David emerged on the Sunday morning, bedraggled and blue with cold. Had they only known it, Lucy was giving Donald his breakfast at that moment and wishing she knew where they were.

"I've run out of money," said Dorothy. She tipped up her purse and out came a twenty-pence piece. Her pockets were empty. "Have you got enough for breakfast?"

David felt in his pockets. He had a pound. "We can get some rolls from the supermarket when it opens," he said, "or a couple of apples."

"We can wash in the public loos. We might feel a bit better then."

Their shoes had gone hard and seemed to have shrunk.

"My feet really hurt," said David.

"At least we survived the night," said Dorothy in an attempt to sound positive, "and I actually slept quite well."

"So did I. Perhaps we're getting used to it. And the sun's shining. Look at the blue of that sky!"

They had to wait for the supermarket to open, and wandered through the empty backstreets shivering and miserable.

"Well, I'm sorry to say this," sighed Dorothy, "but I feel extremely non-positive. We've either got to ask someone for help or we've got to hitch a lift to London. At least we'll find food behind the restaurants and shelter under the railway arches — a backward step to where we were last year!"

David took out his mobile phone. "I'll try Mr Lovett. You never know, he might work at the weekends."

"I don't see what he can do. He's so far away."

"Perhaps he knows someone here we could trust."

There was a recorded message saying Mr Lovett would be out of the office till Tuesday. The phone gave a ping. David groaned. "See that little picture at the top? We're nearly out of battery."

"We're just going to have to ring Mrs Jones. Quick! Before the battery runs out."

David nodded. He found the number, but paused before pressing the button. He looked at Dorothy anxiously. "Shall I? It's such a cheek – she hardly knows us."

Dorothy didn't feel comfortable about it either. "I don't know what else we can do," she said. "We've slept rough two nights and we've got no money, our clothes are all damp, and we're both so cold we're numb all over. If we don't do something we'll be ill and the police will pick us up, and they might be infiltrated." She sneezed. "Do it. At least we can trust her and we can't live like this forever. I feel disgusting even though we did have a wash."

David pressed the button and waited. He was just saying, "Supposing the grandfather answers?" when there was a little click, and Gwen's soft voice, with its gentle lilt, said, "Hello?"

"Hello, Mrs Jones. It's David here."

She sounded pleased. "Oh, David! How nice to hear you. Oh, of course, you haven't got school. It's Sunday. Are you coming to see us today?"

David's eyes filled with tears as he heard the kindness in her voice. His own voice cracked as he said, "Can you help us, please?"

Dorothy could hear Gwen saying, "What's the matter, love? What's happened?", but David couldn't speak. She took the phone from him.

"It's Dorothy here, Mrs Jones. We daren't come to visit you in case we're seen going in and it might get you in trouble. We've had to escape from Miss Clements's house because of those people – the Magnifico's people – and they might still be around."

They could both hear Gwen's gasp of horror.

"And we're embarrassed, but we have to ask you for food or money, and some dry clothes or something," gabbled Dorothy. "We'll pay you back somehow, one day. And can you tell us somewhere safe to go?"

There was a silence on the other end of the phone, then, "Where are you?" Gwen's gentle voice had become firm.

"On the prom."

"Of course I'll help you. Go up to the playground by the cas—" The phone went dead.

"It's run out. The battery. She must have meant the castle. Let's go!"

Half an hour later, they were still sitting on a bench by the swings, with their hoods pulled up and shivering despite the sunshine.

"One good thing about anoraks," said Dorothy, "is that everyone looks the same."

David sneezed. He looked around anxiously. "I just hope we're in the right place."

As he spoke, they heard the scuttling of feet behind them and an excited yelp. They turned to see Paul hurtling towards them. Gwen and Evan were more sedate. Dorothy and David stood up as they approached, and pulled back their hoods.

"Hello, dear boy!" cried Evan, shaking David's hand vigorously. "My goodness, your hand's like a lump of ice! Fancy seeing you here! No school today?"

"No sir, it's Sunday."

"Ah, so it is." Evan turned to shake Dorothy's hand. "And how are you, my beautiful young friend?"

"Very well, thank you, sir," said Dorothy.

Paul ran off to the swings.

"Do you think you could go and give him a push, Evan?" said Gwen. "My back's a bit stiff today."

"Gladly!" he said, and ambled away.

Gwen pulled two bacon-and-egg sandwiches and a flask of hot coffee out of her bag, and sat down on the bench.

"Come on you two, have something to eat, and you can tell me all about it. Though I suggest you pull your hoods back up while you're here. Evan and I won't be offended."

They gave her a detailed account of what had happened, and to their relief, she remained calm and collected. When they had finished she sat silent for a while, and was obviously thinking.

"Well," she said at last. "You can't go back to the big house, in case they're watching it. I've no doubt that Miss Clements and Miss Marilyn took fright and have gone off for a few days. I expect they'll call the police as soon as they feel safe. When is Lucy due back?"

"We're not sure," said Dorothy, "but probably tomorrow or Tuesday."

"Now, you're both to come back with us, and you can stay in our house till all is well. No one will recognise you

189

in those clothes. Just keep the hoods up, but don't stoop as though you're afraid to be seen. Walk proudly with all the confidence in the world." She looked up at the sky as she spoke. "One good thing about our weather is that it's changeable. It's going to rain again any minute, so of course your hoods will be up, as will Evan's and mine."

It did indeed start to rain five minutes later, and Evan and Paul returned to the bench.

"I've invited Dorothy and David to come and stay with us for a few days, Evan," said Gwen. "They're living with that Miss Clements and her sister up at the top there, but they've had to go away on business."

His face lit up. "That will give both of us great pleasure," he said. "Maria will be back soon, and will be so pleased to see you."

It was decided that they would walk back separately, "Because of the narrow pavements," Gwen told her husband. She and he and Paul would reach the house first, followed shortly after by Dorothy and David.

"I doubt if those horrible people know we have any connection," said Gwen quietly to Dorothy, "but it's just a precaution."

*

The hallway was narrow and the living room small, but the house was warm and prettily furnished in an old-fashioned way.

"I've never been anywhere so cosy in my life!" exclaimed Dorothy. "I'd just love to live in a sweet little house like this."

Evan was pleased. "And so you shall, my dear; at least until those two ladies come back. Where did you say they were, Gwen? Oh, I remember – gone away on business. I wonder what sort of business they're involved in?"

There was just enough hot water for Dorothy and David to have hot baths one after the other, and they were wrapped in ancient dressing gowns and pyjamas while Gwen put their clothes in the washing machine.

"The one luxury we do have is a tumble dryer," she said. "There's not room for much of a line in the back."

A mattress was laid on the floor in Paul's room for David to sleep on, and some suitcases were moved to one side in the box room so that Dorothy could reach the little camp bed in the corner.

"This must be what heaven feels like, if there is such a place," said Dorothy, as they sat down at the kitchen table and watched Gwen ladle out platefuls of steaming lamb casserole.

★

Lucy took Donald out on the Sunday afternoon. They wandered about the town for a bit, and walked the length of the prom and back, with frequent rests on one bench after another to give Donald a chance to recover his breath. When it began to get chilly, they made their way slowly back to the house. It was nice to have a dog for company. She didn't have to wonder if she trusted him. He didn't make her suspicious, but was simply there, as glad of her company as she was of his. She opened the front door with Miss Clements's spare key, and stopped to listen. It didn't feel as though anyone was there. She shut the door and bolted it, top and bottom.

She gave Donald his supper, and made herself some bacon and egg. Tomorrow would be Monday, so the next decision she had to make was whether to go to school or to stay in the house all day on her own. She weighed the pros and cons. If she went to school there was a small chance that Dorothy and David might be there and had simply been staying at a friend's house while Miss Clements and her sister were away. But it was unlikely. The risk of staying with strangers would be too great. And, it wouldn't explain Paul's disappearance. Also, if she went to school, Donald would be on his own all day and might howl, and the neighbours might send for the cruelty to animals people to come and take him away.

It could be that instead of bringing Paul back from school as usual on Thursday, Mrs Jones had been allowed to take him home and keep him there till Lucy came back. He did sometimes go there to tea, and she knew that the 'devil's spawn' man there liked him and thought he was a neighbour's child. Maybe Mrs Jones had asked Miss Clements if he could stay for the weekend because he was missing Lucy. That was a very real possibility.

A wave of relief swept over Lucy as she considered it, until she remembered that Mr Lovett had told Miss Clements she'd be back on Friday. Mrs Jones would surely have brought him back to the big house so that he could see Lucy. Even so, it was worth a try. After all, although Lucy couldn't think of Mrs Jones as a grandmother, that's what she was and they should be able to trust her. She racked her brains. What had they done with the bit of paper with her address and phone number? It had been in David's anorak pocket when they went down to look for the house.

Lucy ran upstairs. The anorak had gone. He would have been wearing it when he left. She shuffled through some homework papers on his chest of drawers and looked through his drawers. Nothing. There was a book on *How to Invest Wisely* next to his bed. Lucy smiled. They'd all had a look at the book, thinking of their housing fund, but they hadn't been able to make head or tail of it. David had been determined to keep on trying, and his page was marked with a scrap of paper. Sure enough, there were the grandmother's instructions, including the phone number.

She ran back downstairs and dialled. A man answered, and her voice stuck in her throat.

"Yes?" he said.

"May I speak to Mrs Jones, please?" Her voice came out in a squeak.

"I'm afraid she's popped out for a minute. Can I take a message?"

Lucy thanked him hastily and said she'd phone back later. She checked her watch. It would be too late to ring again. They'd be going to bed as soon as Mrs Jones came back. She had another idea. If Paul was at Mrs Jones's they'd both be at the school gates tomorrow. She'd get down there early, before half past eight, and she couldn't possibly miss them. If they didn't come, she'd put a note through the letter box and hope that man didn't see it first.

Having made that decision she felt slightly cheered. When she went up to bed she took Donald with her, and his snuffles and snorts kept the noise of the silence away.

★

Lucy and Donald were outside Paul's school by half past eight. Children and parents and grandparents, of all shapes and sizes, streamed towards the gate.

"What a sweet little dog," said one mother as her child ran into the playground. "What breed is he?"

"I think he's half a Westie," said Lucy, bending down to stroke Donald. "He's quite old for a dog. He's fifteen."

The woman smiled. "That's a good age, but he looks very fit."

Lucy was pleased and smiled back. People were friendly here, she thought – not like London.

"Yes, he is fit. He can be quite fierce sometimes," she said proudly.

She hadn't noticed her grandmother hastily pushing Paul through the school gate and rushing off. The flow of children continued and Lucy returned to her vigil, but there was no sign of Paul or Gwen. When the last child disappeared indoors, she turned away disappointed and terribly weary. She had so convinced herself that she'd see Paul at the school that she'd forgotten her alternative plan of dropping a note in Gwen's door. Really, her brain seemed to be useless these days. She hadn't even had the wit to bring a piece of paper and a pencil with her. Now she'd have to go all the way back and write something and come back again.

*

The house was too quiet, and Lucy's heart was heavy. Without Paul and Dorothy and David she was just a pointless, unconnected speck in the universe. Aunt Sarah's voice rang inside her head – *Stop feeling sorry for yourself. You've got a dog to look after. Get some fresh air and take him for another walk – and wipe that miserable look off your face.*

She pulled herself together and almost laughed. Aunt Sarah had been a pain when dealing with the soul, but she was so often right in other things. She bent down to stroke Donald.

"Later, after you've had a rest, we'll go out again. We'll deliver our letter to Mrs Jones and then we'll walk from one end of the prom to the other, very briskly."

If Donald had understood what she said, he might not have wagged his tail. He was old and fat, and was rarely exercised. He'd had to puff hard to get himself up the hill once already that morning.

Lucy searched yet again for Mr Lovett's number, without success. She looked through the shelves in Miss Clements's sitting room, and even rummaged through some of the mess in Miss Marilyn's room. Why on earth did Miss Clements keep a phone book right next to the phone if she didn't put really important numbers in it?

"You haven't had your breakfast yet," she said to Donald eventually, "and nor have I. We'll have something to eat, and then we'll go out again."

She would drop the note in Mrs Jones's door asking her to ring the big house, and just hope that her husband didn't catch her doing it.

Donald's appetite had improved, Lucy noticed, as she watched him gobble down his food. He heaved himself out through the dog flap, and returned a few minutes later and settled down in his bed for a rest. By the time she had boiled herself a couple of eggs and buttered some toast, she felt almost optimistic. There was plenty of food in the freezer and a roof over her head, and she still had this feeling that Paul might be with their grandmother, even if he hadn't gone to school. She wrote the note and put it in her pocket.

When she had cleared up her breakfast things, she went upstairs and tidied Dorothy and David's bedrooms so that there would be decent beds to get into when they came back. Better not touch Miss Clements's room, or Miss Marilyn's. They might not like to think that she had been in there.

At last she and Donald were ready to go. She put on his lead.

"Come on boy!" she said. "Walkies!"

As she took the key off its hook by the door, the front gate squeaked.

CHAPTER EIGHTEEN

The gate gave another squeak. Lucy's heart soared. At last, someone was home. Before she had a chance to pull back the bolts on the front door, the sound of uneven footsteps on the path brought her down with a bang. Nobody she knew had a limp like that – one heavy step, followed by the drag and scrape of a shoe on the path. She pressed against the door unable to move. The bell jangled and she held her breath. A key jiggled in the lock and turned, but the bolts held fast. Somebody swore under his breath, and turned away. She could hear him trying the side gate. That was still locked. Thank goodness Miss Clements had asked Mr Nicholas to nail a strip of barbed wire at the top.

She ran to the dining room and peeped through the curtains, but whoever it was had gone. It wouldn't be safe to escape through the front in case he was waiting for her round the corner. Best to stay put. No one could get in if the door was bolted.

Had she locked the back door?

She hurried to the kitchen. Thank goodness, the key was still in the door and it was locked. Donald shuffled after her, dragging his lead. It made a clattering noise and she bent to take it off.

"You'd better go back to bed," she whispered, throwing the lead on the table. "We'll go out later."

As she straightened herself up, there was a clunking sound in the yard outside and she dashed to the window. She should never have left the ladder there! A leg had already appeared over the wall and was waving about before locating the top rung. A peculiarly twisted foot followed it, searching painfully with its toe for the rung below. The ladder gave a jerk and righted itself.

Lucy looked around her. The boiler cupboard was the obvious place. She crawled into the space at the bottom, and Donald shuffled in next to her. Supposing the boiler collapsed on top of them? She kept the door slightly open, and they both watched through the gap.

There were sounds of movement out in the yard – a scraping noise as the storeroom door was pulled wide open over uneven concrete, the clanking of a bucket kicked across the yard, the rattling of the backdoor handle – and then silence. Lucy held her breath. Perhaps he'd go away.

Then there was a puffing sound and a thump.

Lucy's eyes were fixed on the door. An arm slid slowly through the dog flap. It withdrew for a moment as the body behind it adjusted its position on the ground. Reappearing at a different angle, the arm reached upwards, its fingers feeling for the key in the lock.

She should have taken the key out! If she was quick enough she might get to it in time. She started to wriggle out from under the boiler, but the fingers had already reached the key.

What would David do? Lucy glanced at the dog lead dangling over the edge of the table. She could tie the wrist to a chair. As she leaped forward she remembered Donald. "Go for it, boy!" she whispered, giving him a shove.

He shot across the room and buried his teeth into the invading flesh. There was a howl of pain from outside the backdoor, and the arm hastily pulled itself back. Donald leaped out after it.

Lucy crouched next to the window and peeped out. The man had his good foot on the ladder while Donald tried to cling on to the other. With a mighty kick, he was sent flying. Before she had time to think, Lucy had unlocked the door, dashed across the yard and grabbed the ladder with both hands. The man was already near the top. The ladder tilted and rocked as he clambered up. Lucy shook it, and gave it a hefty pull. It twisted and fell towards the house. The man lurched sideways and hit his head on the open door of the storage cupboard.

Lucy watched as he fell to the floor, twitched for a moment and lay still. The face was familiar. It was Bernie. She couldn't move. The world went black. Lucy Copse, murderer – or was it murderess? The fire of the melting flesh flickered around her. She could feel the flames. The Magnifico had caught her after all.

*

"We'll sit down and have a little rest," Lucy said to Donald when they reached the bandstand, "and then we'll go back and you can have a nice sleep." She had completely forgotten about the note in her pocket. She sat on a bench with Donald at her feet, and tried to calm the thundering in her head. She watched the people go by. How lucky they all were, not to have just done something so dreadful that they couldn't bear to think of it. Her heart leaped and jerked with the horror of it all. She should never have left the Magnifico. Life would have been structured and secure. She would have known her place and kept to it, like Aunt Sarah.

She waited for Aunt Sarah's voice to tell her what to do, but there was nothing. Even she had given up on her. Tears ran silently down her cheeks. No one seemed to notice her, and after a while she mopped her face and sat upright. There was no point in running away, because the Magnifico would always find her. All she could do was face the consequences – and, you never knew, if she went back to the house she might find that the man wasn't dead after all. He might have stood up and walked away. Sometimes things weren't as bad as they seemed.

"OK, Donald," she said. "Time to go back. You've got your breath back now."

Donald puffed reluctantly to his feet and they returned the way they had come, along the prom and up the hill. As they turned into the far end of the road they stopped dead. There was a police car in front of Miss Clements's house (parked on double yellow lines, Lucy noticed) and an ambulance. Her instinct was to run, but she managed not to panic. She walked as sedately as her trembling legs would let her. If she could get there before anyone appeared she would nip up the hill path and peep over the wall. She heard men's voices, and slipped sideways onto the path just in time. The wall was lower here near the gate. Peering through the shrubs, she could see that the front door was wide open. Two paramedics emerged, carrying a body on a stretcher. One arm was bandaged and the face wasn't covered. Surely, if he were dead, they'd have put a sheet over his face? Gladys, the cleaner, appeared in the doorway. A policeman stood beside her, and they watched the stretcher's journey down to the ambulance and away.

"Well, another housebreaker hits the dust," said the policeman.

"Good riddance," snorted Gladys. "Serve him right. Have you got time for a cup of tea?"

They went back into the house, and Lucy watched and waited. Donald lay on his side on the rough path. He was glad of the rest. It seemed an eternity before the front door opened again, and the policeman came out. Gladys stood on the step.

"The two ladies must have been taking a break while the kids were in London," she said. "I'll tidy up a bit downstairs, and then I'll be off home. There's no point coming in again till they're out of hospital. Anyway, I'm away tomorrow for a week. We're doing a peace vigil outside the Houses of Parliament."

"Good for you, Gladys, old girl. And thanks for your help. If you see anything odd while you're tidying up, let me know."

"Will do. Ta-ra."

Lucy took a deep breath. She swallowed hard, smoothed her expression to one of concerned curiosity and stepped out onto the pavement just as the policeman came through the gate.

"Oh, hello, sir!" she said, sounding surprised. "Has something happened at the house?"

"Nosy, aren't you!"

"Yes sir. Is everything alright? Because I know the ladies who live there. They're my granny's friends."

"Yeah, well, they've had a car accident, and now while they're in hospital they've had a break-in, except he knocked himself out before he could take anything. So, now you know as much as I do about it."

"Thank you, sir."

201

"It's a pleasure." The policeman climbed into the car. As he drove off, he remembered he should have asked her why she wasn't at school. Oh well, he thought. She must have had a good reason, she seemed a pleasant kid – called him 'sir'. You didn't get that often these days.

It wouldn't be safe to go into the house now. Gladys might be doing the downstairs for hours, and she'd be sure to phone the policeman if Lucy appeared from nowhere. Donald reluctantly followed the tugging on his lead and they walked down to the town to the long, wide avenue next to the station.

Lucy sat down on the first bench they came to. At least Bernie wasn't dead and that was a tremendous relief, but even so, she'd done him harm. She leaned back and closed her eyes, and tried to work out if there was any way she could contact one of the holy leaders and beg the Magnifico's forgiveness. Donald wheezed away at her feet. Passers-by noticed a sad young girl with olive skin and a wind-blown mass of soft brown curls, and they wondered why she wasn't at school.

"Maria?" said a voice. Lucy opened her eyes. A tall, elderly man stood in front of her. He was speaking to her in Welsh, and she didn't understand. She stared blankly at him. When he spoke again, it was in English.

"What are you doing here, when you should be in school? Aren't you feeling well? Come home now, *cariad*." He switched again to Welsh, and Lucy didn't reply. Taking her hand, he pulled her gently to her feet. "Why have you got a dog with you?" he asked.

By now Lucy had realised who he was, and she of the spawn and the devil's blood didn't dare speak. He chatted to her as they went along, but she understood little. As he opened the blue front door she knew she couldn't go in. She looked up at him, and gave a shaky smile. Would her voice sound all wrong to him?

"I'll have to take the dog back first." She released her hand from his, and walked away as fast as Donald's legs would go.

"Don't be long," he called after her. "Mam will have the dinner ready."

From the window in the front room, David saw her retreating figure.

"It's Lucy!" he hissed. "She's supposed to be in London!"

Dorothy jumped up and peered over his shoulder. They both made for the hall, but it was narrow, and they would have had to push rudely past Mr Jones to get out.

Dorothy ran to the kitchen. "Mrs Jones," she whispered urgently. "We've just seen Lucy going past."

"Run after her then, and bring her back!"

Evan ambled in and filled up the kitchen doorway. Dorothy gritted her teeth as she waited for him to move out of the way.

"I just saw Maria, my love," he said. "She must have missed school. There's a dog with her, and she's taking it home. She'll be back in a minute."

Gwen's heart was beating fast, but she spoke calmly. "She'll be just in time for dinner. She doesn't like school food. Run after her, Dorothy, and tell her to hurry or the meat will be cold. Did you manage to get your newspaper, Evan, dear?"

By the time Dorothy had squeezed past Mr Jones as politely as she could and dashed out of the front door, David was halfway down the street. He could see Lucy and Donald easily, despite the crowded, narrow pavement. When they reached the corner, they turned right towards the sea. At the crossroads they waited for the traffic to pass, and David caught up with them.

Lucy flinched as he grabbed her arm and then she nearly collapsed with relief.

"Flaming flesh! You gave me such a fright. I thought you were the Magnifico. Where have you been?" she wailed. "I've been really worried. There was no one in the house. I've been on my own since Friday."

"We'll explain it all. Mrs Jones said to bring you straight back for lunch."

"I can't! He thinks I'm Maria! What will he do when he realises I'm not? He'll go berserk if he finds out the devil's spawn is in his house."

"Take a chance," said David. "We can't go back to Miss Clements's place."

"Nor can I," said Lucy, "The police were there. And Gladys. Meet me on the castle after you've eaten."

They were joined by Dorothy and, after some persuasion, Lucy agreed reluctantly that as soon as Mr Jones had gone for his afternoon sleep they would come and take her back to the house. All three, and Donald, were watched with interest by the drab woman with the pink-rimmed glasses and permed hair, standing on the steps outside the station.

CHAPTER NINETEEN

Isobel followed the children to the house with the blue door, noted the number, and went up to the end of the road before turning back. What a stroke of luck, she thought. For the past three days she'd been tramping round this dreary town, and there they were, only a hundred yards up the road from her hotel.

She phoned head office and gave them the address, with instructions to find out who lived there and what connection they had with the children. Then she took out her private phone and had a satisfying chat with Drax.

"I've told them to send down an abductor again. I wanted two, but the only other one available was that Robin, and Dorothy would recognise him straight away. I'll have to make do with one. As soon as I've had the info about the household I'll decide how to approach things. This time it'll really have to work."

Drax agreed. "Don't waste time bribing anyone. Just get the kids away to some quiet spot, do what you have to do and tip them out, or chuck 'em over a cliff. Have you still got your equipment with you?"

"Yes, of course. I never go anywhere without it."

"There's been a further hold-up on my visas," he said. "Head office says they're short of staff, and even the holy leaders are melting away. I don't like to say this, but it looks to me as though the Magnifico is on the way out."

"Never!" said Isobel. She blew him a kiss down the phone. "Once the children are sorted, things will die down and there'll be a mighty resurgence, you'll see! They're still hoping to use Paul. See you soon, lover boy, with a bit of luck."

They rang off. She sat in the hotel room with her phone on a nearby coffee table, waiting to hear who lived at the house with the blue front door. Half an hour later the information came through. A Mr and Mrs Evan Jones lived there. They were the parents of Copse's deceased fifth wife, Maria, and grandparents of two of his fifteen children, Paul and Lucy Copse.

So that was Lucy Copse, right under her nose – the Jones girl in the computer class with the pre-Raphaelite hair and big, wary eyes! She certainly bore no resemblance to the scraggy, squinting child in the photograph.

There was a change of instructions from the holy leaders, and it was a very tall order. She was to try and get the three older children all at the same time if they were still at that address. If the little boy was there, she was to leave him. They'd had their eye on him, even before the night of the fire. Copse's boasting about his special powers had certainly borne fruit.

OK, she'd leave Paul. The holy leaders would keep track of his whereabouts and send Robin for him in a few weeks' time. He would have to be assessed, of course, but if he did indeed appear to have special powers, they would groom him as the next messiah and reignite the Holy Cause.

She had enough on her plate dealing with the three others.

★

The family round the Joneses' kitchen table was on tenterhooks, apart from Evan. He was remarkably cheerful.

"Maria will be here any minute," he said. "She said she had to take a dog back. I don't know whose it was. I expect she got chatting – though she shouldn't neglect her guests like this. I'll have to speak to her about her manners."

He stood up and stretched. "Time for my nap. I'll see you all at teatime."

A few minutes later they could hear him snoring. His wife looked in on him. He lay back in his brown leather chair, with his legs propped up on a matching stool. She shut the sitting-room door quietly.

Dorothy and David rushed towards the front door.

"You go and have a cup of tea." Dorothy whispered to Gwen. "We'll do the washing up when we come back."

They were back in less than fifteen minutes, with Lucy and Donald. Gwen had cleared up already and had the kettle on when they arrived. She put down an old blanket in the corner for Donald.

"I don't have to pick up Paul from school till three," she said, "so there's plenty of time for a cup of tea. Now, Lucy, tell us what happened."

Lucy sat down at the table. She spoke quietly, one ear straining in the direction of the front room. "Donald and I waited for you outside the school this morning, but I didn't see you go in."

"Oh my goodness, what a shame! I was in such a rush. Now I remember, I did see a little white dog on my way out, but I didn't know it was Donald and I didn't see you. Was there a woman talking to you?"

"Yes. She was nice and was admiring Donald. I must have got distracted just at the wrong moment."

"Well, thank goodness you're here now."

They all related their stories.

Gwen was thoughtful, and stood up to put the kettle on again. "If Miss Clements is in hospital," she murmured, "Social Services will take charge and put you somewhere else."

Three faces stared at her back in horror.

"I wonder if they'd let you stay here – though not in this house, of course, because of Evan – but somewhere nearby. Otherwise, you might be sent to Birmingham or Bristol, or anywhere, and we could lose contact – especially if they change your names again."

"No. It's alright," said Lucy hastily. "They think we're all in London. I heard Gladys tell the policeman. And obviously I can't stay here. When Mr Jones wakes up he might realise I'm not Maria. I'll have to go before he wakes up."

"We'll think of something. We can talk about it as soon as I get back with Paul. Evan will be out of this world till four o'clock on the dot"

As if to prove her wrong, there was a bellow from the front room. Gwen leaped up, and pushed Lucy out through the back door. "Wait in the yard till I say," she whispered hastily, locking the door and putting the key in her pocket.

Evan appeared in the kitchen doorway. Tears trickled down his cheeks. "I had a beautiful dream that Maria was with us," he said, "and then I woke up and remembered."

Gwen put her arms round him. "Sit down, *cariad*," she said. "I'll make you a cup of tea and get one of your tablets, and then perhaps you can finish your rest while I go and fetch Paul from school."

He sat down and looked at Dorothy and David, and wondered aloud who they were. They didn't know what to say. He sipped his tea.

"There's a dog in the corner," he said. "Sometimes I think I'm seeing things. My beautiful daughter," he wept, as he shuffled back to his chair in the other room.

"Would you like me to go and fetch Paul, Mrs Jones?" whispered Dorothy.

Gwen thought for a moment, and then shook her head. "I don't know how wise that would be," she said. "We can't be sure that their spies aren't still around. I'll go myself." She unlocked the back door and let Lucy in. "You must be freezing. You'd better go upstairs to warm up, just in case he wakes up in one of his violent rages."

She took off her apron and hung it up on the back of the kitchen door. "He can't remember afterwards, but at the time he can be frightening. I do have sedation for him, but I've had to hide it away upstairs while Paul is here."

She had quick look in the sitting room. "He's sleeping deeply now. That tablet's working, so you won't have any trouble while I'm out. Even so, I'd just feel happier if Lucy was out of sight. I'll be about twenty minutes."

She hurriedly pulled on her old beige mackintosh, grabbed an umbrella from the hall stand and left.

Dorothy took Lucy upstairs and showed her the bedrooms. "You could sleep here tonight," she said. "We could ask Mrs Jones. She's really kind."

"I can't stay in the same house as that man," said Lucy. "It's too risky. I could set him off at any time. You two had better stay here just for the moment, because you're the ones who had to escape. I doubt if the holy leaders know I'm back from London yet, so I'm alright. Donald and I will be fine up at the big house now they've caught Bernie. Gladys isn't coming back for a while, and if anyone comes to the door I won't answer it."

Dorothy had to agree. "But I think you should stay just for tonight – in case the police go back to the house."

"I don't think they will, from what Gladys said. Not unless she rings them."

There was no room to stand in the tiny box room, and they sat down on the bed.

"I wonder how they are," said Dorothy, "Miss Marilyn and Miss Clements, that is."

Lucy ran her hand over the faded old candlewick bedspread. It felt soft and comforting. "At least it sounds as if no one was killed. I don't think the policeman really knew what had happened, unless of course he was being discreet and not passing on gossip. If I go back to the house, I could go up to the hospital and see if I can find out anything."

Dorothy thought about it. "Well, that might be a good idea," she said, rather doubtfully. "I don't like to think of you in the house on your own, but I suppose you'll have Donald. He's been such a hero!"

★

Isobel was standing in front of the station, on constant watch. Every now and then, she would stroll back and forth, and look up at the clock as though she was waiting for someone – a friend perhaps. There was hardly any need, because she was so nondescript as to be barely noticeable.

At a quarter to three the blue door opened, and Gwen Jones emerged. She called a farewell into the house, and closed the door behind her. It was easy to follow her to the school, where she greeted Paul with a hug and a kiss.

Ah, so the little boy was there after all, thought Isobel. Everything was falling into place now. Copse's son and daughter were both in that house, as well as Drax's children. What a prize collection! For a moment her ambition soared. It was a pity she'd been instructed not to take Paul, but she could at least let head office know where the school was. Just as well. To get the other three all in one go would require careful planning and a lot of nerve too. She felt a buzz of excitement. It was so stimulating, this work!

She'd always been meticulous. Even as a student, her policy had been to plan, prepare and practise, leaving no room for failure.

Recalling her first public disposal always made her smile. Sitting next to a heavily pregnant woman on the underground she had smiled and chatted, and the woman had told her she was expecting twins. "How thrilling!" Isobel had said as she slid her hand sideways and pricked the woman's thigh. The train was slowing to a halt. "My stop," she said, standing up. "It was lovely talking to you. Bye."

The woman sat with her mouth suspended in mid-goodbye, and Isobel stepped off the train. The carriage was full, yet no one had noticed. Isobel was exhilarated. She couldn't wait to tell her tutor – three gone in one jab. That must be a record.

So, three was no problem. Now she watched as Gwen and Paul turned down the street that led towards the sea. They went into a bank on the left and came out again after about five minutes. The Joneses will be short of money, Isobel thought, with that lot in the house to feed. They certainly didn't look well off, judging from that shabby mac the grandmother was wearing, but a bribe was out of the question. It hadn't really worked with the two old birds, and it was even less likely to work with grandparents. But Isobel had never been short of ideas. Something would come to her.

★

"Where's Maria?" The grandfather had woken up in a benign mood.

"She popped out," replied his wife, "Her friends are upstairs with Paul. She'll be back soon."

He was surprised to see Donald lying comfortably on a blanket in the corner of the kitchen, with a bowl of water and the remains of a bone next to him.

"Why did she bring the dog back here?"

"The people were out. They'll come for him later. Now, help yourself to some *bara brith*." She put a plate of fruit loaf in front of him. "I made it last night, and it's nice and moist."

★

Upstairs, the four of them were all squashed up, sitting on Paul's bed. Lucy wished she'd left the house before he came back from school. It would be much more difficult to leave now, especially if he made a fuss, but she would definitely have to go before Mr Jones woke up. Paul was happily cuddled up to her, telling her about some naughty boy in school, but her ears were straining for Mr Jones's voice.

She hadn't heard his sitting-room door opening. All seemed quiet downstairs. Perhaps she could slip away now before it was too late. She'd wait round the corner, and one of the others could bring Donald to her. Just as she was pushing Paul gently off her lap, the doorbell rang. All chatter stopped immediately.

"It can't be about us," said Dorothy. "No one knows we're here. Paul's the only one who's here officially."

In a hurried, whispered discussion it was decided that Paul should go downstairs to stand next to Mrs Jones while she opened the door.

Dorothy gave him his instructions. "Don't speak at all while you're there," she hissed. "Not a sound. But listen to every single word."

They silently leaned over the banister as he hurried down on his important mission.

"Good afternoon, Mrs Jones," chirruped a briskly pleasant voice with a slight Welsh accent. "How do you do? My name is Sandra Williams, and I'm from Social Services. This is my identification."

There was a silence.

"We've had a report that you have several children in the house who were put into the care of a Miss Clements."

Lucy and Dorothy simultaneously clapped their hands over their mouths to suppress a gasp of horror. A vision of the social worker who had whisked David off to the disposal cells flashed before his eyes, and he felt sick. He leaned further over and could just see the hem of a long, khaki mackintosh and lace-up shoes with sturdy, round toes. Then, the top of Mr Jones's head

213

appeared as he emerged from the kitchen and joined his wife at the front door. Paul squeezed in between the two of them. He was looking at the woman's ankles, and then up at her face.

"Oh," Gwen was saying uncertainly. "Well, I suppose you had better come in."

"What does she want?" said her husband, blocking the way and studying the visitor. "I'm sorry, I didn't catch your name."

As Sandra Williams started to speak, Paul began to hum. Dorothy clutched Lucy's arm. The humming got louder. Gwen and Evan both looked down at Paul in surprise.

He burst into song. "Beware the ankles, and the chin. Beware the voice. Beware the new T-shirt," he sang.

"Paul! Don't be so rude!" said his shocked grandmother. "Just stop that! Go in the kitchen."

The song collapsed into a hum again, as Paul backed into the kitchen.

Miss Sandra Williams, for once in her life, was speechless. She stepped backwards, and Mr Jones shut the front door firmly in her face.

The little group on the landing clung to each other.

"Miss Morris!" whispered Dorothy.

They could hear Gwen speaking crossly to Paul. "I hope you never do that again, Paul. You wouldn't like it if you had a job to do and someone started humming at you."

"You two go down," whispered Lucy. "I'll stay up here till I get a chance to leave."

As Dorothy and David entered the kitchen, they could see that Gwen was upset. They guessed she would be worrying about not co-operating with Social Services.

Mr Jones sat down and pulled Paul onto his lap. "I thought he hummed very nicely," he said. "I didn't like that woman. We don't want busybodies coming to our door."

"It's not so much the humming," said Mrs Jones, "but the fact that Social Services called at the house. Who could possibly have reported us?"

"Nobody," said Dorothy, firmly. "Paul is always right when he hums, and she was a bad woman."

Evan nodded his head in agreement. "This boy can sense things," he said. "Same as me. I could feel it my bones."

The grandmother gave Paul a kiss. "I'm sorry I sounded cross, *cariad*. I was just so nervous that's all. I was afraid she was some sort of an intruder. You were quite right to warn us."

Paul was pleased with the kind attention, but he longed to be with Lucy. He had been told he mustn't mention her name.

"I think I'll go to bed now," he said, getting down off Mr Jones's lap. Dorothy and David guessed immediately what was in his mind, as did his grandmother.

Mr Jones looked at the clock. "We haven't had supper yet."

"He is looking a bit tired," said his wife. "It's all go at that school. Perhaps an early night would do him good, and we'll stay away from school tomorrow. You go up, my darling, and I'll bring you up some supper later, when you've had a bit of a rest."

"Where's Maria?"

"She's still out. I expect she bumped into a friend on the way back."

Dorothy and David looked at each other. Too many lies could make things confusing.

Gwen hurried upstairs after Paul. Lucy was sitting on his bed, listening to a story he'd heard at school. She stood up as her grandmother entered the room. "I'm just about to go, Mrs Jones," she said. "That is, if I can get down without Mr Jones seeing me. I can't stay."

Gwen knew she was right, but Paul started wailing. "I want you to stay with me."

"Hush, Paul," said Lucy anxiously. "You'll disturb Mr Jones. He's not at all well."

"He's very well. He was eating *bara brith,* and now he's going to have a nice sleep. He sleeps all the time."

"He does seem to be alright at the moment, but I'm afraid it doesn't last, and he can change at any minute – when you're least expecting it," said Gwen. "And then he becomes very cross, which is not at all like him, because he's a very nice man, but it can be upsetting for everyone."

"Don't worry. If one of the others lets me know when he's back in his room, then I'll leave," said Lucy. "And Paul, you're going to have to be good and quiet about it, because I'll see you again very soon. Remember, I'm with you in spirit."

"I don't like the idea of your being alone in the big house," said Gwen. "I'll try to try to think of someone who'd let you stay just for a night or two till we get this sorted."

"No. I'm fine on my own, honestly."

Gwen racked her brains, but unfortunately her closest friend was away, and another had German measles in the house. She simply did not have the money for a bed and breakfast, and nor did the children.

"I'll be perfectly alright," Lucy insisted, "and I'll have Donald with me. He's been so brave. I'll feel absolutely safe with him."

Paul clung on to Lucy. "Don't leave me," he wailed. "Don't leave me."

In the end, it was agreed that she'd stay upstairs with him while the others had their supper, and she'd sleep one night on Dorothy's floor. Gwen would try to make arrangements for all of them in the morning – on the strict understanding that she would not contact Social Services. Lucy spent the rest of the evening trying to concentrate on Paul's chatter, while listening for the sound of slow footsteps on the stairs.

Luckily, bedtime always came early in the Jones household. Lucy hid under Dorothy's bed when Mr Jones came upstairs. She heard him asking Paul if he felt better. He called goodnight to the others, and closed his bedroom door. Gwen came up ten minutes later. She cleared a space on Dorothy's floor for Lucy and spread a duvet over it. "You'll have to lie on this," she whispered. She smoothed two blankets over it and threw down a pillow. "Sleep well, both of you."

Lucy crawled under the blankets. The duvet was thick and soft. It was very comfortable, and it was nice not to have to listen out for the Magnifico.

★

In the front bedroom Gwen padded around, laying out Evan's clothes for tomorrow, while he tossed and turned, and muttered in his sleep. She was worrying about Sandra Williams's visit. Now that she'd had time to consider, she was confident that none of her nearest neighbours had reported her to Social Services. They would never have done such a thing.

The terrifying thought was that if Social Services were involved, not only would she lose the children, but Evan might be taken away too.

Thanks to her nursing background and training on how use the tranquilizing syringes, the doctor had agreed to let her keep him at home despite his terrible rages; but neither she nor the doctor had expected her to have a house full of children. She couldn't possibly turn them out into the street when they were in danger but, at the same time, she had no right to keep them if they were at risk from her own husband.

Their dread of the police and Social Services was understandable, considering their past experiences, and the last thing she wanted was to betray them. That Mr Lovett was supposed to be back in his office by tomorrow, so she'd get hold of him in the morning. He'd know what to do. She climbed into bed and switched off the bedside light.

*

In the next room, David lay on a duvet on the floor, half-listening to the movements as Mrs Jones prepared for bed. He knew he'd sleep well tonight, now that Lucy was back. They were all together again and the world felt full of hope, despite today's visitor.

Just as he was dropping off, there was crash.

CHAPTER TWENTY

David shot upright and listened. There was another crash, a bang and a clatter, all interspersed by bellows of rage. He could hear Gwen softly pleading, and then a terrible roar.

"I will not have that man's blood in my house!"

Gwen's soft voice rose and fell, but David couldn't catch the words. The roar began again.

"I knew there was something wrong. I felt it. We've been tricked. Tricked by the devil's spawn," bellowed Evan. "I can sense it. The devil's spawn is in my house, this very house!"

Gwen's voice became clear. "You're having a nightmare, Evan, there's no devil's spawn."

"It's not a nightmare. It's real. The voice was wrong!" There was another crash. "It wasn't her voice."

David scrambled out of his makeshift bedding. It was all his and Dorothy's fault. They should never have come. A kind grandmother had taken them in, and this was her reward.

Paul was sitting up. "It's the frogs," he whispered.

David pulled him out of bed, and shoved him into the girls' bedroom. "Stay with Lucy," he hissed.

He shut the door and crossed the landing. Should he interfere? Supposing he made it worse? He had to do something, but he was afraid. His hand was on the door knob. He hesitated. What did Aunt Bertha say about difficult situations? "Behave like a gentleman. Manners give you a structure. They hold you together."

He knocked firmly on the door and stepped inside. A stool flew across the room. Gwen was ducking and holding out a tablet at the same time. A bedside lamp lay upside down. It flickered and died. David switched on the main light.

Mr Jones stopped in mid-bellow, and turned. David circumvented a broken chair and put a shaky hand on his arm.

"Are you alright, sir?" he said. "You must be having a nightmare. If you lie down, I'll sit with you for a while, and we'll think of something pleasant to make it go away."

Gwen pushed a tablet into the side of her husband's mouth and held a glass of water to his lips.

He stared at David's pyjamas and drank without noticing. They reminded him of Maria. "Who is this boy?" he said.

"I'm David, sir, a friend of your daughter's."

"Have we met before?"

"Yes, sir."

As they spoke, Gwen hastily snatched something out of the dressing-table drawer, tore off its wrapping and then plunged a syringe straight into the back of her husband's left thigh.

He rubbed the spot. "I think something just bit me," he said drowsily. "We'll have to get the spray out tomorrow." He lay down on the bed. "Maria's friends are always welcome," he mumbled as he fell asleep.

Gwen pulled the blankets over him, and gasped with relief. David clenched his teeth together to stop them chattering.

"Thank you," whispered Gwen.

David found the others huddled together on Dorothy's camp bed.

Lucy was trembling. "I'll have to go," she said. "I should never have come."

"Well, you can't go in the middle of the night," said David. He tried to sound firm, but his voice quavered. He pulled Dorothy's blanket round his shoulders.

"The police would pick you up and ask what you were doing out so late," whispered Dorothy. "Tomorrow, if he's back to normal, David and I will take Mr Jones for a walk up the avenue, and you and Donald can creep out. When we can, we'll join you up at the big house and contact Mr Lovett."

Paul was beginning to object. "I want to go with Lucy."

"Well, I'm afraid you can't," said Dorothy firmly. "But you'll be able to speak to her on the phone."

"But," said Lucy, "if you come to the house, Sandra Williams might come there to look for you."

"She might, but on the other hand she might think we'd not be so daft as to go back there. She'd assume we'd hide somewhere less obvious. Once we're there, we can ring Mr Lovett without upsetting Mr Jones or getting Mrs Jones into trouble. Tomorrow's Tuesday, so he'll be back in the office. He'll know what to do. If he's not there, we'll say it's urgent and for him to ring us back."

Everyone went back to bed, but the only one who slept was Evan Jones. Lucy could hear him snoring. She decided not to wait for the others to take him up the avenue. The sooner she went, the sooner they'd all be safer. Early in the morning, while it was still dark, she got dressed.

"I'll see you later," she whispered in Paul's ear. "Remember, I'm with you in spirit." He mumbled sleepily. She fetched Donald from his comfortable bed, and they slipped out, closing the front door quietly behind them.

If that woman was watching, she thought, well that was just too bad; and if police infiltrators came to the big house and found her there, well that was too bad too. There really seemed no point in life if she always had to be running and hiding. She was fed up with not trusting people, and always being on guard, and worrying about being safe. All those weeks with Miss Clements had been too good to last. It would be easier to give herself up to the Magnifico, and say, "Come and get me, I'm all yours."

She mentally gave herself a good shake. Now that she had found the others, she knew she couldn't give in. They needed her as much as she needed them.

*

Isobel was not watching as Lucy left the house early on the Tuesday morning. She was still asleep, having lain awake half the night formulating her plan. It was really annoying that they had only sent one abductor down this time, instead of two. They just hadn't got the staff, she'd been told. The abductor who had come said that if things got any worse, head office would be closing down. She would have to worry about that later. At the moment, she had a project to carry out.

Sandra Williams would go back to the house with the blue door, accompanied by the abductor. He would be dressed in an official-looking suit, and would carry identification and a court order. The car would be waiting on the double yellow lines right outside the house, with its doors unlocked, ready to leap into. She would show Mrs Jones official-looking documentation requiring her to hand over the following three children, namely Dorothy and David Drax, and Lucy Copse. They were to be taken into secure care for their own safety until they were required for the forthcoming trial of Lucy's father.

All the children, except for that dreadful humming boy, would be ushered out onto the pavement. The abductor would get into the driver's seat and turn on the engine. Isobel would help each child into the back seat, while blocking the view of the child behind. Her handbag would be hooked over her left wrist with the syringes lying in a plastic tray on the top, lightly hidden by a piece of silk and ready for a quick jab as each child climbed in. As soon as she slammed the door after the last child, she would jump in on the passenger side, and the locks would be slammed down. The car would move gently away with three, apparently sleeping, children in the back.

She had successfully carried out similar operations before, and was fully confident that it would work. It was just a matter of detailed preparation and keeping her cool. If she were to produce the bodies of all three children to the holy leaders, her services to the Magnifico would be rewarded handsomely, in this world and the next.

★

Drax rang the following morning after breakfast. He approved the plan.

"Good riddance to the lot of them," he said. "Head office have told me my papers have come through, and I'm off to Chile next week. By the time I reach Mexico, I'll have had a complete surgical make-over. You won't recognise me."

She laughed. It was an effort, because her head was splitting with the sound of the sea. She put on her affectionate-wife act. "I'll always recognise you, lover boy! It's not just your height. It's the way you move."

Their banter turned to argument.

"You wouldn't have recognised me yesterday," declared Drax triumphantly. "I was in full disguise. Hat, moustache and make-up. I took the bus to Regent Street, and wandered round Liberty's and had tea there. Then I went to a concert in the evening."

Isobel tried to suppress a splurge of anger. "I wish you wouldn't! You'll get caught." How often had she said that? He just would not listen.

"Nag, nag, nag! I'm so bored. Cooped up like a battery hen."

Isobel snapped. "Who's fault is that? Whose fault is it that the Magnifico was exposed? Whose fault is it that everyone, not just you, has had to go into hiding?" She didn't wait for an answer. "You and Copse, and your idiotic rivalries. That's who."

Drax was too taken aback to speak.

Isobel's softly-cultured voice had developed into a shriek. "You and Thomas have ruined the Holy Cause with your stupid attack on Copse's house. If it weren't for you, the Holy Cause would never have become public knowledge, the communes and the schools would still be thriving, and the breeding rooms would be producing future followers at a rate of knots. And all you do is moan like a spoiled brat."

She slammed the phone down and switched the ring tone to mute. There were more important things to think of than that idiot on the other end.

Drax sat silent with shock. No one had ever spoken to him like that in all his life. Indeed, it was unlikely that any wife had ever spoken like that to any Father. His head surged with red-hot anger. Isobel would have to be disposed of immediately. Almost blinded with rage, he stood up, stumbled to the bathroom, and took the box of syringes down from the top of the cupboard. She thought she was so clever, so efficient, always keeping her stocks well supplied. Well, she'd been a bit too clever this time. He grabbed a syringe, tore off its packaging and removed the safety tip. Then he laid it carefully on the coffee table in the sitting room and covered it with his handkerchief. He was huge and she was tiny. She would never escape him.

CHAPTER TWENTY-ONE

Breakfast in the little terraced house was a subdued affair. Mr Jones was still asleep. Lucy and Donald had gone, and Paul was anxious. Gwen Jones was deeply upset by the night's events, as they all were, but at least she was used to it, she thought, whereas these poor children were not. Thank goodness she'd had the syringes handy. If it weren't for them Evan would have had to be put away, and she just couldn't bear to think of it.

"Have Mr Jones's frogs gone?" asked Paul.

"Yes, they've all gone, *cariad*. They won't come back."

"Mrs Jones," said David. "What was in that syringe you injected Mr Jones with?"

"It's a tranquillizer, love. The doctor gave me them. Just in case of emergency. Sometimes the tablets are enough, but not always, so then I use the syringe. It's very quick and makes him go nicely to sleep for hours, and when he wakes up he's forgotten everything. He'd be terribly upset if he knew what he'd done."

Her eyes filled with tears. "He's always been such a lovely man – so gentle and good to me and Maria." She fished in her pocket for a handkerchief, blew her nose and added bitterly, "I don't believe in hell or things like that, but if there is a hell then I hope those people who did this to him, and to our Maria, will go there forever."

She wiped away her tears, and stood up briskly. "Now I'm off to the supermarket before it gets busy. He'll be sleeping for hours yet. Paul needn't go to school today. I've phoned the school. He can come shopping with me, and we'll be very quick. Don't open the door while I'm out. You can answer the phone. It'll probably be Lucy calling to let you know she's alright. By the time we're back, Mr Lovett should be in his office and we can give him a ring."

Lucy rang just after they left. Yes, everything was fine. She and Donald had slept well. Later on she'd go to find out about the visiting hours in the hospital. Was it too early to ring Mr Lovett yet? What would they do if that woman came back?

"Don't worry," said David. "If she comes we'll sort it, and Mrs Jones is going to ring Mr Lovett. See you later." He put the phone down, and looked at Dorothy.

"I'm going to get one of those syringes," he said quietly, "I've got a plan, just in case."

He tiptoed up the stairs and listened outside the front bedroom. The door was ajar. He pushed it slowly and peered into the room. Mr Jones lay on his back, his head turned slightly away towards the window. He was breathing heavily. David tried to see his eyes. They seemed to be shut.

The dressing table was to the left, just behind the door. It was still covered with broken glass. Silently, David slid out the drawer. There was a row of slim packages, each holding a syringe. He took two, just in case something went wrong with the first one, and shut the drawer quietly. It gave a little click. Mr Jones moved his head and his eyes opened. David stood still. The eyes turned in his direction.

"Good morning, sir," he said. "Did you sleep well?"

Mr Jones raised his head slightly and dropped it back again. "Like a log, boy. Thank you for asking."

"I'll go down and fetch you some coffee," said David.

"Thank you, dear boy. I'll have it in bed, and then I'll be as fit as a fiddle."

David's head was buzzing as he ran down the stairs.

"I nearly passed out when he looked at me," he whispered to Dorothy. "Quick, pour him a coffee, and I'll take it up. Then I'll tell you my plan."

When he took the coffee up, Mr Jones was fast asleep and snoring gently.

Back in the kitchen, David and Dorothy examined the syringes.

"I saw her doing it last night," whispered David. "You flick off the tip, and then you just stick it in the back of the thigh and press the flat bit down."

Dorothy picked one up one and inspected it. She ran her thumb gently over the flat top. "We'll have to be careful not to stab ourselves. I'd just love to stick this needle into Sandra Williams."

"Now, hear my plan. We'll keep watch from the window – all day if we have to. If she comes before we've got hold of Mr Lovett, we'll invite her into the front room, unless Mr Jones is in there, in which case, it's the back room. We'll ask Mrs Jones to take Paul to the kitchen, because we'd like a quiet word with Sandra Williams on our own, without the humming. We'll each have one of these syringes. Whichever one of us manages to get behind her will stick it in the back of her thigh. She should conk out pretty quickly. Mr Jones flopped straight away last night."

"He's much bigger than she is," said Dorothy, "so it should work even better on her."

"Where did you put our anoraks? We can say we were just about to go out."

They put on their anoraks and laid the syringes carefully along the bottom of their pockets, so as not to press them accidentally. Then they wrote out Mr Lovett's number and put it next to the house phone on the table by the window.

"Right," said David. "Now let's practise. We can't afford to fail. Planning, preparation and practice. That's the secret." He stopped, surprised at his own eloquence. "Hey, that sounded good," he said, "I wonder how I thought that one up!"

Two hours passed before Mr Jones woke up properly. Paul and his grandmother returned from shopping. She phoned Mr Lovett and was told he was in court. By eleven o'clock, Mr Jones was seated at the kitchen table devouring a late breakfast with gusto. David and Dorothy were still in their anoraks, keeping watch at the front window.

"Perhaps she won't come," muttered David. "Perhaps Sandra Williams isn't Miss Morris after all. Perhaps she's a harmless old biddy and we're getting paranoid."

Just as he finished speaking, a car drew up and parked outside on the double yellow lines. They both tensed. A woman emerged from the passenger side. She was carrying a large handbag. Their hearts thumped.

"There she is. Flaming flesh! There's a man with her," whispered Dorothy. She dashed to the kitchen just as the doorbell went. "I'll get it Mrs Jones, you stay there," she said breathlessly.

Paul scrambled down from a chair and tried to come out, but she gently pushed him back.

"I want to answer the bell," he said indignantly.

"Not this time. You go and help Mrs Jones get the lunch ready," she said.

Gwen gave her a quick nod. "Come on, Paul. I want you to stir this pudding mixture for me."

Dorothy gave him another little push, and shut the door after him.

David was already opening the front door. There stood Sandra Williams and an official-looking gentleman in a dark-blue suit, with a clipboard in his hand.

"We've come to see Mrs Gwen Jones," said Sandra Williams in her crisp, business-like voice.

Gwen appeared in the hallway.

A second later Paul's face peeped round her legs. "My feet are still in the kitchen," he called.

"Good morning, Mrs Jones. It's Sandra Williams. We met yesterday. This is my colleague, Mr Preston." She was already in the hall as she spoke, and Mr Preston was close behind her.

"Oh," said Gwen. She was at a loss for words.

"Paul go back in the kitchen and talk to Mr Jones," snapped Dorothy. She shoved him in once more and said fiercely under her breath, "and don't come out till I tell you."

"We have been informed that you have four children here who are supposed to be in care, and we have documentation from the court ordering you to hand three of them over to us for safe custody," said Sandra, pushing her pink-rimmed glasses firmly up on her nose. Damn these things, she thought. They kept slipping, and the wig was itching. She hoped this wouldn't take long.

Dorothy stepped forward. "Good morning, Miss Williams. Good morning, Mr Preston. I'm Dorothy. Of course we'll come with you, if the court orders it."

230

A humming sound floated out from the kitchen, and Mr Jones was laughing. "You're a good hummer." The humming got louder and louder.

"Shall we go into the sitting room, Miss Williams," said Dorothy, ushering her in to the front room. "We can talk quietly in there. Would you like to come through, Mr Preston? Then you can show us the court order. This hall's too narrow for us all."

As they filed in, David turned to Gwen who was standing speechless, almost ready to faint. "You go into the kitchen, Mrs Jones," he said quietly. "Dorothy and I will look at the papers, and we'll call you if we need you."

He turned her gently and held the kitchen door open for her. When he came back Dorothy was carefully scrutinising the court order. He slipped his hand into his pocket.

"Yes, you've got all the names right," Dorothy was saying, "though Lucy Copse isn't here. She left early this morning and we're not sure where she is at the moment. David and I will come. Should we go and pack?"

Miss Williams was just in the process of saying, "Come as you are," when David jabbed his syringe into the back of her thigh.

"What on earth?" she exclaimed, slapping her leg. Then she swayed.

"You're faint," said David. "Let me help you into a chair."

Mr Preston realised at once what had happened.

"Why you little devil!" he snarled, and grabbed at the syringe in David's hand. As he did so, he felt a sharp jab in the back of his leg and swivelled round to face Dorothy. He lunged at her. She stepped back, and he fell forward. He made a feeble effort to rise, and then his

231

head dropped face-down on the floor. The humming in the kitchen stopped.

"He's gone," whispered Dorothy.

David waited for the buzzing in his ears to die down before slipping out of the room and putting his head round the kitchen door. "Would you like to come in now, Mrs Jones?" he said, trying to sound calm. "Paul you stay where you are. Mr Jones might want you to make him some more toast."

Gwen stood transfixed in the sitting-room doorway. Dorothy and David stared in awe at their handiwork.

"I cannot believe that we did that," said David eventually.

"Nor me."

Sandra Williams lay sideways across an armchair. Her permed wig was askew, and her real hair, pinned in little circles close to her scalp, gleamed silver against the lifeless brown. Her bag had fallen to the floor and burst open.

"Fire of the melting flesh! Just look at that!" cried Dorothy, pointing at the three syringes that had spilled out onto the carpet. "Those were for us!"

The hairs rose on the backs of their necks.

Gwen Jones's soft voice cut across the shocked silence. She had recovered just enough from her initial horror to realise that some sort of action was required. "Don't touch anything," she said. "I'll ring the police."

"No, we can't!" chimed Dorothy and David in unison. "Infiltrators!"

"Mr Lovett will know who to trust," said Dorothy. "He'll send someone. How long should the drug last?"

"About four hours," said Gwen. "It lasted longer on Evan because I gave him a tablet as well."

Dorothy shuddered. "Well, let's hope we don't need to do that! I'd be sick if I had to shove a pill into their disgusting mouths."

Paul's face appeared round his grandmother's legs. He surveyed the scene with satisfaction. "Good," he said. "She was bad. She made my hum come."

There was a sound of shuffling chairs in the kitchen.

Gwen darted off. "You can sit in the back room this morning, Evan," she said. "I'll put the gas fire on for you. David and Dorothy are giving the front room a good spring clean, so you won't get any peace in there."

She waited for him to object, but he was in an amenable mood today.

"That'll make a change for me," he said affably. "Sometimes I get tired of that front room without Maria to come and sit with me. I shall sit by the fire and read my paper, and Paul can keep me company and do some drawings at the table."

While Gwen was settling her husband, David picked up the scrap of paper by the telephone. His fingers fumbled as he dialled Mr Lovett's number.

"Their car's on double yellow lines," he remarked as he waited for a reply. "I wonder if the traffic warden's seen it. Ah! Hello. May we speak to Mr Lovett please?"

Mr Lovett was not available, said the receptionist.

"But it's urgent!"

"He's in court all morning, and he won't be back till half past one."

"Could you please tell him to ring us back as soon as he gets in?" said David. "It's urgent. Tell him it's David who was a witness in the arson case when the Copse house burned down." He gave the number, stressed the urgency, and put the phone back in its cradle.

"I bet she won't tell him," he said despondently. "She sounded as though she didn't care. She said he won't be back till half past one. That's in an hour and a quarter. They shouldn't have woken up by then. If he doesn't ring back we'll ring again, and just keep ringing."

"Were there any more syringes in the drawer?" asked Dorothy.

"Yes. Two."

"Good. If one of them stirs before he rings, we'll give them another dose." She eyed the three syringes that lay on the carpet next to Sandra Williams's handbag, and David followed her gaze.

"There's something very tempting about those particular syringes," she said with a nervous little laugh. "So humane!"

David gasped. The blood rushed to his head. "Don't even think it!"

"No, no. Of course not. It was just a joke." Dorothy herself was shocked. "Holy fire!" she said, "I'll turn into one of them if I'm not careful. Now that's something that really would frighten me!"

CHAPTER TWENTY-TWO

Gwen was white-faced and shaking and moving aimlessly about, wondering whether she should peel some potatoes, or try to hide the bodies, or ring the police.

David hugged her. "You've been good to us," he said, "and we've brought you nothing but trouble."

Dorothy put her arms round them both, and for a moment they held each other close.

"Right!" said Gwen, eventually detaching herself. "I must pull myself together."

They decided on a cup of tea, and sat silently round the table. Time seemed to stand still.

"It'll never be half past one," sighed Dorothy. She tossed her head and stood up. "I'll find something to do. It'll help pass the time."

She popped her head in the back room. Mr Jones was asleep in the chair. Paul held up his picture and whispered, "It's Lucy."

Dorothy admired it. In fact, it did look very like Lucy – and very like the twelve-year-old Maria in the photograph.

"That's exactly how she stands, and how her hair floats away from her face," she said, genuinely impressed. "I don't know how you do it!"

Paul wrote his name at the top of the paper and put his crayons back into his pencil case.

"That's a tidy boy," said Dorothy quietly. "And now I'd like you to come up with me to make the beds. Don't thump on the stairs because we don't want to wake Mr Jones."

David helped Gwen finish preparing the lunch, not that any of them felt like eating. He scraped some carrots and peeled the potatoes, and put some washing in the machine, but whenever he looked at the clock the hands had hardly moved. Every now and then, he or Dorothy would unlock the sitting-room door and check the contents. The two bodies lay exactly as they had left them.

When one o'clock came, the time seemed to go even more slowly.

"If we can't get hold of him straight away," said Dorothy, "we'll just have to give in and call the local police, and keep our fingers crossed that they're genuine. Someone simply has to come before they wake up."

At twenty past one, Dorothy and David told Paul to stay in the kitchen and help Mrs Jones lay the table, and they locked themselves in the sitting room. Mr Lovett rang just before half past. Despite the anticipation, they nearly jumped out of their skins. The bodies didn't move.

David took the call. Mr Lovett knew at once who he was. David tried not to gabble as he explained the situation.

"So they're still asleep here in the sitting room," he said finally, "But they might wake up in an hour or two."

Mr Lovett was already on another phone. Dorothy had her ear right up against David's head. They could hear him speaking urgently.

"Get on to him double-quick, but no one else," he was saying.

Back to David, he said, "Stay put. Someone local will come. You can trust him. He'll give you a code name of Peter Pan. Don't let anyone else in, except for the men he brings with him, and don't leave the house. I'll get hold of Beverley. If she's free she'll come for you today, and if she's not, it'll be tomorrow, Wednesday."

Lightheaded with relief they squeezed each other tight.

"Let me speak to Mrs Jones," said Mr Lovett.

David unlocked the door and called Gwen in, and locked it again behind her.

She trembled as Mr Lovett explained the instructions he had given to David. "It's going to be alright," she assured herself as she put the phone back in its stand. She averted her eyes and stepped round Mr Preston's body. "Once they take these dreadful people away, we can relax."

A hand rattled the door knob.

"What dreadful people?" came Evan's voice. "What's the matter with this door? It's stuck. It's not locked is it?"

As Gwen's shaking hands unlocked the door, Dorothy positioned herself beside her to block any view into the room.

"It's alright dear." Gwen's voice was steady. "Dorothy and David didn't want Paul to come in before they finished the cleaning. He was laying the table for me, so we can eat now." She put her hand on her husband's arm, and gently turned him towards the kitchen.

Dorothy clenched her teeth for a moment to stop them chattering and then took a deep breath. "Did you have a nice nap, Mr Jones?" she called after them, as brightly as she could. "You've woken up just in time for lunch."

"It's not lunch, it's dinner," he said rather grumpily. He didn't like having doors locked in his own house, especially by people who didn't belong there. His wife could see the early signs of a rage, and was silently praying that it wouldn't erupt.

Dorothy tried to smile, but he turned away from her and didn't see the horror in her eyes.

"I'm sorry, Mr Jones. It's dinner," she said. "I've got to get it right. I'm really grateful when you tell me how to do things properly."

His face cleared. "Now, tell me your name again, you pretty girl," he said, as they settled themselves around the table. "I've forgotten why you are here."

Gwen had difficulty eating. Her hands trembled so much that Dorothy jumped up and served the meal for her.

Her husband was concerned. "You must go and lie down, *cariad*," he said. "There's something wrong with you. Somebody had one of those modern bugs around here the other day, but I can't remember who it was."

"I'll be alright in a little while," she said. "I'm just a bit shaky, that's all. I think I might have been overdoing things lately."

"You do too much. You should get them to change your shifts at the hospital – or perhaps you could ask them to let you go part-time. I don't how you do it, working full-time and running this house, and looking after me and Maria."

She smiled at him and patted his hand. "It's never too much for me to look after you, *cariad*."

The atmosphere round the table relaxed, and the children tried to eat.

"I like to see good appetites," said Mr Jones.

The doorbell rang before they had finished the first course. David jumped up. "I'll go," he said hastily.

They heard him open the front door. There were voices and someone went into the sitting room. David poked his head into the kitchen.

"It's alright. Please don't disturb yourselves. Just carry on eating. It's visitors for Dorothy and me." He could see the look of puzzlement gathering on Evan's face as Dorothy scrambled to her feet. "I do apologise, sir. I know it's a cheek having visitors at your house, but they'll be gone in a minute," he said.

"Off you go, my dear," said Evan to Dorothy. "Maria's friends, and their friends, are always welcome in our house."

He carried on eating, and Paul had a second helping, while Gwen toyed with the food on her plate.

CHAPTER TWENTY-THREE

Someone took photographs. The bodies were quickly removed into a waiting van, and the handbag and its spilled contents were taken away, together with an interesting assortment of clothes and wigs that were found in the boot of the car. Peter Pan waved off his helpers, and both the van and the car drove off. Dorothy straightened the cushions in the sitting room, and the whole thing was over in less than ten minutes.

"That's it then," said Peter Pan. "Well done, you two. You can relax now. I'm told your escort will contact you and tell you what to do next. Don't leave the house till you've spoken to her."

Mr Jones heard a familiar voice, and appeared in the hall. His face lit up. "Well, hello there, Sam, old boy! How are you? I haven't seen you for months. Are you still rounding up all the crooks?"

Peter Pan shook his hand warmly. "Yes. I'm still at it, Evan. As soon as we round up one lot, there's a fresh supply coming in. I was just passing, and thought I'd pop my head in to say hello and see how you were."

Evan was delighted. His wife smiled nervously behind him, always afraid of what he might do next.

"This house is getting just like the old days, when people were always in and out," he said happily. "Our young friends had visitors only a few minutes ago, and now you're here. Come in and have a coffee."

"Just a quick one then. Thank you."

He followed them into the kitchen, where Paul was on his third helping of pudding. Sam gave him a big wink.

Paul inspected him with interest, and then smiled. "The hum's not coming," he said, to no one in particular.

"Maria's not here," Mr Jones was telling Sam. "She's away at university somewhere." He turned to his wife "Where is her college, *cariad*? Oh, I remember. It's in London. She'll be back in a few weeks. You'd never recognise her, old boy, she's so grown up. Such a little beauty!"

When Sam stood up to leave he patted his old friend on the shoulder and gave the others a cheery wave, but his face was sad as he left the house. He turned and gave Gwen a card with his private number on. "Ring me any time if you need help, Gwen, love," he said. "Lovett and I will be keeping each other informed."

He gave her a kiss on the cheek and left. She went back to the kitchen and warmed up a plateful of cottage pie in the microwave.

"I'm glad you're feeling better, my dear," said her husband as he watched her eat. "It does us both good to have all this company. We've missed Maria while she's been away."

As soon as Mr Jones had gone for his afternoon nap, Dorothy rang the big house to give Lucy the news, but there was no answer.

"She's probably gone to the hospital," said David. "We'll try again later."

They didn't have the chance, because Mr Jones hardly slept a wink. He woke up revitalised and sat in the kitchen chatting non-stop about old friends and happy days gone by. He went upstairs a few times to look for Maria. "She must have popped out," he said each time when he came down. "I expect she was feeling better. She'll be back in a minute."

★

David ran his long fingers softly over the piano keys. He liked the feel and the sound.

"It feels kind of therapeutic," he said. "I wish we could have learned music at the Mag's school. We don't even know any tunes. Everyone at this school knows all sorts of music, and all we know is a couple of hymns and chants to the Mag."

Dorothy was sitting in Evan's chair, and hoped he wouldn't mind. She had avoided the chair over which Sandra Williams's body had been draped. They were supposed to be relaxing, but they hardly knew what to do with themselves after the day's excitement.

"Well, you can have piano lessons when we've bought our own house. Perhaps you've got a talent. Look how long your fingers are!"

It was peaceful in the front room, and both felt drained. When the phone rang, they guessed it was unlikely to be Lucy. She wouldn't risk having to speak to the grandfather. Gwen hurried in to answer it, and handed it over to David.

"Wrong number," she said to her husband when she

went back to the kitchen. He was telling Paul a story about the adventures of his great grandfather, the sea captain, and took no notice.

It was Beverley on the phone. She couldn't make it tonight, she told David, but would be down the following day, Wednesday. She'd be taking them all back to London, where they would be placed in secure care.

"We don't want to go to London," said David. "We're secure here now that woman's been caught."

"Well, I'll see what I can do, but those are my instructions at the moment. I'm told you need money, so I'll bring some with me, and we'll have to give Mrs Jones something for your keep so far."

"That's great, thanks."

"I hear you've done a fantastic job, so congrats. They've been trying to catch Isobel Drax for months. She's supposed to be the most dangerous of all the Good Doctors, and she's the cleverest. Brilliantly clever. It's a bit ironic that she was caught by a dose of her own medicine. She laughed. "Except, of course, your injection wasn't lethal."

"Yeah, OK, we'll see you tomorrow," said David trying to ring off politely.

"Righty ho! You must be made of tough stuff to be able to turn in your own mother like that. I'll be off now. Toodle-oo."

"Stop! Don't go! What do you mean, my own mother?"

"Isobel Drax, of course."

There was a silence.

"Oh, didn't you know? It was in the commune records."

Dorothy watched the colour drain from David's face as he dropped the phone back onto the stand, and collapsed into the nearest chair.

"What is it?" she cried, but he couldn't speak.

She ran to the kitchen. "Mrs Jones, come quickly! I think David's passed out."

By the time they reached the sitting room, David was on his feet, white-faced and shaking.

"I must go," he mumbled. Grabbing his anorak off the peg in the hall, he stumbled out into the street and took several deep breaths of fresh air. Then he pulled the door shut behind him.

"I'll go after him," cried Dorothy. "I don't know what she said to him, but it was something about his own mother."

She turned right out of the house and ran up to the corner, and looked down towards the sea. The pavements were fairly clear, but there was no sign of David. She ran back up to the other end of the street and then crossed over towards the avenue. He could be anywhere. She returned to the house, but he hadn't come back.

"It was a happy phone call," she told Gwen. "I heard him say, 'That's great,' and thanking her, and he sounded really pleased. Then suddenly he went as white as a sheet."

"He'll be back soon, I expect," said Gwen, trying to reassure herself as well as Dorothy. "He knows this town well by now, and he's not going to get lost. Once it starts getting dark, he'll be back."

Evening fell, and still David did not come back.

"Of course!" said Dorothy. "I should have thought! He'll have gone up to the big house to be with Lucy — though Peter Pan did tell us not to leave this house. He's probably gone to tell her that the Ginger Witch has been caught."

She picked up the phone and dialled with shaking fingers. There was no answer.

★

Lucy knew where the hospital was because she passed it every day on her way up the hill to school. She put a dried pig's ear into Donald's basket, and he dutifully followed it in and curled up comfortably to have a satisfying crunch.

"I'll be back soon. Be a good boy and guard the house," she said.

Donald gave a little twitch of his tail and concentrated on his treat. She left the kitchen light on to deter burglars, switched on the radio softly, and let herself out through the front door.

Five minutes later, she was up at the hospital asking where she would find Miss Clements. The receptionist looked in the book.

"We have two Miss Clementses," she said, "a Marilyn Clements and a Primrose Clements. Which one are you visiting?"

They were both alive! Lucy's spirits soared. "Both of them, please. Are they in the same ward?"

"No, but I can tell you their wards." The woman gave Lucy directions, and she set off along the corridor to find the proper Miss Clements first. She'd go and see Miss Marilyn after.

As she approached Miss Clements's ward, the boiler man emerged. Lucy was so used to seeing him in Miss Clements's kitchen it took her a second to recognise him out of context.

"Oh! Hello, Mr Nicholas," she said brightly as he walked past.

He stopped and looked hard at her, and wondered who she was for a moment. All kids looked the same, but she seemed familiar. One of those London children.

"Hello," he said, "are you on your way to see Miss Clements?"

"Yes," said Lucy. "You'll be pleased to know the boiler's working properly. The house is lovely and warm at the moment."

He smiled. What a nice girl! A credit to Primrose and her careful upbringing of children. "That's good. I like to be useful," he said.

"Bye," she said cheerfully.

She found Miss Clements looking very much alive, sitting in an armchair, knitting. There was an open tin of Quality Street on the bed next to her, and she had a peaceful smile on her face. As soon as she saw Lucy, she put down her knitting needles in pleased surprise.

"Why, Lucy!" she exclaimed. "I thought you were still in London. How lovely to see you, dear! Mr Lovett did ring to say when you were coming back and I should have written it down, but what with one thing or another and life's so hectic, is it not, I completely forgot,"

She seemed genuinely delighted, but then she looked anxious. "Tell me, dear," she said in a whisper. "Are David and Dorothy alright?"

"Yes, they're fine, Miss Clements. So is Paul. They're all with Mrs Jones at the moment," confirmed Lucy.

Miss Clements gave a long slow sigh of relief. "I'm truly thankful to hear that," she said. "I've been so anxious about them, and now I don't need to worry any more. Worry puts so much pressure on one, does it not, dear?"

Lucy agreed.

"I'm coming home tomorrow, you know. We had a nasty accident, Miss Marilyn and I. The car went over a cliff." She sighed. "It's most disturbing to remind myself of it. I must think of something else. Would you like a Quality Street? Mr Nicholas, the boiler man, just brought them for me. So kind, don't you think? Have more than that, dear. Take a handful and put them in your pocket. I can't possibly eat all those by tomorrow."

"Thank you. I'll take some for the others," said Lucy, filling her pocket. "What happened?"

"Well, I was knocked unconscious for forty-eight hours, concussed you know – which was a good thing really, because it saved me having to worry about why no one was coming to rescue us for such a long time. No one noticed the car until two days later, because it went into the gorse bushes, and it's that dreary, brownish-grey colour that Marilyn insisted on when we bought it. So dull. 'Mole', I think it's called. It was raining so hard no one saw it. So, being unconscious helped to pass the time. But poor Marilyn broke all sorts of bits and pieces, and it did put her in a very bad mood. In a way, I'm quite relieved that she's in a different ward."

"You poor things!" cried Lucy. "It must have been really frightening! But I'm so glad you're both going to be alright. When I was walking Donald, a policeman told me there'd been an accident, but he didn't know any details about it."

"Donald!" exclaimed Miss Clements. "I will never forgive myself, but I forgot all about him until after we left, and then it was too late. The policeman said there wasn't a dog in the house when he went round, and I thought the RSPCA must have taken him away. And he was with you all that time!"

Tears of guilt and relief trickled down her face, and Lucy passed her a tissue from the box on the bedside table.

"Well, he's alright now," she said, "because I've been looking after him, and he's been looking after me."

"I can never thank you enough, dear," said Miss Clements, taking her hand, and Lucy knew that she was sincerely grateful.

"I'd better go now, if I'm to see Miss Marilyn as well," she said. "Is there anything you want me to get for you before you come back tomorrow?"

"Just take a loaf out of the freezer, there's a good girl, and there should be ten pounds in the housekeeping drawer, so get me a pint of milk and some eggs. It'll be lovely to be home again."

"I'll see Miss Marilyn," said Lucy, "and then I'll have to get back because Donald will be wondering where I am."

"Don't spend too much time with Marilyn, dear. I wouldn't like Donald to be upset."

★

Lucy found Miss Marilyn trussed up in bandages, with her leg in a hoist.

"Oh, you're here are you?" Miss Marilyn's tone was no more gracious than it had ever been, but Lucy did sense that she was pleased to see her. "Tell me what's happened to David and Dorothy," she said anxiously. "Did they get away?"

"They're fine, Miss Marilyn. They're at Mrs Jones's house with Paul."

"I told them to try and get to London"

"Yes, I know, but they turned back because there was a bad storm, and they're safe with Mrs Jones – my grandmother, that is. They're truly grateful to you for helping them escape."

Miss Marilyn sniffed.

Lucy changed the subject. "Is your leg very painful? I hope you're not suffering."

"I'm on painkillers, so that helps. But they're all so slow here. I'd be up and about by now if only they'd get a move on."

She didn't look as though she'd be up and about for a long time, thought Lucy. Not with that leg in the air. "Would you like me to bring you some books or something?" she asked.

Miss Marilyn's face lit up. For once in her life she smiled. Lucy was surprised – she looked quite pretty.

"I can tell you straight away what I'd like. In my sitting room on the first floor there's a desk. On that desk is a laptop, and to the right of the laptop is a file full of notes. If you could bring me that file and the laptop, I can get on with some work that I was just about to complete when all this happened." She waved at her hoisted leg.

Her cheeks became flushed with excitement. "If you can do that for me, I've a chance of meeting a very important deadline. I must say I'd given up hope of finishing it in time. That would be such a tragedy, because, while I was trapped in the car, and while I've been lying here in this bed, my mind's been working, and I've found the very answer I've been trying to find for the past six years."

She was so animated that Lucy hardly recognised her.

"I'll try and bring them tomorrow," she said. "At the moment, there's no reason why I shouldn't be able to come, but things seem to change so quickly in our lives that I can't promise anything." She put a handful of Quality Street on top of the bedclothes, and stood up. "Would you like some of these? I'll have to go now, and I won't forget."

Miss Marilyn was looking pink and cheerful as Lucy left. She was quite transformed.

★

While Lucy was up at the hospital, David was already on the path that led over the cliff at the far end of town. He didn't feel the sharp wind or the stabbing rain. Nor did he notice when he stumbled over the rough ground. He pressed forward away from the lights of the streets and the houses, his teeth clenched and his fists tight.

At last he reached the highest point of the cliff. He stopped on the edge and looked down at the swirling waters below. The tide was high, and even the tallest of the rocks had disappeared. Huge waves boomed against the cliff, fell back and boomed again.

He stared at the white clouds of foam. Spray hurled itself upwards and hit him in the face. It flew over his head and soaked him, but he didn't feel a thing. The more he stared into the angry water, the more it seemed to invite him in. It offered him peace – no more running, no more hiding. The son of two monsters – two murderers – he was tired of it all. He put his head back and let out a loud cry, but there was no one to hear it. With his eyes closed, he fell to his knees at the very edge of the cliff.

Minutes passed by until the thumping in his head quietened, and the cold of the earth and the rain penetrated his mind. He opened his eyes and saw where he was – on the brink of oblivion. On his knees, he shuffled backwards and then rose slowly to his feet. What on earth did he think he was doing? He had a family. They would be worrying about him, and he had to go back.

Now the wind tormented him. It blew so hard in his face that he could hardly breathe, and he hurried, tripping and stumbling in the dark. He found the golf course and cut down at the edge of the wood until he came to the narrow path that led down past the big house. He peered over the wall that he had climbed over only last Friday, and saw light streaming into the yard from the kitchen window. His ankle twisted on the rough stones, and he limped as fast as he could down the path. Within seconds, he was pulling on the old metal bell.

"It's David," he shouted.

The door opened a crack, and Lucy's cautious face appeared. Donald barked from the kitchen and waddled out to greet him. David staggered into the big, square hall and felt the warmth wrap itself around him like a blanket.

Lucy was frightened. "What's happened?" she cried.

David didn't answer. He hobbled over to the stairs and sat on a step and rubbed his ankle. His hair fell in black tendrils like seaweed over his ashen face, and round his mouth was a rim of blue. He looked up at Lucy, distraught and speechless.

All Lucy could think about was Paul. Had something happened to Paul? She was afraid to ask. Her voice came out in a croak. "Are the others alright?"

David nodded. The sense of utter relief brought strength with it. Lucy shut the front door and bolted it, top and bottom. She tugged off David's soaking wet anorak, grabbed Miss Clements's Sunday-best coat off its hook on the wall and wrapped it round him. Then, she sat down next to him on the stair.

"Now tell me," she said quietly. "What happened?"

"Beverley rang. She's coming to fetch us tomorrow. She told me who my mother was."

Lucy waited.

"You'll never guess who it was." He had to breathe deeply before he could bring himself to say it. "It was that woman," he whispered. "That woman who made Paul hum."

Lucy gasped. Her hand flew to her mouth. "Miss Morris? Sandra Williams?"

"Yes, Isobel Drax – wife number eight – who gave me up at birth. The cleverest and most dangerous of the Good Doctors."

He covered his face with his hands. Lucy didn't know what to say.

"I wish she'd put me down at birth, like all the other defective babies she's disposed of," he moaned.

"Oh, poor David! Don't say that. You're not defective. You're the complete opposite. What would we have done without you?"

"If you reckon the devil's blood flows through your veins," he said, "well, I've got a double dose."

Lucy was horrified. "Stop it! Neither of us has the devil's blood. If you don't believe in the Magnifico, then you don't believe in the devil." Did she believe in him herself? No, she certainly did not. "We both know he absolutely does not exist."

She pulled herself up straight and twisted her hands in agitation. Donald had crept out of the kitchen and now he licked her ankle. It distracted her for a moment, and she bent down to stroke him.

"Listen," she said, more calmly. "You and I both had wicked fathers, and you also had a wicked mother, but

252

that doesn't make us wicked. We've already disowned our fathers. Now you can disown your mother."

"But I've got her hair. I saw it when the wig came off and it was silver, and my eyes are just like hers."

"No, they're not. Hers are hard like diamonds. Yours are piercing. It's not the same thing."

He hardly heard her. "And I've got Drax's looks and height. However much I disown them, I can't disown my genes. I've got their genes."

Lucy longed to put her arms round him and comfort him, but Aunt Sarah's voice had returned – *not allowed! Comfort is a sin.*

"Everyone has good genes and bad genes," she said at last. "That's what Dorothy said that day on the castle. Maybe you've inherited their good genes."

She thought for a moment.

"If she was able to kill all those people and babies," she said slowly, "her chief bad gene must be lack of compassion or empathy, or whatever it's called. That's what's wrong with all the Magnifico's people – lack of compassion. They don't care how other people feel. You've got compassion, absolutely loads of it. Why, you wouldn't even let Paul drop a stone on a shrimp!"

If only Dorothy were here, she'd know how to put things properly.

"Oh, and one more thing," she added. "Both of them were probably brought up in a commune, so perhaps it's nothing to do with genes after all – just brainwashing. Goodness knows what we'd have ended up like if we hadn't escaped."

She stopped. What on earth was she rabbiting on about? The Magnifico didn't exist, so who was he to tell Aunt Sarah that comforting wasn't allowed? She tentatively put her hand on David's shoulder. He didn't shove her off, and she slid both arms round him and held him tight.

It was a nice feeling. How on earth could this be wrong? For several minutes, they clung to each other. She could feel the tension draining out of him. When he lifted his head the blue line round his mouth was fading, and the colour was returning to his cheeks.

"Well," he said at last. "One thing's certain, I definitely disown them both."

He sat up. "Anyway, we've caught her! I've been so full of myself and my stupid genes, I haven't told you. We caught the Ginger Witch – that Sandra Williams."

"What?" Lucy gasped. Joy, amazement and incredulity surged through her. Then her skin prickled as she listened to the details of Isobel's visit, the syringes, Mr Lovett's instructions, Peter Pan's arrival and finally, Beverley's phone call.

She sat silent with shock. Dorothy and David would be dead by now if Isobel's plan had worked. The sense of loss was too horrible to contemplate.

"How could they do this to us?" cried David. "Their own children – anyone's children! We'd done nothing to harm them."

Lucy had no answer.

David rubbed his ankle and stood up slowly.

"I must ring Dorothy to tell her I'm alright. I should have done it as soon as I came in. She'll be worried."

Lucy tried to smile. "See?" she said shakily. "You care how she feels. Compassion!"

CHAPTER TWENTY-FOUR

Miss Clements arrived home mid-morning in a taxi. Donald wagged his tail and shuffled up to her, and turned round and round, making little whining noises. She picked him up, with great difficulty, and clasped him in her arms.

"My poor Donald," she puffed. "Did I give you a nasty fright leaving you on your own like that? Goodness, you're heavy." She put him down and took off her coat and said briskly, "I'll make us all a nice fluffy cheese omelette for our lunch, because Donald loves that, and then we'll think about what sort of cake I should make for tea. I'll do some scones, and Lucy, if you would be so kind, I'd like you to go down to the shop and get some double cream."

"There wasn't any money in the housekeeping drawer for the eggs and milk," said Lucy, "but I used some that Beverley had given me."

"Oh, I wonder what happened to it. I must have put it somewhere safe. Never mind. I'll pay you back, dear," said Miss Clements. "Here, take my purse and the shopping bag with you, and perhaps Donald would like a little walk to the shop and back."

She didn't question David's presence in her house, remembering with embarrassment that she was the cause of his having to flee on the Friday. She had handled things badly with that Miss Morris, and it would be distressing to dwell on it.

"It is so pleasant to be home, is it not?" she said.

David was rubbing his ankle with some liniment he'd found in a kitchen drawer. Wishing that it really was his home, David agreed that it was very pleasant but, he said, he had to go back to the other house. He told her that Miss Morris had been caught, and he had to say goodbye to Mrs Jones because Beverley was coming to take them all back to secure care in London. He would bring Dorothy and Paul up to the big house later to pack their things, and Beverley would pick them up from here.

"Well, I don't want to go," said Lucy when she came back from the shop. "I don't want some other secure care. I feel secure here. Now that they've caught her, they'll be able to track down Father Drax, and all the danger should be gone."

As soon as they had finished their omelettes, David left for the little house in town, and Lucy went up to Miss Marilyn's sitting room. The laptop and the folder were exactly where she had said they would be. It was amazing how Miss Marilyn could remember where anything was in all that chaos of documents and books, and scraps of paper. Taking care not to touch anything else, in case it was in a specially remembered place, Lucy put them in a plastic carrier bag and left them by the front door ready for visiting time.

Miss Clements took some fairy cakes out of the freezer and put them in a Tupperware box for Miss Marilyn. "These will have defrosted by the time you get there," she said. "They don't take long."

★

Lucy carried the box of fairy cakes upright in one hand and the plastic carrier bag in the other, and went up the hill to the hospital for the afternoon visiting time. She hoped nobody would ask why she wasn't at school. Miss Marilyn's eyes were fixed anxiously on the door when she arrived. Her mouth was pursed and twitching round and round. Her leg had been lowered to a lying position, and she was propped up in the bed.

"What a relief!" cried Miss Marilyn. "I thought you'd never come!"

"It's only just visiting time," said Lucy. "I'm not late."

Miss Marilyn wasn't listening. She leaned over to take the plastic bag out of Lucy's hand and pulled it up onto the bed.

"Dare I hope you've brought the right one?" she muttered as she emptied out the bag. She shoved the laptop to one side, and opened up the file, and rifled through pages of notes and cuttings and photocopies.

Lucy put the Tupperware box on the bed, and sat down and waited.

"It's all there." Miss Marilyn was smiling.

Good gracious, thought Lucy, she'd smiled two days in a row.

"You don't need to stay. I'll get started straight away."

"Miss Clements came home today," said Lucy. "She sent you up these fairy cakes."

Miss Marilyn pushed the box to one side.

"She'll probably come up to see you, when she's settled back in again."

"Tell her not to bother," said Miss Marilyn.

She already had three sheets of notes spread out on the bed, and was mumbling to herself as Lucy said goodbye.

★

Beverley arrived at the big house that evening. The car pulled up outside on the double yellow lines. Beverley climbed out and her heels click-clacked up the path.

"They're not here, dear," said Miss Clements. "They're all down with Mrs Jones. Her husband was all agitated and had a turn or something, and fell down the stairs. You'd think she'd want them all out of the way at a time like this, but no, they all insisted on being there. She sent for Lucy because he was calling for his daughter, and Mrs Jones thought it might help. I gave Lucy a cake to take down. Food can be such a comfort, can it not?" She smoothed her apron down over her stomach.

★

"We're not leaving Mrs Jones," said Dorothy when she opened the blue front door to Beverley. "She needs us here. The doctor's been and he said there's nothing he or the hospital can do, and the best place for him is at home either in bed or, if he prefers it, in his comfy chair."

Mr Jones was in his chair in the front room. Lucy was sitting on a stool next to him, holding his hand. He seemed to have shrivelled, and she was no longer afraid. His eyes were closed, but every now and then a faint smile would light up his face and he would whisper, "That's my good girl, my little pretty, my Maria."

"Right," said Beverley, briskly, but in slightly lower tones than usual. "I'm off to my hotel, and we'll have to sort this out tomorrow."

Dorothy held the front door open.

"Won't last the night, if you ask me," whispered Beverley hoarsely as she went out.

★

Evan felt very comfortable. This chair had always been his favourite. Dear me, that was quite a fall, but here he was, all in one piece – just sleepy. No pain, nothing, and the two most beautiful faces in the world floating in and out in front of him. He must be the luckiest man alive. His eyes wanted to close, but he wouldn't let them. No way! Gwen, his beloved, was asking him something. He could see her lips moving but couldn't quite catch what she was saying. For some reason his own words wouldn't come out so he smiled and she smiled back, the love of his life. It was nice to feel drowsy. Maria was still there, holding his hand. She'd been away, he couldn't remember where, and now she was back. Something about a dog. His lips were dry. "My Maria." Had he said it out loud or was it just in his head? He wasn't sure.

★

Beverley informed them that they were allowed to remain in Wales for an extra fortnight, so that they could attend Mr Jones's funeral. They were to stay in Miss Clements's house, and someone called Peter Pan would be keeping an eye on things. There would be no need to go back to school after the holidays, because they would be in London for the rest of the academic year.

Lucy went up to the hospital every day, and came back each time with instructions to look for a particular book or document, or to bring up the battery charger for the laptop. Miss Marilyn described the whereabouts of each item, in its obscure hiding place, with meticulous accuracy, and Lucy never ceased to be astonished at the contrast between the orderliness of her brain and the disorder of her room. Her final instruction was to take the laptop back to the house and print out a lengthy document, in its entirety, and to bring it back with a large envelope which would be found in a cardboard box under the bed.

David knew how to use the printer, and the mission was accomplished.

"Sit there while I check through this," said Miss Marilyn, when she was handed the printed pages. Lucy sat for some time and then went over to chat to the woman in the bed opposite. She was in the middle of an informative conversation about gallstones when Miss Marilyn called her back. She was looking pleased.

"It's an excellent piece of work, though I say it myself."

"That's good," said Lucy. "I'm afraid I won't be able to come again because it's Mr Jones's funeral tomorrow, and then we go back to London."

"It doesn't matter." Miss Marilyn was putting the document into the large envelope and addressing it with a typed sticker. "I can buy a stamp here, and use their post. I'll get this off tomorrow."

"Well, goodbye then," said Lucy.

"Goodbye."

As Lucy left, Miss Marilyn was checking the address on the envelope, and looking very satisfied.

★

The funeral was over, and the children were sitting round Gwen Jones's kitchen table. Neighbours had called in for a cup of tea and some of Miss Clements's cakes. Now, everyone had left, and the children had washed up the cups and saucers, and put them away. Gwen sat upright in her chair, as always, and the signs of exhaustion in her face had slightly softened. Paul climbed onto her lap and covered her face with kisses.

Lucy watched him, thinking sadly that she would never be able to do that. Something inside her would always hold her back. Aunt Sarah's voice was clear – *Demonstrations of affection weaken you, and lead to favouritism, nepotism and corruption.*

Gwen smiled at them, over Paul's head. "I'll go back to work," she said.

They looked at her in astonishment.

"I know I look old to you, but I'm only fifty-five. That's young these days. There's plenty of go in me yet. I stopped nursing when Maria died, because I had to look after poor Evan, but that was only a few months ago, and they'll probably be glad to have me back. They're always short-staffed. I'll go up to the hospital tomorrow and find out if they need me. If not, I can always get work in a care home."

She looked at them fondly. "As for all of you, it's back to school! You've missed a lot, but you'll soon make up for lost time if you work hard. And, Dorothy, you'll probably be allowed to come back in May to do your

261

exams, so perhaps they'll let you stay with me while you're here. I'm sad that you're going back to London, but I'm sure you'll be allowed to visit me sometimes."

"Can I stop calling you Mrs Jones now that Mr Jones isn't here?" asked Paul. "Miss Wyn Lloyd says you're my *nain*."

Gwen's eyes filled with tears. "Of course you can. You all can."

Paul turned to the others, proud to be able to demonstrate his superior knowledge. "It's spelt n a i n," he said, "but you say it like the number nine and it means 'grandmother.'"

Lucy liked that. She didn't think she would ever be able to say 'grandmother' without remembering how she had once thought Gwen was a trap.

"Yes, well, Nain, once the next lot of trials are over, we want to be allowed to come back here to live," said Dorothy. "Then I'll get a job and look after us all."

"And we'll get an education and good jobs and buy our own house and be safe!" chanted Paul.

"We'll be safe sooner than that, I hope," said David. "They'll track down Drax now, unless he really is abroad, and then that'll be the end of it all, and we should be OK."

"Oh! By the way," said Dorothy. "You'll never guess who I saw in town today – that creepy Robin. Yuk!" She shuddered. "He was coming from the station. He saw me too, and came over and asked how I was."

"What did you say?" asked Lucy anxiously.

"I just said, 'Very well, thank you,' and walked away. To make sure he didn't follow me, I went through a shop on the high street and out through a storeroom at the back."

David groaned, "Let's hope he's nothing to do with the Mag. I don't think I can bear any more frights at the moment. We need time to recover from the last lot."

Dorothy changed the subject. "We have to go back to the big house now," she said, pushing back her chair. "Come on, everyone. Miss Clements will be waiting."

"Would you like one of us to stay, Nain, just to keep you company for tonight?" asked David.

"No, *cariad*. Thank you. The funeral's over, and I must start as I mean to go on."

CHAPTER TWENTY-FIVE

Dorothy was right. Miss Clements was waiting for them with a great feast for their last night. There were flowers in the centre of the gleaming mahogany table, the cutlery shone and the best crystal tumblers sparkled.

"Only one more day," she said, "and then goodness knows what they'll feed you on in London. Make sure you stick to proper food – you should be safe with French or Italian."

They ate in silence. The thought of tomorrow weighed upon all of them. No one had told them where they would be staying, and there was always the possibility that they would be separated or constantly moving from one foster home to another. Miss Clements had gone to so much trouble with the food, thought Lucy, it was really sad not to be able to enjoy it. She was trying to think of some sort of conversational topic when the phone rang and made them all jump.

David answered it. "Yes, she's here," he said, handing the receiver over to Dorothy. "It's Mr Lovett's secretary," he whispered. "She's putting him through to you. It must be really important for them to be working so late. Perhaps they're going to let us stay here."

Three interested faces were turned in Dorothy's direction.

"You may prefer to take this call in private," said Mr Lovett.

Dorothy tensed up. What bombshell was going to be hurled at her now?

"It's OK," she said. "I can talk to you here."

"We have some news for you."

The others watched Dorothy's face anxiously.

"We've managed to obtain a lot of information from some of the aunts who used to work in the Drax commune."

"Yes?" said Dorothy. He was speaking incredibly slowly, she thought. The suspense was horrible.

Mr Lovett was trying to think how to put his news. His voice was less fruity than usual. "I'm afraid it's a bit late in the day now, because she's in an old people's home, and of course one never knows how the elderly will react – or youngsters for that matter – though I don't think that she is elderly – especially if they have dementia." There was a pause. "So I don't want to raise your hopes."

For Bag's sake, thought Dorothy. He's a lawyer. They're supposed to be articulate.

"Who's in a home, Mr Lovett?" she asked rather sharply. If David or Lucy had been as dumbstruck as this, she would have told them to pull themselves together. "I'm afraid I don't know what you're talking about."

"We've followed up some of the information we've been given, and we've found that you have a grandmother."

Dorothy gasped. Her head flushed hot and the room spun round.

David jumped up, shoved a chair behind her legs and pushed her into it. He caught the phone as it was falling from her hand.

"Are you there?" Mr Lovett's voice was calling from the other end.

"She's here, Mr Lovett," answered David. "She's just had some sort of a turn, but she'll be alright in a moment. Can I help?"

"Well, it's supposed to be confidential, but it obviously isn't going to be if you're all there together, so I might as well tell you. We've tracked down her grandmother in an old people's home in South West London. If you have a piece of paper handy and a pen I'll give you the address, and when Dorothy's recovered, she can ring me to say what she wants to do about it."

David remained calm. There was a notepad on the mantelpiece with a pencil attached. He wrote down the address and thanked Mr Lovett politely.

"Don't forget, Beverley will be picking you up tomorrow at midday," said Mr Lovett, relieved that the sensitive purpose of his phone call was dealt with, and that he could return to more mundane arrangements. "She'll explain where you're going. I'm afraid it wasn't possible to accommodate you all in one place, so you and Dorothy will be with one foster mother, and Paul and Lucy with another."

David barely digested the information. His mind was swimming with the grandmother news, and he had to force himself not to collapse like Dorothy.

"I can't remember their names," continued Mr Lovett, "but I'm told they're very efficient about security. Much more efficient than that disastrous lot you've just been with. Goodbye."

★

The next day, after Beverley had taken the children away, Miss Clements sat in her kitchen, stirring a pudding. There would be no one to eat it, except herself. She would have to cut it into quarters and put them in the freezer. Donald was in his basket, so she wasn't alone, but the house was huge, and it was sad to have no one to cook for.

Even so, it was a relief they'd gone. They were nice children, very considerate and their manners were impeccable, but there had been an awful lot of hassle with all that security business. She really couldn't face going through that again. It was too disturbing.

Somehow, the cottage in Greece didn't appeal to her any more. It was a dream that had caused her to lose her judgment, and the thought of it filled her with shame and embarrassment. She scooped the pudding mixture into an ovenproof dish, scattered it with brown sugar and popped it into the Aga. So satisfying! Straightening herself up, she smoothed down her apron and reached a decision. She crossed the hall to the dining room, checked in the mirror over the fireplace to make sure that her hair was tidy, and then picked up the phone and dialled Mr Nicholas.

"Hello, Primrose! How nice to hear your voice. Have you thought about my offer?"

"Yes," she said. "I had to think about it very carefully, because marriage is such an important step, don't you think?"

"It is indeed," said Mr Nicholas.

"Well, I've decided to accept."

The thought that the pudding would not go uneaten flashed through her mind, while delightful visions of sponge cakes and casseroles and roasts danced before Mr Nicholas's eyes.

"You've made me a very happy man," he said.

CHAPTER TWENTY-SIX

"I do hope Beverley won't get into too much trouble," said Lucy, as all four of them huddled together against a wall under Waterloo Bridge. "But we've told them over and over again that we won't be separated."

They had slipped away quietly while Beverley was upstairs inspecting the bedrooms with Paul and Lucy's prospective foster mother. They did feel guilty and horribly mean, because they knew she'd be in a panic searching for them, but their worst fear was that once they were separated they might never see each other again. They had made a pact that if they ever did lose contact, they would make their way back to Nain Jones's house. But supposing it had burned down, or she'd gone away, or one of them didn't manage to make it back there and the others never found out what had happened?

"We're insecurity in human form," Dorothy had commented, "but it can't be helped. That's the way we are. It'll get better with time, but in the meantime we have to stick together."

Now it felt like old times, on the run in London. It was all so familiar. There was a small fire burning near the opposite wall, and a strong smell of marijuana. A girl was crouching a few yards away, injecting herself with something, and a group of men were drinking out of cans and chatting among themselves.

"This takes us back a bit," whispered David. "Remember the night we saw Father Drax with his briefcase, fast asleep under the railway arch"

"Will we ever forget it!" said Dorothy. "And he's got my birth record in that briefcase, according to Mr Lovett. I wish I'd known then. I'd have pulled it out from under his head while he was sleeping and stamped on his face."

"Ugh!" exclaimed David. "You're gruesome!"

Dorothy shrugged. "Ugh to them! Anyway, let's try and sleep. And keep as clean as you can. We don't want to look like tramps tomorrow."

★

When they woke, the traffic was rumbling overhead. Respectably dressed people were hurrying through the tunnel, taking a shortcut to work and skirting nervously round the dark, lurking figures.

"They're afraid of us," whispered Paul, and they felt ashamed.

"Well, we're afraid too," said Dorothy, "but at least no one knows us. Come on, let's get out of here."

They washed in the public lavatories on Waterloo station and cleaned their teeth, and checked each other over to see if they were tidy.

"My anorak's filthy," said David.

They brushed each other down as best they could, and then went off to look for some coffee and a sandwich. They studied the underground map and worked out their route, and half an hour later they found themselves walking towards a large sign announcing, "The Laurels Residential Home".

Lucy stopped short and stared at the house. It was identical to Father Copse's house, and her stomach did a somersault.

"I can't go in," she said.

Dorothy stood stock still. "I don't think I can either. She may not want to see me, or she may be too demented to understand who I am. Or it may make her more demented if she does know who I am – like poor Mr Jones with Lucy."

"You three go and sit on that bench over there," said David, "and I'll go and knock on the door and ask if we can visit."

He rang a security button and a woman appeared.

"What do you want?" she said crossly.

"Is it possible to see Mrs Ferranti?"

"It's much too early," she snapped. "We haven't got them all up yet. Visiting's at two." She shut the door in his face.

"Why do London people have to be like that?" sighed Lucy when he reported back. "It's so much easier to be nice."

They sat on the bench to rethink. Lucy looked at her watch. It was only half past nine.

"Tell you what," said David. "We've got loads of time. Let's go back to the tube station and see if we can get to our old commune. There won't be anyone there. They've all been arrested or escaped by now. And we could have a look at Father Copse's old house while we're there, and the Mag's school."

★

270

"Let's go up the High Street to look at the communes first," said David as they climbed the steps from the underground station, "then the school, and then we'll go over the common to look at Father Copse's house."

The Drax and Copse communes faced each other from opposite sides of the High Street. They were boarded up.

"They can't hurt us now," said Dorothy quietly. "We're free."

It was a while before anyone spoke, as the old memories hit them. But they had to move on if they were to face up totally to the past.

David was the first to speak. "Let's see if they've blocked up the passageway to the disposal cells."

They crept up through the Drax House garden and out into the woods beyond. The entrance to the passageway had a cordon round it and a no-entry sign, and a new, barred grid with heavy padlocks. They stood and stared in sober silence. Then they turned and ran.

"Good riddance to the lot of them," said Dorothy bitterly when they reached the High Street. "I hope they all rot in the fire of the melting flesh."

When they reached The Mag's school it was boarded up as well. They went round the side to the bicycle shed.

"It's not even a year since Lucy and I used to hide behind there," said Dorothy. "It's like another life."

Lucy said nothing. She was remembering how Dorothy had tried to persuade her that there was no such thing as the Magnifico, and she had refused to listen.

"Come on. Let's go and look at Father Copse's house," said David.

271

They followed their old path over the common, and came out at the pond where Paul and Lucy used to play.

The house had been flattened, the land had been cleared, and even the old garage had gone. There was no sign of the fire. All the events of last September flooded back into Lucy's mind. She was glad there was nothing left. The appropriate word was 'cleansing', she thought – or was it 'closure'? That's what people said on television.

"That land must be worth a fortune," said David. "Look at the size of it! Somebody will build a block of flats there one day, and sell them for hundreds of thousands of pounds. If Father Copse dies, you and Paul – and I suppose all his other children – will inherit it, and you'll be rich."

"Ugh!" exclaimed Lucy. "We wouldn't want it, would we, Paul?"

"No," he said. "The ghosties would make me hum."

They made their way back to The Laurels, and sat on the bench waiting for two o'clock.

"Do you know what?" said Lucy after a while. "I feel better now I've seen those places."

The others nodded their heads in silent agreement.

At two o'clock on the dot, they crossed the road to The Laurels and rang the bell. A voice crackled, "Yes?" out of a box in the wall. Creepy!

David put his mouth to the box and said, "We've come to see Mrs Ferranti."

There was a buzzing sound and the door clicked. David pushed it open, and he and Paul stepped inside. Dorothy hesitated. Lucy took her hand as they followed the boys.

The hall was wide with patterned tiles on the floor, just like the hall in Father Copse's house, but there the similarity ended.

Aunt Sarah would never have allowed the place to smell like this, thought Lucy.

Paul put his hand over his nose and mouth, and tried not to breathe. David approached the reception desk and asked a woman where they could find Mrs Ferranti. She pointed wordlessly to the second door on the left and waved her hand.

They stood in the doorway and stared, embarrassed, at a semi-circle of white and bald heads, gazing awkwardly up at a blaring television or lolling forwards in sleep. To one side, a very upright old gentleman sat at a table reading a newspaper. A woman on a sofa nearby was counting the stitches on her knitting needles. Another slept in the window overlooking the side garden.

Dorothy turned away. "If I told her who I was, she wouldn't understand," she said sadly. "Come on. Let's go."

"Don't be silly," whispered David. "Most of them are just ordinary people like you and me, sitting down because their backs are bad or their legs are tired. Of course they can understand."

Paul didn't move. He was looking round the room studying each individual intently. Two of them stared at him and smiled.

One elderly lady stretched out her arm and tried to touch him. "Hello, darling," she said softly. "How nice of you to visit."

"It's a pleasure," said Paul. "I hope you're happy and comfortable."

"Very," she replied. "Are you looking for someone in particular?" But, before he could answer, her eyes had closed.

"Come on, Paul," said Dorothy nervously. "We're disturbing them."

Ignoring her, he crossed over to the woman in the window. He studied her carefully as she slept. Her bone structure was fine but emaciated, and her face was surrounded by soft, silver curls. The long hands that lay in her lap were bony, but had once been slender and graceful. Paul inspected the ankles. These too had once been elegant. Now they sprouted likes sticks from the depths of her sheepskin slippers.

Paul put his hand on her knee and whispered, "Mrs Ferranti?"

When visiting time was over, the children were back on the bench outside, flushed with success. Dorothy was still trembling.

"She said her name was Dorothea, just like me, only Italian," she said, as tears streamed down her cheeks. "My mother named me after her!"

David was already on his mobile phone to Gwen Jones.

"Can you come?" he asked her urgently. "We need you fetch Mrs Ferranti and take her back to Wales."

"How is she? Is she ill? Can she travel?"

"She's not exactly ill, but she's been broken-hearted for a long, long time — ever since Dorothy's mother was taken."

"Ah, the poor, poor soul! I can't come tomorrow, but I'll get the train the day after, and I'll go and see her and find out what she'd like to do. She may prefer to stay where she is."

"No. She won't. It's horrible. They don't smile, and it smells, and I think she pays a lot for it, though she didn't say how much. She's very thin. Maybe Miss Clements would have her as a lodger and feed her up."

"Miss Clements told me she's getting married – but if she can't have her, she can stay with me till we find her somewhere better."

David gave her the address, and instructions how to get there.

"By the way," she said anxiously. "Someone from Mr Lovett's office rang to see if you were here. She said they rang The Laurels this morning and asked if four children had turned up there, and they told her you hadn't. Are you alright? What about Paul?"

"We're all fine, so don't worry about us. They shouldn't have tried to separate us. We explained to Mrs Ferranti that we can't go back to The Laurels because Mr Lovett is sure look for us there. We told her to expect you – I hope you don't mind, and I hope the train isn't terribly expensive. When we found her, she was really drowsy and far away, but she seemed to come alive, and she certainly hasn't got dementia as Mr Lovett seemed to think. She said she was going to give them notice as soon as she'd discussed things with you."

"I'll be there!"

★

Dorothea Ferranti got up from her chair, bent and stiff. She stretched slowly. What on earth was she doing wasting her time sitting down all day? Idling her life away wouldn't put her poor old heart back together again. Her eyes brimmed with tears. It wouldn't bring back her beautiful daughter.

She put her shoulders back, and stood up straight and tall. Back in her room, she burrowed in a drawer and found her mobile phone. She wondered when she had last used it. The battery was empty, so she burrowed a bit more and found the charger and plugged it in. She pressed a number and rang her brother.

"Mario. Come and see me." She spoke in Italian, and her voice sounded strange to her. "Get on the first plane out of Rome. Such news! I have a granddaughter!" Her legs buckled and she dropped down into her armchair. Mario's voice crackled anxiously. Was she still there, was she alright? She took several deep breaths and tried to still the galloping of her mind.

"The business – I need to be brought up to date." She paused. I'm incoherent, she thought. He'll think I've gone mad. "And can you send me a lawyer. I want to make a will – two wills, one Italian and one English. Come tomorrow if possible. I'm thinking of moving to Wales. Such a beautiful girl!"

Rising shakily to her feet, she left the phone to charge fully and crossed the room. With wasted arms, she pulled her suitcase out from the bottom of the wardrobe. Her sheepskin slippers squeaked on the vinyl flooring, and she looked down.

"Good heavens!" she said aloud. "What on earth have I got on my feet?"

In the back of the wardrobe she found some pretty shoes with elegant little heels. She sat down to put them on. Her feet were a bit loose in them but never mind.

"That's better!" she said.

CHAPTER TWENTY-SEVEN

They were too elated to go back to Waterloo Bridge.

"We'll go to Piccadilly Circus," said Dorothy. "I went there last year. We can sit on the steps all night if we want to and no one will care. And there are plenty of snack bars, so we can eat. Tomorrow, we could stroll around Soho and places, and I might even be able to get a job as a waitress or something."

"It might be difficult to get work without identification," said David. "And, remember, until Mr Lovett sorts out your birth registrations, you and Lucy don't exist in the eyes of the law."

"He's had all my details for ages, from Father Copse's file," grumbled Lucy. "I don't know why it has to take so long."

"Bureaucracy," said Dorothy. "Red tape. Anyway, I don't see that it should stop me getting a job, because they employ immigrants all the time in Soho. I could pretend I'm an immigrant." Her face lit up. "Hey, do you realise, I'm half Italian!"

They strolled cheerfully along, and then took a bus. It was still light when they found themselves on the steps in Piccadilly Circus.

★

Father Drax paced up and down in the flat on the Cromwell Road. Something must have gone wrong. Isobel had not contacted him for three weeks or was it four? The syringe was still lying waiting for her, under the handkerchief on the coffee table. Head office hadn't replied to his phone calls, and its website had disappeared from the internet. He had rung its travel department, but the phone number was unavailable, and although he had been told weeks ago that his documents were ready, they had not turned up.

The flat had become a prison. He was a caged animal – an enraged animal. It was the ingratitude that got him. He'd been a good Father to his commune, made sure the children were kept clean and well-fed. He'd even given the aunts a little pocket money now and then. He could understand the Copse kids turning against their Father because he'd bullied and starved all his children, including those two in his own house, and he never gave Aunt Sarah a penny. Everyone knew that floral dress she wore in the summer had been made out of old curtains. Copse had deserved to have his house burned down. This was entirely his fault.

There was no food left in the freezer and he had to get out before he starved or went mad. The white-and-chrome furniture and ice-blue walls, which had once seemed so sharply stimulating, now closed in on him, clinical, cruel and hard. What a fool he'd been to allow vanity to stop him dyeing his wonderful golden-blond hair. He stood in front of the bathroom mirror and put on the dark-brown wig that Isobel had bought him, and pressed the hat down over it. His head felt as though it was suffocating. He stuck a thin moustache over his upper lip. It was slightly darker than the wig, but looked quite authentic. A bit of make-up on his eyebrows darkened them nicely to match the moustache. He did look different.

First, he would have to get money out of a cash machine. He mentally ran through the various pin numbers of his many bank accounts. Once he'd got the cash, he would go to the cinema. His heart lifted a little at the thought. A meal in a restaurant was out because he would have to remove his hat and the wig might shift, but he'd find a snack bar. Anything would be better than these four walls. He put on his coat, pressed the hat further down over the wig and quietly closed the door behind him. It was good that London was so impersonal. The neighbours were all foreigners. They didn't know him and he didn't know them. He took the lift to the ground floor. There was no sign of the caretaker, and he let himself out without being seen.

*

On the steps in the middle of Piccadilly Circus, Lucy felt safely anonymous as traffic and people swirled around them.

Paul lay with his head on her lap. "I'm hungry," he said sleepily.

"Just be patient," she said. "David will get us something to eat."

She watched Dorothy and David counting out their cash. They still had most of the money that Beverley had brought them. There might even be enough to rent a room for one or two nights, as long as they shared. If it weren't for the exhilaration of having found Mrs Ferranti, she reckoned she could sleep right now on these steps. It was exhausting trekking back and forth across London on the tube, with the foul air and pushy people. But, holy fire, it had been worth it!

David went off to buy burgers and fizzy drinks. Paul fell asleep, while she and Dorothy chatted happily about their visit to the old people's home and the newly acquired grandmother.

"When I get my job, she can come and live with us," said Dorothy. "And I'll cook all those recipes Miss Clements showed me, and build her up again till she's fit and strong."

Their faces were alight with pleasure as they embellished their plan for Mrs Ferranti's future comfort, and they were unaware that they were being observed.

"Hey, look at those two stunners!" muttered a man in a sharply cut, light-grey suit.

He and his friend studied the scene on the steps. The friend crossed himself over his open-necked white shirt and black jacket.

"They remind me of the Madonna and child, that one with the boy in her lap," he said. "I don't know that it would be decent."

"You and your stupid superstitions," said the other one, giving him a thump on the arm. "Come on, I'll take the Madonna if it worries you, and you take the one with the black hair."

They climbed the steps and approached the two animated girls.

"Excuse me ladies," said the grey-suited man smoothly. "We're talent scouts from a modelling agency, and we're wondering if you happen to be looking for work. We have jobs available in Paris, Rome and other glamorous venues."

The girls looked at him in astonishment, and were immediately on their guard.

"We would have no trouble in finding work for two such beautiful ladies – and for the little boy too – in photographic modelling."

As the man spoke, David came up the steps behind them with his arms precariously full of canned drinks and plastic boxes. His face turned scarlet with rage as he caught the last sentence. He jumped two steps and landed alongside them.

"Get your filthy selves away from here before I call the police," he growled, and with an almighty shove he knocked them sideways. He was thin and wiry and half their weight, but they lost their balance and fell, and all his shopping fell with them. Paul woke up with a look of surprise. The men picked themselves up and, with snarled threats and oaths, they disappeared into the crowd down Haymarket.

"Phew! Let's get away from here," said David. "That's put me off this spot for the rest of my life."

Within five minutes they found themselves in a nearby square and sat down on a bench to recover.

"As Miss Clements would say," muttered Dorothy, "that was so disturbing, was it not?"

"And we lost all our food!" wailed Paul.

"Never mind," said Lucy, "David will get us some more in a minute, but I've lost my appetite now. Can we just sit quietly for a little while?" She turned to look at Paul. "Pull your hood up, it's getting chilly. See? I'm pulling mine up."

They all pulled up their hoods and sat studying the queue of cinemagoers waiting to buy their tickets.

"Flaming flesh!" exclaimed David, clutching Dorothy's arm. "Look at that! Don't turn and stare, but look at the fifth person from the end of the queue." They turned and stared. "For Bag's sake, don't all look at the same time!"

He needn't have worried, because the man in the queue had his hat pulled well down over the side of his face and could see nothing except the back of the person in front of him.

"It's not just his height. I'd know that way of standing anywhere," said David hoarse with suppressed excitement. He turned to Paul. "Who's that man? The one with the hat."

Paul stared quite openly at the cinema queue. He stood up and went closer to have a better look. David pulled Lucy back as she tried to stop him. They all held their breath. Paul moved forward slowly, almost unnoticeably, until he was right next to the man. He glanced quickly up into his face and neck, and then studied his hands.

The man looked down at the hooded child and muttered, "Clear off!", and brushed him away with an irritated movement.

"It's the Drax with the yellow hair," said Paul when he returned. "I recognise the big, brown freckle near the bottom of his thumb. I could see his hair sticking out from under his hat and it's dark brown, but he has yellow whiskers on the back of his hand, just like Father Drax."

They watched the man go into the cinema. There was no point in following him because they would never find him in the dark. They would just have to wait.

David fetched more food and they ate it on the bench. Paul wanted to go into the arcade to look at the slot machines, but was strictly forbidden.

"You stay with us," said Dorothy sternly. "There are rough men in there."

The film seemed to go on forever. Paul slept, and the others passed the time discussing the best way to follow Drax without being seen, and arranging how and where to meet up if they lost each other. By the time the film ended, it was night, yet the square was still full of flashing lights and noise and people. The four youngsters sat in the midst of an unsleeping world of colour and movement, and watched the cinema crowd emerge.

"It's lucky you and David are so tall," remarked Lucy. "People will think you're adults. Otherwise, they might wonder what we're doing here this time of night."

Dorothy gave little laugh. "They probably think we're a pickpocket gang."

"Look!" whispered David.

A very tall, elegant man with brown hair and a little moustache stepped out into the square. He pressed his hair down hard and put on his hat. They followed him. He walked with the same firm but easy grace that Lucy recognised in David. Despite the hat, he held his head high as though he had no doubts as to his own worth. They watched through the window of a snack bar as he sat slowly eating a sandwich and drinking coffee. The manager was moving towards the door to turn them away, when the man paid for his food and left. David followed him. The two girls trailed a few yards behind with Paul.

At the tube station, the man bought a ticket. David stood as near as he could behind him and watched, and then bought four.

"Try not to look as though we're together," he said quietly, as he handed them out, "but don't lose sight of me or him."

In the carriage the crush was oppressive. Lucy couldn't reach the hanging strap. She clutched onto the back of Paul's jacket with one hand and Dorothy's sleeve with the other, and swayed with the movement of bodies. Months and months ago, when she had been so lonely in Father Copse's house, she used to wonder what it would be like to be one of the crowd on a bus or in the tube. Now she knew – it was smelly, sweaty and suffocating.

At South Kensington, the carriage door opened and spewed out its contents. When they emerged onto the pavement they breathed deeply, and even the traffic fumes felt good. Drax was already turning into the Cromwell Road, and they hurried after him. He walked briskly towards a block of flats. The front entrance was down a side road and faced a garden square. They turned the corner just in time to see him press a coded security button, and a big glass door slid open. He stepped into the foyer and it closed behind him.

David swiftly took command. "We'll know which flat is his when he puts the lights on. You all stay here and look for lights, and I'll run round the side and look from there." He dashed off and turned right into the Cromwell Road. Dorothy and Paul pressed their backs against the garden railings, and stared straight up at the front of the block, while Lucy watched from the right-hand side.

Within seconds, David reappeared. "Second floor on the main-road side!" he said triumphantly. "Quick! We need to find out where we are."

"That was the Cromwell Road," said Dorothy. "And look!" She pointed at a sign. "We're here."

David took out his mobile phone and rang Mr Lovett. A recorded message referred him to another number, 'for emergencies only'.

Their hearts sank. None of them had a pen or paper.

"Keep saying it," said Dorothy.

David put his hand through the railings that surrounded the garden square and scrabbled in the earth of a flower bed. He found a little stone, rubbed it dry on his sleeve and scratched out the emergency number on the pavement. In the light of the street lamp, it showed up white and clear.

By the time the building had been cordoned off and surrounded by police, Beverley had turned up.

"We want to watch," protested David.

"OK, but you'll have to stand right back, outside the cordon, or you'll annoy the police. We'll go over to the other side of the Cromwell Road, well out of the way."

"We don't need our hoods any more," said Dorothy, pushing hers back as they crossed at the lights. "There's nothing to stop us having a good look now!"

★

Up in the flat Father Drax switched on the light and then hastily switched it off. Curtains first, he reminded himself. One night out and he was getting careless!

He closed the curtains, switched the light back on, and took off his hat and wig. What a relief! He gave his head a good rub and peeled off the moustache, and then threw himself into an armchair to think about the film. He would have enjoyed his evening more if he hadn't been so conscious of his height. The wig had been uncomfortable, and he'd had to take the hat off in the cinema because some stupid woman said she couldn't see. It wasn't his fault he was so tall.

He daren't stay in London any longer. Tomorrow, he would take out large quantities of cash from his bank accounts and fly to Europe, and then he would look for a crooked official willing to provide him with a visa for Australia. Head office might have let him down, but money would never fail him. He stood up and pulled the briefcase out from behind the sofa and put it on the table. Which coat should he take? He threw a jacket down next to the briefcase, ready for a quick start in the morning. Perhaps it would be better to take a raincoat. He peeped out between the curtains to see if it had started raining.

For a moment, he could not move. Staring up at him from the other side of the Cromwell Road were four young faces that he recognised. Their hoods were thrown back, and each face shone with excitement and expectation and – how dare they! – with triumph. The familiar red-hot rage exploded.

He could see the cordon and the halted traffic. Then, someone started hammering on the door and voices were bellowing. He switched off the light and dashed from room to room. Police swarmed below every window. The hammering changed to crashing, and he knew that there was no escape. On the coffee table the syringe still lay, awaiting Isobel. So humane! And the Magnifico would welcome his loyal servant with open arms.

★

Four youngsters watched the arrival and departure of an ambulance and a stretcher, and then a policeman came out with a briefcase.

Dorothy clutched Lucy's arm. "My existence may be in that bag!" she whispered.

CHAPTER TWENTY-EIGHT

Beverley was taking instructions from someone over the phone. She switched it off. "Time to move on," she said, shooing the children along the Cromwell Road. She waved her hand at a passing taxi, and it stopped a few yards up Queensgate, just beyond the lights.

"OK, kiddos," she said, as she held the door open. "That's it! Show's over. Get in."

"Can't take more than four," snapped the driver nastily. "Insurance."

"Rubbish!" snapped Beverley back. "This is a police emergency, so you watch out or you'll lose your licence for interfering with the course of justice."

She gave them all a good push from behind, and they clambered in. They squeezed into the back, while she perched on a little fold-up seat facing them.

"I'm to put you all in a hotel for two nights," she said, holding tight to the sides of the seat to stop herself from falling off. "Or it might be three, depending on whether they've had the chance to check the flat and go through the briefcase. And don't worry because you'll all be together in the same place. Once they've had a good poke around, Mr Lovett will want to see you – and don't you dare run away from me this time, or I'll get the sack."

★

Two days later, the four of them were sitting in brown leather armchairs and two upright chairs, facing Mr Lovett. Beverley sat in her usual corner, wondering whether to look for another job. She'd had enough of pesky kids who ran away and hid under bridges.

Mr Lovett was shuffling through his papers. At last, he looked over his enormous desk and smiled kindly at his young audience.

"We found confirmation of your birth in the briefcase, Dorothy, and registration will not be a problem. Both you and Lucy will be now be able to have birth certificates, which will mean that you exist in the eyes of the law. Apparently, the reason girls weren't registered was because they were usually expected to be aunts or wives and never leave the communes. Also, it made it easier to dispose of them once they were no longer useful."

Dorothy and Lucy looked at each other in indignation. What a cheek!

Mr Lovett seemed unperturbed. He continued, "The Magnifico's boys were always registered legally at birth because they had to have careers and infiltrate companies and so on. So David and Paul exist officially already. Even so, we're going to get new identities for all four of you. There's a risk that these people – the holy leaders and so on – might try to track you down if they ever come out of prison, so we can't be too careful."

He noted the look of dismay on their faces.

"Don't worry," he said hastily. "It won't happen. The ones they've caught will probably get life and it looks as though the rest have disbanded, in this country at least.

We just want to be extra cautious. You can keep your first names if you like, because they're ordinary enough. We'll give you two weeks to choose your new surnames, and if you can't decide, we'll choose some for you. Then we can get you all the documentation you need, new birth certificates, national insurance numbers, passports, and so forth."

They looked at each other in pleased surprise. The possibility of a passport and being able to travel abroad was exciting, but even more so was the prospect of choosing their own surnames.

"Can we go back to Wales?" asked Lucy.

"Yes, I don't think there's anyone left for you to hide from now," said Mr Lovett. "Miss Clements told us she'd given up fostering because it's all been too upsetting, but now that Drax and Isobel are out of the way she's willing to have you just until Copse's trial – if it goes ahead – and then Isobel's. After that, there will have to be other arrangements because she's getting married."

They looked at each other and giggled. Miss Clements getting married! So old!

"I bet it's that nice Mr Nicholas," said Lucy. "I wonder if we'll be invited to the wedding"

"By the time the trials are over, we'll be registered with birth certificates and I'll be old enough to work," said Dorothy. "So then I'll be able to look after everyone."

"Ah, Dorothy! That's something I was going to mention," said Mr Lovett, shuffling again through his papers. "It seems you were misled about your date of birth."

Dorothy stared at him, "What do you mean? Don't say I'm only fifteen!"

"No," he said. "According to Drax's records in the briefcase, you are seventeen, and your birthday was in December, not September. You'll be eighteen on December the ninth."

"Ancient!" said Paul.

"We're taking Father Drax's records as correct," continued Mr Lovett. "One of the aunts in the Drax commune told us they changed the dates in the commune records so that no one from outside could trace your mother."

Dorothy caught her breath. Something seemed to swell inside her and burst. "The pigs!" she exclaimed, tears streaming down her cheeks. "My poor mamma! They took me away from her, and they didn't even leave her my birth date!"

There was a shocked silence. Dorothy never cried. Then they all joined in.

Mr Lovett looked at the four weeping children. He couldn't understand it. After all the horrors they'd been through without turning a hair! Passing over a box of tissues, he wondered if he should postpone the meeting. Beverley stood up, and the wailing stopped immediately. The last thing they wanted was her poking her nose in and telling them what to do. Dorothy sat up straight and mopped her face.

★

Ten days later, Miss Clements had prepared yet another feast. The leaves of the mahogany dining table had been pulled out and it was no longer round. Miss Clements sat at one end and a stout Italian gentleman sat at the other. The children sat with a grandmother halfway up on each side. Gwen Jones wore her best summer dress, stitched on her sewing machine more

290

than sixteen years ago, and Dorothea Ferranti's skeletal frame was draped loosely in fine, black velvet appliquéd with roses.

"Such happiness!" exclaimed Paul.

Mrs Ferranti smiled at him. Her soft silk scarf threw gentle colours up into her haggard face, and her skin seemed to glow. "You are right, Paul," she murmured. "I never thought I could be happy again, but now I have new blessings."

Her brother, plump and genial, looked round the table at the four children. "You and I have found a family, Dorothea," he said, "and now we can go forward." He tucked his napkin into his collar. "This meal is delicious, Miss Clements. If this is how you intend to feed my sister, she will soon find that her clothes are no longer too large for her." His eyes fell on Dorothy. "Your *nonna* was once a great beauty like you," he said, "and she will be again if Miss Clements has her way."

"That's enough about me, Mario!" said Nonna Ferranti. "Perhaps this is a good time for the children to reach a final decision on their new name."

Gwen agreed. "You only have two weeks, remember, and time is nearly up."

Despite days of constant discussion, the only thing the children had managed to agree was that they should all have the same surname.

"Now we're all here round this table, let's make one big, final effort," said Dorothy, as she passed up the Cumberland sauce. "As you already know, I want it to be something really glamorous. What about Mariabella, or Vanderbilt?"

David was horrified. "No way! Imagine being called David Mariabella! I want something plain, like Jones.

And Jones would be convenient because that's how we're already known at school."

"You can't have that," said Dorothy. "There are too many David Joneses, and we wouldn't know which one was you. There are two in my class."

"I'd like something in the middle," said Lucy, "not so different as to make us stand out too much, but enough to make people know us from other people." She turned to Paul. "What would you choose for our family name?"

He thoughtfully chewed a tender piece of honey-roasted gammon and followed it down with a bit of roast parsnip and some potato *gratin dauphinoise*. The others waited. All faces were turned towards him.

"Two grandmothers, two names, like my teacher," he said at last. "Ferranti and Jones. Dorothy, David, Lucy and Paul Ferranti Jones. One family."

There was a long silence.

"I like it," said Mrs Ferranti, "but it's a bit long. Does it have a hyphen?"

"We don't use hyphens for surnames in Wales, Mrs Ferranti dear," said Miss Clements. "It's so that you can use either one or the other, or both together — whatever you want."

"Good!" exclaimed David. "I'll use Jones most of the time and Ferranti Jones for special occasions — like when I'm an ambassador, or something like that."

"Paul and I could be Ferranti," said Lucy. "It's more unusual than Jones, but not too noticeable."

"No!" Paul was firm. "My name is Paul Ferranti Jones, in full."

"Same here," said Dorothy.

When they had finished savouring their new family name and were starting on a summer pudding with cream, Miss Clements remembered something. "Lucy, I forgot! You've got a letter. It came while you were up in London, so that was a few days ago. It's from the United States of America, which gave me quite a turn, and it looked like my sister's writing. I put it in a safe place." She pushed her chair back and heaved herself to her feet. "Now where did I put it?" she asked herself.

Lucy had never had a letter in her life. She and the others waited on tenterhooks. Miss Clements found it eventually, in a jug in the kitchen, and returned triumphantly to the dining room. "I knew it was safe," she said proudly, "No one would have found it there."

She had a good look at the writing before handing it over to Lucy. "It definitely looks like Marilyn's writing, but it can't be if it's from America."

For a moment her usual bland expression was replaced by one of terrible hurt. "She wouldn't speak to me after she came out of hospital, and then she went away. Found it all too distressing, I expect. Such a shake-up to the system, don't you think?" she said sadly. "I heard she won some important prize for her work, but I've not seen her since our accident and that was many weeks ago."

Lucy didn't know anyone in America. The others crowded round as she opened her letter and read it aloud.

"Dear Lucy," it said *"Thank you for visiting me in hospital and bringing me my work. It won me an award. I am now a university professor and am very happy. If you ever come to the States I'd be pleased to see you. I have a husband called Dwight, who is also a professor. We are soul mates. Yours sincerely, Marilyn Clements.*

They all looked at each other in wonder.

"Such a relief!" said Miss Clements, her face clearing. "A married woman! Now I can stop worrying about her. So disturbing, you know. Dorothy, dear, please will you pass the cream up to Nonna Ferranti. We must build her up, must we not?"

CHAPTER TWENTY-NINE

Dorothy burst into the sitting room.

"I've found a job," she announced triumphantly.

Three pairs of eyes looked up from their various tasks. David put down an incomprehensible article on stocks and shares, and Lucy set aside her book. Paul added two more strokes to his drawing of the house and then gave Dorothy his full attention.

"I'm going to be a chambermaid!" Dorothy's face was flushed with excitement. "I went into all the hotels along the promenade asking if they needed someone to help cook and, when I'd nearly given up, this woman said I could be a 'kitchen-stroke-chambermaid'."

The others were impressed.

"Wow!" said David. "The first step in our plan is achieved! When do you start?"

"Next Monday. I have to be there by seven o'clock in the morning to help with the breakfasts, then work in the kitchen from half past nine to half past ten, and then help clean the bedrooms – which is the chambermaiding bit – and I'll work in the restaurant from half past twelve to two, and then clear up in the kitchen and help with the dinner, and I'll finish at five."

"That's a lot of work," said David. "It's ten hours."

"I know, but she said I'd have a coffee break, and lunch and tea breaks, if they can fit them in, so it's really only eight hours. I'll be on three months' probation, but I'm sure I'll be OK. I've got a feeling that this is the job for me. I'd love to run a hotel, but I've got to learn all about it first – like an apprenticeship."

She was too excited to sit down.

"Thank goodness I've finished my exams! They won't be hanging over me all the time, unless of course I've failed. Now I can really look forward – especially to helping in the kitchen. Perhaps they'd let me do some of Miss Clements's pudding recipes. They're going to pay me minimum wage, even though I'm not eighteen yet, provided I work as hard as an adult. I thought that was very fair."

There was considerable excitement. Lucy ran upstairs to fetch the box with the housing fund, and they counted out their money. They had just over fifty pounds.

"If I put in a bit of my wages every week," said Dorothy, "It'll grow."

"We shouldn't keep it in a box," said David. "We should invest it. I've just read a book which says you should invest one tenth of your earnings each week and forget about it, so that it grows and you become rich without even noticing."

For weeks now Lucy had noticed that, ever since David had discovered the truth about his mother, he'd had an increasing obsession with how to make money. He used to love doing practical things, like mending Miss Clements's shopping trolley or changing the light bulbs, but now he was too busy for that sort of thing, always with his nose in a book on finance. She supposed there was no harm in that, but he didn't seem the same. The life had gone out of him somehow.

"How do we find out how to invest something?" she asked. "Obviously we've heard of stocks and shares, whatever they are, but I suppose you have to have quite a lot of money to start with before you can do anything."

"I've been reading about these things," said David, "but I don't really understand them yet. I really do want to learn because it could be useful to us. It could help us buy our house. We can ask Great-Uncle Mario when he next comes over from Rome."

★

Dorothy's alarm went off at six. While the others were just getting up for what was left of the school summer term, she was already being shown where everything was kept in the hotel kitchen and how to set out the breakfast buffet. Her day flew past, and the conversation that night at supper revolved around the new job. She was full of stories about difficult guests and grumpy staff, and she lectured her attentive audience on the various ways in which the hotel could be run better if only they would take note of her suggestions.

Her grandmother smiled at her enthusiasm, but Miss Clements anxiously shook her head. "You must take care of yourself, dear, and not overdo things," she said. "All things in moderation, isn't that right, Mrs Ferranti?"

"Now that we've reached step one of our plan," said Dorothy, "we must find somewhere to rent, so I can look after everyone."

"Oh, but you don't have to do that yet, dear!" Miss Clements was quite hurt. "You can stay here till I marry Mr Nicholas. I'm not sure what happens after that, because he wants me to live at his house, and I can't keep putting him off forever. But, you know, dear, I do think you might have difficulty finding anything that you can afford if you're only getting the minimum wage."

"Oh," said Dorothy, slightly dampened. "It seemed like a lot of money to me."

"And so it is, dear, for someone just starting, is it not Mrs Ferranti? But when you have to pay for rent and bills and food, nothing goes very far."

Mrs Ferranti nodded agreement, and Miss Clements briefly noted how much better she looked these days – and only after a fortnight! Or was it three weeks? Or a little more? Never mind. She was living proof that good food was a wonderful medicine.

"Now I mustn't sound negative must I, Dorothy dear? Help yourself to some more apple tart. You'll need all your energy for work tomorrow."

After supper, the children cleared the table and filled the dishwasher while Miss Clements worked out her menus for the following week. They wouldn't let Mrs Ferranti help.

"The doctor said you've got to build yourself up gradually, Nonna," said Lucy ushering her into the children's sitting room. The empty fireplace had been filled with vases of roses, and Lucy put her next to it in a comfortable chair. "Now you can smell the roses," she said. "Just another month, according to the doctor, and you'll be fit for next year's Olympics, and we could all go to Athens to watch you with our new passports." She laughed. "We'll be in as soon as we've cleared up in the kitchen."

When they had finished their chores and were gathered in the sitting room, Nonna Ferranti asked them to explain their plan to her – unless, of course, it was a secret, she said.

"No, it's not a secret. It's our motivation, and we're always talking about it," said Dorothy. "It's just that, because we've all missed such a lot of schooling, except for Paul, we've got no education except in maths and languages and praying. So I'm going to get a job – well, I've got one now, so that's step one – and the others will work really hard at school to catch up."

She embarked on a convoluted explanation of the plan, but stopped when she noticed the confusion on her grandmother's face.

"So you see," explained David, hoping to put it more coherently, "step one was for Dorothy to get a job so she can look after us – and you, of course, because you'll come with us and we'll all look after you. Finding somewhere to rent is important, because we have to leave here when Miss Clements gets married and we don't want to go into care again. But step two is for us all to get an education and good jobs; and step three is buying a house of our own, so we can feel safe."

"I suppose we'll still get money from Mr Lovett till after the other trials," said Lucy, "but things will probably change after that. We'll have to find out so we can plan it all properly."

"Perhaps I can help you," said Mrs Ferranti.

The children were shocked.

"Oh, no! It's we who're going to help you," exclaimed Dorothy. "You must concentrate on getting well again, and when we get our own place you'll live with us, and we'll take care of you. And – when you're really strong, and if we've got enough money – we can all go on a holiday to Italy, and you can show us where you were born."

Mrs Ferranti smiled. She looked at the four eager young faces and her eyes filled with tears.

"And we can go and visit Great-Uncle Mario in Rome," added Dorothy.

★

David was alone in the upstairs sitting room. He needed to think.

So, minimum wage wouldn't be enough! Well, it wouldn't be fair to put all the burden on Dorothy. There must be a way of making money while he was still at school. It was surely just a matter of finding an idea and working out a strategy. There was a book in the charity shop which told you *How to make a million in ten easy steps*. That was absurd, of course, because if you could do that, everyone would take the ten easy steps and make a million. But there was something irresistibly exciting about the possibility of making money quickly. He just had this feeling he'd be really good at it if only he knew how to start.

CHAPTER THIRTY

On a beautiful, breezy morning at the beginning of July, the two grandmothers sat in the sun on the promenade and looked out to sea. They made a contrasting couple, one supremely elegant in a light wool Italian jacket and linen trousers, and the other in an old washed-out floral dress and shapeless cardigan.

Gwen Jones was working shifts at the hospital and had Tuesdays off.

"I'm thinking of selling the house," she said. "It's got such sad memories for me, and I need to start afresh. I'll get something smaller up the hill near the hospital. Then I won't have to walk all that way down into town at night when I've finished a late shift. Also, it'll release a bit of money for me. I really do need some new clothes, but I'll have to make sure the children are all right first."

Mrs Ferranti lifted her collar up to keep out the sea breeze, and looked over her shoulder. "Is that the hotel where Dorothy's working?" she asked. "I do hope they don't exploit her."

"Not Dorothy!" laughed Gwen. "She's strong. They all are – even little Paul. She won't be put upon! Have they told you about their three-step plan?"

"Yes. I could help them, but they seem so concerned about helping me that it hasn't occurred to them that they too could do with a little help."

"Well, they've had to think for themselves for so long, I don't suppose they expect anything from anyone else."

"I could make things a bit easier for them, though," said Mrs Ferranti, "and they don't need to know anything about it. I too have a plan, but I thought I'd discuss it with you first."

Gwen was interested. She listened quietly while the idea was put to her. If Miss Clements were to sell the big house to Mrs Ferranti after the wedding, there would be no need to tell the children. Miss Clements could go and live with Mr Nicholas, and the children would be under the impression that Mr Lovett was still organising their accommodation while they stayed on in the house.

"And," said Mrs Ferranti, "I don't know what you'll think of this suggestion, but if you do decide to sell up, and if Miss Clements does let me buy her house, perhaps you would like to come and live with us? There are so many rooms, and you could have your own sitting room and bathroom."

Gwen was taken aback. For a moment, she didn't know what to say.

"It would be very handy for the hospital," added Mrs Ferranti.

"It would indeed," murmured Gwen. "Also, there would surely be no need for the children to go into foster care if there were two grandmothers in the house. I think it's a wonderful idea! I'd pay you rent, of course."

★

Isobel was in court awaiting sentencing. She had pleaded guilty with tremendous pride. The police had found the holy leaders' records when they raided head office, and even she had been astonished to hear the actual number of disposals she had performed throughout her career. Purifications, she preferred to call them, and over the years she had performed purifications in the hundreds, even thousands. The Magnifico's world was a purer place thanks to her unflagging loyalty and diligence.

A whole life order! That's what the judge said. Her cup of joy ran over when it struck her that the Magnifico had bestowed a great honour upon her. As soon as she was settled in prison for the rest of her life, she would have the privilege of being in a position to set up His mission. There would be an endless influx of souls for conversion to the Holy Cause, and she would ensure that when their time came to return to freedom, they would carry His word with them and broadcast it to the outside world. She would even be able to teach a few carefully selected disciples the theory and techniques of lethal injection. That fool, Drax, had taken the coward's way out. She was the Chosen and her future in Paradise was now assured.

As she left the court, she turned to thank the judge, and he felt the warmth of her smile.

★

"So many murders must be a record!" exclaimed Miss Clements. "And to think she was in this very house!"

Well, at least it had given her an excuse to make this magnificent celebratory gateau. She'd had her eye on the recipe for a long time.

"And then, that Father Copse being found unfit to plead! Would you like a bit more cream on it, Dorothy, dear? All these months of worrying, and now no more trials! I can't think why David won't join us. He normally loves gateau."

Lucy guessed why David had gone to his room. He needed to be left alone. After all, Isobel was his mother, and Lucy sensed that, in a way, he felt tainted by her guilt. Copse was her father, and she certainly didn't feel at all tainted by his guilt, but having both Isobel and Drax for parents was a double dose. Maybe, now it was all over, he'd be able to find his old live-wire self again and move on. With Copse locked up somewhere for the criminally insane, Isobel in prison for life and Drax dead, they might actually be free at last. There must be a catch!

★

Now that Copse and Isobel were safely out of their lives, Miss Clements felt she had no further excuse for postponing her wedding, and she fixed a date for the last Saturday in August. She found the prospect of marriage disturbing.

"Mr Nicholas wants me to live in his house," she said one morning at breakfast, after Dorothy had left for work. "He says this house is too big. I won't be sorry, because it is a lot to manage, but it won't be the same only cooking for two, and I've worked all my life and would really prefer not to be a kept woman – so restricting, you know. I do like to have my independence. I've always been in charge of myself and Marilyn, and I've supported her through all her education. But there you are. I said I'd marry him, and I won't go back on my promise. Maybe I'll get a part-time job in one of the hotels on the front."

No one could think of anything appropriate to say in response to this uncharacteristic outpouring of private thoughts. The dish of bacon and scrambled eggs was passed up the table in silence. Mrs Ferranti unobtrusively sniffed at the delicious smell that rose from her cup of very good coffee, and wondered how she should put her plan to Miss Clements.

"I suppose it will be time for you children to move on anyway, and I shall miss you," said Miss Clements sadly. "I do hope they don't send you away to Birmingham or London, or some such remote spot. So distressing, don't you think? It would be nice if you could stay here somewhere, so I could see you often and make sure you're eating properly."

She wiped a tear from her eye.

"Oh dear, oh dear," she sighed. "In all my life it never occurred to me that I might get married, and our parents warned us about it and told us not to, but it's too late now. Mr Nicholas is such a lovely man, and I can't let him down. And Dorothy is getting on so well with my cookery lessons."

"We hope Dorothy can rent a house here," said Lucy anxiously. "We don't want to stop seeing you or Nain Jones. And Nonna will be living with us. Everyone we trust is here, and Dorothy's cooking lessons are really important because one day she's going to be a famous cook on television and write cookery books."

Miss Clements sighed, and there was gloom around the table until a rat-tat on the front door told them that Gwen had come to fetch Paul for school and they were all going to be late. There was a mad rush, and suddenly the table was empty, apart from Miss Clements and Mrs Ferranti.

"Another cup of coffee?" asked Miss Clements. "Do help yourself to a croissant."

Mrs Ferranti passed up her cup. She pulled her rose-coloured *peignoir* tightly around her and sat up very straight. What a beautiful woman, thought Miss Clements. Now that she was filling out and the colour was coming back to her cheeks, it was easy to see what Dorothy would look like when she was sixty. Perhaps I'll stop wearing grey once I'm married, she thought. She loved red.

There was a clattering and banging as the children rushed down the stairs and out through the front door.

Mrs Ferranti sat up even straighter. "Miss Clements, I have a proposition to put to you," she said, as soon as the house was quiet. "I'll come straight to the point. How much are you asking for this house?"

It was quite late when the two ladies rose from the table, after a very pleasant and fruitful discussion. Miss Clements went off to her kitchen to think about lunch and the large sum of money that would shortly be coming her way, and Mrs Ferranti went upstairs to what had once been Miss Marilyn's bedroom suite. She put on a crimson shirt and her straw-silk trousers. Thank goodness they almost fitted her again, she thought, instead of hanging off her like a scarecrow.

She could hear Gladys, the cleaner, clearing up the dining room and was glad that part of the agreement was that she would stay with the house — provided she was willing, of course. Also, for a generous fee, Miss Clements was to come in on Dorothy's days off from the hotel and, together, the two of them would plan and cook a week's menu to put in the freezer.

"It may not exactly be a day of rest for Dorothy," Mrs

Ferranti had said, "but it'll be wonderful training for her. And, perhaps, sometimes the two of you could prepare enough for a month, if the freezer will take it, so that she has practice in cooking for large numbers."

Miss Clements had agreed wholeheartedly. "She can help me do the cooking for my wedding buffet," she said. "It may be a good thing if she has something to occupy her mind on her days off," she added, "because she does attract an awful lot of young men."

Mrs Ferranti had laughed. "She'll never be too busy for that, I'm sure."

Now, here she was, fit and well, dressed in the elegantly classic clothes she had forgotten about in her dark time – and buying a lovely house in which to live with her beautiful granddaughter and that granddaughter's adopted family. Life could begin again. She picked up the phone and rang her brother.

"Mario, I think I've got us a really promising trainee," she said. "Someone who may well be fit to take over the business from us one day."

★

"Miss Clements has kindly agreed to let us to stay on in the house once she's married," Mrs Ferranti announced at supper that night. "That is, provided Mr Lovett or the court or whoever it is agrees, of course. And your *nain* has decided to sell her house and will move in with us."

There was a silence as the children digested the information.

Lucy pinched herself. It must be a dream. She would have to wait for it to happen before she could believe it was true.

CHAPTER THIRTY-ONE

Robin stood on the pavement outside the primary school and watched the children in the playground, all screeching and yelling and bumping into each other. He was looking for brown curly hair and olive skin, but all the kids looked the same to him.

Patience was a virtue, and Robin had plenty of it. The only two holy leaders who hadn't fled abroad had promised him a fortune if he could bring this prize home to them. The hot July sun beat down on him, and he longed for the cool water of the nice blue pool at the Spanish *finca*.

His patience was rewarded at last. A teacher blew the whistle and, as the children lined up, she shouted something incomprehensible in a foreign language.

Robin was irritated. "At least everyone speaks English in Spain," he muttered to himself. He studied the lines of children carefully. Good! There he was – that boy at the back of the queue. He'd seen him before, trailing down the road after Dorothy.

At three o'clock, he came again, and stood well back several yards up the road to watch the children run out to their parents. He saw Paul take hold of a woman's hand and, when they moved away, he followed them. So that was the grandma. They went through the town towards the sea, and waited on the promenade, near the pier. A few moments later, Dorothy emerged from one of the hotels. Robin held his breath. He had almost forgotten how lovely she was. She picked up Paul for a second, gave him a big, cheerful kiss and plonked him down again.

So, that was definitely the right Paul. Next thing was to check the pick-up point. 'Be prepared' was his motto, just like the boy scouts. At least they couldn't pretend he wasn't an efficient abduction agent, whatever they said about his brains. He walked back to the school to survey the road access. 'Research' he called it, just like those big-heads who went to university.

He couldn't believe his luck. The situation was perfect. The road leading down from the main road to the school was marked with a white line, indicating permitted parking for parents. Most parents would approach that way. The beauty of it was, when it reached the school, the road looped round some bushes and back towards the main road. So that was the departure route. It was separated from a graveyard by a thick privet hedge, and marked with double yellow lines. No parking there, but plenty of discreet hiding spots on benches set into recesses in the hedge. Or, if he needed to run, a fit and agile individual like himself could easily slip into the graveyard through a weak spot in the hedge.

Robin knew his driver well. He was as highly experienced and efficient as Robin himself, which was saying something. Give credit where credit was due. All the driver had to do was stop the car dead on time on the double yellow lines, while carefully selected local yobs caused a diversion. Robin would deliver the goods. The car would drive off, and Robin would either be running through the graveyard or resting with his eyes closed in a recess in the hedge, having not seen a thing.

He ran over the plan in his mind. Foolproof. The next task was to find the local yobs to create the diversion. That should be no problem. There were plenty of idiots if you knew how spot them, and they were always glad of the extra cash.

When all this was over he would concentrate on Dorothy. If there were any other abductors left he might pay one to come back later to help him, and then he would take her to Spain.

★

The evening sun streamed through the sitting-room window from a brilliant-red sky and all was peaceful. David and Lucy sat on the sofa, poring over Miss Clements's *Radio Times*, looking for suitable programmes to enhance their cool image. Paul lay on the floor with a book, and Dorothy was stretched out on the window seat with her eyes closed after a hectic day full of summer visitors.

Paul was mouthing the words as he read to himself. Suddenly he sat up. "I saw Dorothy's Robin today," he said, "and he made my hum come."

"He's not mine!" said Dorothy indignantly, without opening her eyes. "Anyway, you never got close enough to have a good look at him."

"I saw him talking to you that time on the pier, and then afterwards when he was going away down the prom. He had a funny walk. Lucy couldn't see it, but I did."

Dorothy's eyes flew open and she sat up. "Where did you see him today?"

"He was watching us in the playground. Miss Wyn Lloyd came out and he went away, and I could see him walking. His foot swings out."

Alarm bells rang. The three older ones looked at each other. Perhaps Dorothy's instinct had been right! Perhaps he was more than just creepy.

"Then I saw him again," added Paul. "He was waiting at the end of the road when we came out of school, but he disappeared."

Lucy's throat tightened. What was he doing near the school? Surely he couldn't be after Paul?

"It's the last day of term tomorrow," she said slowly. "It would be his last chance to catch Paul coming out of school."

"We mustn't jump to conclusions," said Dorothy unconvincingly. "After all, he might be one of the parents." She sat thinking. "No, I'm sure he's up to something," she continued. "It's not just the creepiness. There definitely is something fishy about him. Izzy really fancied him when she saw him on the pier. She said if I didn't want him she did, so she checked in the admin office and they said there was no one called Robin working there, and that they were all women."

David picked up his mobile phone. "I'm going to ring Nain, and ask her to call in on her way down from the hospital," he said. "We won't say anything to Nonna, in case it makes her ill again."

Fortunately, there was no need to say anything, because after supper Miss Clements took Mrs Ferranti down into town with her to visit her friend Mary.

Gwen arrived just after Paul had gone to bed. The older three were huddled around the empty summer fireplace discussing their strategy. Eventually, with Gwen's agreement, they decided that Paul should go to school as usual.

"Keeping him at home won't help," said Dorothy. "Robin may be innocent, but if he's not, we'll have to trap him or he'll try another time."

Gwen had a shift in the afternoon, but would try to find cover for the two last hours. If she couldn't make it in time to pick up Paul, David and Lucy would definitely be there, because they finished school early on the last day of term. When Gwen dropped him off in the morning, she would warn Miss Wyn Lloyd not to let him go near the school gate unless she, or his sister, was there.

"And I'll ask if I can leave work early," said Dorothy, "for important family business. If they say I can't, I'll leave anyway."

It was agreed that the three of them would be outside Paul's school by three o'clock, all in different strategic positions. Lucy would be at the gate in case Gwen didn't get there in time. The others would be a few yards away, David to the right of the crowd of parents and Dorothy to the left.

"If he does come," muttered David, through gritted teeth, "whichever way he runs one of us will be there."

"Supposing he doesn't come and leaves it till we've all relaxed?" asked Lucy.

"Well, we'd certainly never relax," Gwen Jones replied. The sad lines that had so recently faded from her gentle face had returned. "We'll just have to be on guard, always. Now, assuming that it could be tomorrow, I'll ring my friend Sam – the one you call Peter Pan – and he'll have someone in among the parents, just in case."

★

The next day, Paul set off for school, his ears ringing with dire warnings not to go off with anyone except Lucy or his grandmother.

Just before three the parents started gathering outside the gates. Dorothy, David and Lucy checked the street from a distance. They were looking for a handsome, young man with a head of gleaming black hair. There was no sign of him.

"Come on, quick!" said Dorothy. "It's nearly time. Let's get in position. He may come at the very last minute." She pulled her straw hat well down and pushed her sunglasses higher up on her nose.

★

Robin stood surrounded by parents. He wore a baggy old tracksuit and the peak of his baseball cap hid his face. He looked around. An insignificant little car was waiting on the double yellow lines next to the graveyard, facing up towards the main road. It wasn't the only car parked illegally, so it didn't stand out like a sore thumb. His unsavoury-looking yobs were poised for action on opposite edges of the crowd, waiting for his signal. Everything was in place except for one thing. He swore to himself. No sign of grandma.

Just in time! Here she came, puffing and panting. Thoughtless old cow, giving him nerves like that.

Gwen wriggled her way through the crush of bodies and reached the gate just as the bell rang. The teachers carefully scrutinised the crowd before releasing children one by one. Paul pointed at Gwen and said something to Miss Wyn Lloyd, and she waved him off. As he came through the gate, two youths suddenly charged into the crowd from different directions and there was havoc. With screams of fear and outrage, parents and children fell back and landed on top of each other, while the youths ran off.

Robin slipped into the mass of bodies and took Paul by the hand.

"It's alright, Paul," he said soothingly. "I'll look after you. I've got some sweeties in the car. We'll wait there till your granny's picked herself up."

There was no time to hum. Paul kicked out fiercely. Robin picked him up, clapped a hand over his mouth and walked briskly to the waiting car. He shoved him in the back seat, slammed the door and slipped through the hedge into the graveyard. Lucy scrambled to her feet and looked around. She heard David shouting, "He's in the car!", and was just in time to see Paul's face, mouth wide open, pressed up against the back window.

Lucy ran. The car moved out, but was blocked momentarily as the car in front of it swerved away from the double yellow lines and cut across it. David reached it first and tugged at the driver's door handle. It was locked. Lucy threw herself onto the bonnet and banged on the front window. The car lurched forward and she fell off. It reversed, lurched forward, bumped and stalled, and would not restart. David pulled Lucy to the side of the road, and Dorothy grabbed the door handle and hung on. The engine restarted, juddered and died. The driver flung open the door with a shove that sent Dorothy toppling and he ran round the front of the car towards the hedge. David was still crouching over Lucy as he passed. He shot out his hand and grabbed an ankle, and the driver fell into the arms of one of Peter Pan's men. By the time he had been handcuffed and taken away, Paul was sitting on the pavement next to Lucy, howling.

Gwen bent over them. "Hush now," she said gently. "They've caught the driver. The ambulance is coming for Lucy, and everything's going to be fine."

A tall figure appeared beside her. "Are you alright love?" said a familiar voice.

She straightened up and smiled "Hello, Sam." She took his hand in hers. "Thank you."

CHAPTER THIRTY-TWO

"Dear Miss Marilyn," wrote Lucy. *"You'll never guess, but I'm in hospital in the same ward you were in, and my leg is up in the air, just like yours! I was run over by a car, but am getting better every day. One of the Magnifico's abductors tried to drive away with Paul, but we stopped him, and he confessed everything to the police. He told them where to find the holy leaders, and they were all arrested. We're pretty sure that it was Dorothy's creepy Robin who actually grabbed Paul, though it was all too quick for Paul to identify him and the driver said it was someone called Dave. Now that the holy leaders have all been caught, Mr Lovett thinks we shouldn't have any more trouble. He's said that before, so I hope he's right this time. I hope you and Professor Dwight are well and happy. Miss Clements is marrying Mr Nicholas, the boiler man, on the last Saturday in August. Love from Lucy."*

★

Lucy sat, propped up by cushions, on the chintz-covered sofa. Her crutches lay across a coffee table, so that she could reach them easily. It was wonderful to be back! Donald lay snoring in a patch of evening sunlight, and Paul sat on the floor, pressed up against the sofa, reading aloud to her from his school book. As it was in Welsh she couldn't understand it, but she smiled and nodded encouragingly.

A large pot of ferns filled the hearth, spreading a thick, green curtain across the empty fireplace. Dorothy was on the window seat, making a list of recipes, and David was hunched up in an armchair trying to understand his book on investment strategies.

Nonna Ferranti sat quietly at a bureau in the corner of the room, behind David's chair. Her pretty silver curls gleamed with little lights as she leaned over figures in an accounts book. An overnight bag lay against the wall nearby, with her coat thrown over it, ready for a weekend trip to Cardiff with Gwen. She wanted to finish off the books before she left, but it was hard to focus when her mind was half on the accounts and half on the children's chatter.

"Lucy, I didn't mention it while you were in hospital in case it upset you," Dorothy was saying, "but I got the sack because I left early on the abduction day."

"That's too bad!" Lucy was indignant. "Couldn't they see how hard you worked? Losing a couple of hours can't have done them much harm."

"Well, it did make it difficult for them, because they had a wedding party that day and needed everyone. It was still in my probation period, and it's important for staff to be reliable. But there we are. It's done now."

Her grandmother smiled approvingly to herself. She liked that attitude.

"And no one would have cooked as well as you," said Lucy.

"They never let me do any cooking anyway, so that part of it was a disappointment."

Dorothy put on what the others called her let's-be-positive look. "It's not the end of the world. We've had to go back to the beginning of our three-step plan that's all, because I still haven't got a job. I'm still waiting for a couple of places to let me know. I've applied to be a bingo-caller, which might be fun."

David looked up from his book. "You needn't work yet. Wait till you're eighteen. It won't be long, and anyway, we don't have to worry about it until Miss Clements gets married. There's another fortnight yet and, you never know, Mr Nicholas might say she can stay here with us for a few weeks instead of moving straight into his house."

"Perhaps it's a good thing you're not working," said Lucy thoughtfully. "You could go back to school."

"That's exactly what I keep telling her," said David. "She says she let us down by getting sacked, but she hasn't. She'd have let us down if she'd stayed for some silly wedding instead of helping us save Paul. Look at all the information Mr Lovett's lot got from that driver! And if Robin really was involved, there are no holy leaders left to give him instructions, so he'll have gone to look for another job. And good riddance!"

There was silence. Nonna completed the accounts and started sorting some papers in her briefcase.

"Well, I'm pleased about it," said Paul after a while, shutting his book, "because I like it when Dorothy's here and not at work all the time. And now Lucy's back, I'm even more pleased."

Lucy smiled down affectionately at him and tickled the top of his head from her superior position on the sofa. "I'm pleased too," she said.

A moment later, Gladys put her head round the door.

"Phone call for you, Dorothy," she said.

Dorothy's spirits lifted. She swung her legs down from the window seat and hurried to the door. "Perhaps it's a job," she said optimistically.

The others waited on tenterhooks.

A few minutes later, she reappeared, looking troubled. Three pairs of eyes were fixed on her, and Nonna Ferranti swung round in her chair.

"Well?" said David. "Was it a job offer?"

"Yes, in a way, but I don't know where it came from. It wasn't what I applied for. A man with a foreign accent said would I like to work for an international chain of hotels in London, Rome, and…" she paused and her voice shook, "in Paris."

Lucy and David gasped simultaneously, and Nonna watched as panic flashed across their faces.

"It's those men!" whispered Lucy. "The Piccadilly Circus men! How did they find us?"

David jumped up and grabbed Dorothy's arm. "You didn't accept, did you?"

"No, of course not," said Dorothy, shaking him off. She was worried. "I wish I knew how they found us. How did they know I had hotel experience? They must have been following us all this time."

"Did he say his name?" asked her grandmother.

"It was something foreign. I was too surprised to catch it."

Nonna leaned over and rummaged in her overnight bag for her mobile phone. "Excuse me" she said, "while I have a quick chat with your Great-Uncle Mario."

She pressed some buttons, and then spoke into the phone in rapid Italian. The children forgot their fears for a moment as they listened to the beautiful sound of the language.

"I wish I could talk Italian like that!" exclaimed Dorothy when she had finished. "I learned it for years in the Mag's school, but I couldn't understand a word."

"And so you shall talk it, and understand it, my love," said her grandmother.

The face that had been so sadly sunken a few months ago was now smooth over the fine cheek bones, and her skin seemed almost luminous in the late afternoon sun.

Dorothy looked at her and remembered the beautiful woman in her mother's photograph, and she thought her heart would burst.

"It wasn't the Piccadilly Circus men, my dears," Nonna was saying. "Those men could not possibly have followed you. You saw them running away, and you saw that they didn't look back. There's nothing to be afraid of. The phone call was from an employee of the company that my brother and I own together. His name is Alfredo, and he obviously didn't explain himself very well."

She handed Dorothy her phone.

"Take this. My brother is going to speak to him, and he will ring you back on this number in about five minutes – Alfredo, that is. I would like you to listen carefully to what he has to say." She stood up and smoothed down the multi-coloured tunic that floated over her flowing silk trousers. "I'm just going to see if Miss Clements wants any help with the menu for the wedding buffet, and if she doesn't, I'll be straight back."

They looked at her in astonishment.

"We didn't know you had a company!" exclaimed David.

"Yes, I have," she replied as she left the room, "and it's a very interesting one."

Then, almost in chorus, they all heaved sighs of relief.

"Alfredo? Phew! I don't think I could have taken any more," said Dorothy, "whether it was the Piccadilly

Circus men, or the Magnifico, or even that stupid Robin."

In less than five minutes, the mobile phone rang. Dorothy waved her hand for hush as she pressed the green button, and they watched her, rigid with attention. By the time Nonna returned, all four children were squashed together on the sofa despite Lucy's bad leg, discussing the phone call.

"He said he was offering me a trainee position with this string of hotels, to start as soon as I'm eighteen. He said I'd learn everything to do with the hotel trade and how to run a first-class restaurant."

"Wowee!" exclaimed David. "But why didn't you say yes?"

"Because my first year of training would be in Rome."

"Ah!" David understood, and so did Lucy. "It'd mean we'd be separated."

Nonna settled herself back at the bureau and bent over her documents.

The children were quiet as their high mood evaporated.

"Where's Rome?" asked Paul.

"It's in Italy," said Dorothy. "Far away."

"It's not that far," said her grandmother quietly, without moving from her position. "It's under three hours by plane, quicker than from here to London. Great-Uncle Mario is always back and forth."

"I can't leave my family," said Dorothy equally quietly. "We agreed we'd never be separated."

"But," said Paul, "you'd be with us in spirit, same as Lucy when she went to London."

"Yes," agreed Lucy. "You'd always be with us in spirit, wherever you happened to be."

"Also," said David, "if you're in Rome you'll be with Great-Uncle Mario, and he's part of our family too."

Nonna had lifted the lid of her briefcase and was stacking her papers in an orderly pile. She turned round and looked at the children, their faces a mixture of excitement and anxiety.

"You know," she said gently, "it wouldn't be forever, and you could all visit Great-Uncle Mario and Dorothy in Rome in the school holidays. And Nain Jones could come with you if she can get the time off work."

The possibility of going abroad was thrilling. Lucy's mind jumped back to her geography lessons at the Magnifico's school. She had always longed to travel to the exotic places shown on the classroom video screen.

"Well, I think you should accept," said David eventually. "If you don't, you'll regret it for the rest of your life. Just imagine if, in five years' time, you were still working in a bingo hall when you could have been running a hotel or a world-famous restaurant. You'd be kicking yourself."

"Nonna Ferranti," asked Lucy. "Would Alfredo mind if Dorothy rang him back and said she'd changed her mind and would love to be a trainee?"

The grandmother looked at Dorothy. "It's up to you, my dear," she said. "What do you want to do? Would you like to go to Rome, and learn to speak beautiful Italian, and start on a career that you're ideally suited for? It'll be hard work, but you're used to that already. You'd have to start at the bottom, cleaning rooms and washing up, just as you were doing in your hotel on the promenade. If you would like to do that, I'll dial Alfredo and you can tell him you accept his offer. If you don't want to, then we'll forget all about it."

"I'd love to do it," breathed Dorothy, "so long as you all know I'll never leave you. I'll be with you in spirit."

The others nodded their heads vigorously, and Nonna dialled.

"Suppose it's too late?" whispered Dorothy as they waited. "He might not want me because I was indecisive."

Mrs Ferranti was put through to Alfredo, and she handed over the phone.

Dorothy took it from her and her voice was trembling with excitement. "Oh, hello, sir – Signor Alfredo, that is. It's Dorothy again." There was a pause as she wondered how to word it. "Please may I change my mind?" she asked tentatively. "I'd love to be a trainee in Rome."

The children could hear his voice and saw the smile spread over Dorothy's face. "I'll come as soon as I'm eighteen," she said.

She handed the phone back to her grandmother. "Thank you!" she cried, throwing her arms around her, and knocking the open briefcase and all the documents onto the floor.

Paul rushed to pick up the fallen documents just as Gwen put her head round the door and called, "Aren't you ready? The coach is waiting for us!"

"Oh my goodness!" exclaimed Nonna. "I forgot!" She snatched up her bag and coat.

Paul was already busy making a tidy pile. "Put them on the desk just as they are or they'll be muddled, there's a good boy," she called as she dashed out. "I'll sort them when I come back. *Addio* everyone! See you Sunday night or, more likely, Monday morning."

Two sets of footsteps clattered down the path. Paul shuffled the documents into a rather messy pile on the floor and put the briefcase back on the desk. Some loose scraps of paper were trying to escape from a pocket in the lid, and he stuffed them back as tidily as he could.

He was quiet for a while.

"What are you looking at, Paul?" asked Lucy. "You mustn't look if it's private."

"It's not private. It's a photograph. It's two beautiful ladies."

CHAPTER THIRTY-THREE

Dorothy shut the bedroom door behind her and leaned against it. The photograph was still in her hand, but she shut her eyes, afraid that what she'd seen at first glance had been a mirage. She waited for her heart to quieten before she dared to look. Then she caught her breath. There they were. Mamma and Nonna! Euphoria and incredulity spun around together in her head. Could this really be her picture, after all these years? She must be imagining it. Then relief! A great pressure, of which she had been unaware, suddenly lifted, and she felt free.

She sat down on the edge of the bed and stared at the two beautiful women. Nonna, she recognised straight away, even though she was much older and thinner now. But would she have recognised Mamma if she hadn't known who it was? She remembered that hair, so black and soft and shiny – but the face? Her memory was blur. But she would never forget the voice. Tears filled her eyes as she heard it now, and all the other emotions were shoved aside by an overwhelming sorrow. She lay down on the bed and wept.

Three anxious faces appeared round the door.

"Is there any way we can help you?" whispered Lucy as they approached the bed.

There was no answer. David bent down to put his arm round Dorothy's heaving shoulder, but it was pushed off.

"Go away!" she moaned. "All of you! This is private."

As they crept out they could hear her crying for her mother.

★

Miss Clements was preparing a tray of soup, with crusty bread and butter.

"She says she doesn't want it," said David. "She says she's not hungry."

"Well, there we are then. That's how we all feel sometimes. It'll warm up nicely later on when she's ready."

"But this isn't just how we all feel sometimes," said David sadly. "It's more than that, because Dorothy doesn't do this."

"My Dorothy is always smiling," said Paul.

David nodded. "We can't help her, because the photograph's brought it all back. Remembering those men taking her away is like a poison that she has to get out of her system, and no one else can do it for her."

"We mustn't let Nonna hear about this when she comes back from Cardiff." Lucy knelt down and put her arms around Paul. "So not a word, OK? It would upset her terribly if she knew poor Dorothy was so sad, and it would bring back her own great sorrow."

★

On the Saturday night, they tiptoed into Dorothy's room before they went to bed. She was staring silently at the ceiling and didn't seem to notice they were there. David sat on one side of the bed and took her hand. It lay lifeless in his. Lucy sat on the other side and pulled Paul up beside her. The three of them sat in silent vigil.

Half an hour passed, and Paul lay sleeping with his head in Lucy's lap. At last, Dorothy turned her head and looked at them dully.

"Do you know what's the worst?" Her voice cracked. "David and I know what it's like to be in a disposal cell waiting to die, but we didn't die, thanks to Paul and Lucy. She was in the cell and must have been as terrified as we were, but no one saved her." Tears streamed down her cheeks. "My poor, poor mamma! I keep thinking how she must have felt, and I can't live with it. Why should I have been saved, when she wasn't?"

As Lucy and David sat there in silence, the cells seemed to close around them both, and they could feel the horror that Dorothy was feeling. Lucy struggled to breathe. Words of comfort were impossible. What had been done could not be undone.

In the end, she said gently, "I think you had to be saved so that there was someone to help poor Nonna in her terrible grief. There was a purpose."

Too late, she remembered that Aunt Sarah was always going on about 'The Purpose'. But why not, if it helped people to have an explanation? Sometimes, what Aunt Sarah said made sense.

Dorothy turned her head away and closed her eyes. "Go to bed now," she said. "I want to sleep."

Lucy shifted Paul gently onto his feet. She wondered if she dared ask if she should take the photograph and restore it to Nonna's documents before she returned from Cardiff. She thought better of it. Now was not the time. Perhaps tomorrow, when Dorothy might be feeling a bit better.

As they were leaving, Dorothy sat up and called out after them. "I'll get them one day – whoever's left of them. I'll get that old Magnifico!"

She lay back on the bed. Her head was on fire. Calm down, cool down. She must work out a plan. There was no rush. Take things slowly and carefully. Go to Rome. Learn the business. Make enough money to do things properly and then seek them out, every one of them, wherever they were all over the world.

★

It was late Sunday night. Dorothy's head was clear. She swung her legs out of bed, slid her feet into slippers and crept downstairs. Nonna's documents lay on the desk, just as Paul had left them. The briefcase was still open and Dorothy tucked the photograph back inside the lid. As she left the room, she heard whispered voices and muffled laughter on the path outside. By the time Gwen and Nonna had switched on the hall light, she was halfway up the stairs.

"Goodness, Dorothy!" called Nonna. "You're still up! Oh, my darling, you look so tired! Is everything alright?"

"Everything's fine. I was reading late, that's all. Did you have a lovely time?"

"Wonderful!"

Dorothy smiled. "That's good," she said. "We'll all want to hear every detail about it in the morning." She blew them a goodnight kiss, straightened her back and carried on upstairs.

CHAPTER THIRTY-FOUR

Two days before Miss Clements's wedding, Nonna and all the Ferranti Joneses, apart from Lucy, had gone into town to help Gwen pack for her move into the big house. Lucy and Miss Clements were in the kitchen, finishing off preparations for the wedding buffet. One end of the long kitchen table was spread with ingredients and the other with work in progress. The worktops and window sills were covered with Dorothy's finished dishes, cooling down ready for the freezer.

"Dorothy seems to be getting more and more like her old self every day. I think all this cooking is doing her good," said Miss Clements, wiping her floury hands on her apron.

Lucy privately thought that this morning's holiday postcard from Jason might have helped Dorothy just as much as the cooking.

"We can keep some of it in the fridge," continued Miss Clements, "and some can stay in the larder because it's only for a couple of days, and it's always cool in there."

As she spoke, there was a bang on the front door and the bell clanged.

Lucy stood up. "Let me go," she said. "I want to practise on my crutches. It's good exercise." She moved off as nimbly as she could, and came back with a parcel tucked under her chin.

"It's for you," she said, dropping it down on the table in front of Miss Clements. "It's from America."

Miss Clements washed and dried her hands, put on her glasses and studied the stamps. She took the kitchen scissors out of the drawer and carefully cut away the wrapping paper to reveal a book and a letter.

"It's from Marilyn," she said, sitting down. "I'm so pleased! It must mean we're reconciled. *"Dear Primrose,"* she read. *"I enclose a book of American recipes as a wedding present."*

She stopped, and exclaimed, "How on earth did she know I was getting married?"

"I told her," said Lucy, "when I wrote to thank her for her letter."

"That was very thoughtful of you, dear," said Miss Clements. "It made me sad to be estranged from her, though I tried not to think about it because, as you know, I don't like to be distressed."

Lucy nodded, thankful that she hadn't done the wrong thing.

Miss Clements carried on reading out loud. *"What you did was…"* She stopped. Then she continued slowly, *"worthy of a Judas, but I have forgiven you, and so no doubt has the Lord."*

She put the letter down, and Lucy was shocked at the stricken expression on her face.

"What's the matter, Miss Clements? Are you alright? What does it mean – 'worthy of a Judas'?"

Big tears rolled down Miss Clements's fat cheeks. Lucy hopped over to a drawer and pulled out a clean tea towel. She handed it over, and Miss Clements buried her face in it and sobbed.

Lucy was frightened. "Are you ill, Miss Clements?

Shall I fetch one of the grandmothers, or the doctor, or Mr Nicholas?"

Miss Clements caught her hand hastily. "No, no, dear," she spluttered. "Is the door shut? Don't tell anyone." And she put her head down on her arms and cried.

Lucy sat down quietly next to her and waited for her to finish. At last, she sat up, mopped her face with the tea towel and smoothed back her hair. She stood up and went over to the sink and threw cold water over her face.

"Put the kettle on, would you, dear," she said. "I'm going to pull myself together now, and we'll have a nice cup of tea and a caramel biscuit."

Lucy grabbed one crutch and hopped, and managed to fill the kettle and put out the tea cups with one hand. She would have felt quite pleased with herself if the situation hadn't been so troubling.

"I'm very sorry, dear," said Miss Clements, dabbing at her blotchy cheeks. "It will never happen again."

They sat in silence for a while, until eventually Miss Clements said, "I owe you an explanation. A Judas is someone who betrays someone he loves, for thirty pieces of silver. I once did something so dreadful I can't speak of it or even think about it, and that is what Marilyn's referring to."

She passed the letter over to Lucy.

"Miss Marilyn says she forgives you. Doesn't it say in your church that if you repent you'll be forgiven?"

"Yes, but by whom? If the whole world and God himself forgave me, I couldn't forgive myself."

Oh dear, thought Lucy. She was not used to this sort of thing. If she or David were upset, Dorothy would just tell them to pull themselves together, and give them a lecture on positive thinking.

"Can't you go and confess it, or something?"

"No. That might make me feel better, but it wouldn't make the thing I did any better." Miss Clements stood up, gave her face one more wipe and checked her straggled hair in the mirror next to the back door. "No," she said, with a look of determination on her face. "It's something I've got to live with all my life, and that's my punishment."

She turned her face towards Lucy, and already it was almost back to its usual bland expression.

"But how could Miss Marilyn say something so nasty if she's forgiven you!" cried Lucy.

"You see, dear," said Miss Clements. "I'll tell you a secret, which I trust you to keep. Our parents, Marilyn's and mine, were... how shall I put it? They were not at all kind to us. It affected us differently. It turned Marilyn sour – she wasn't always like that, you know. She was sweet when she was a little girl. As for me, I've taught myself the knack of suppressing any unpleasant thoughts and, indeed, I think that has saved my sanity over the years. I don't think I'm very strong-minded, you see."

She had another good wash at the sink, and dried her face and hands on a clean towel. With a final sniff, she returned to the table and picked up a patty tray.

"Right then, back to work!"

They rolled and cut and decorated in silence for a while.

"Oh, and I know everyone's wondering why I'm not marrying in the church," said Miss Clements. "Well, that's the reason why. I've not been to church since I did that unforgivable thing. It would be hypocritical. And even if it weren't for that, I would much prefer to go to the Registry Office and be married by my good friend

332

Mary. She'll wear her lovely red suit – so cheerful, you know – and it'll make me feel much better to be married by a dear friend."

She moved a bowl to make more room on the table, and remembered Marilyn's parcel. "Oh my goodness!" she exclaimed. "I still haven't looked at the American recipe book."

She put a tray of tarts in the oven and shut the door, then wiped her hands. The book was still on the table, underneath a bowl of brown sugar and a bunch of celery stalks. She picked it up and leafed through it slowly. At last, she put it down and turned to Lucy with a look of genuine puzzlement on her face.

"Where on earth does she expect me to find elk and bison in Wales?" she said.

CHAPTER THIRTY-FIVE

It was Dorothy's eighteenth birthday. The residents of the big house were gathered in the hall, while Mr Everard, the photographer, set up his equipment. Nain Jones had arranged the session as her birthday gift. The children were excited. Apart from Thomas's snap of Lucy, and one each for their passports, none of them had had their photos taken before.

First, Mr Everard sat them one after the other against a dark curtain, and took a portrait of each of them individually. Then he positioned them together on the stairs, arranged as gracefully as he could persuade them. He took away Lucy's stick, changed their poses slightly, and stepped back to admire the scene.

"Say cheese!" he said.

They all giggled.

Next, there was to be a formal group photograph. Dorothy, as the birthday girl, was put in the middle of the big square hall in an important-looking carved chair with arms, while Lucy and David sat one on each side of her. Paul leaned against Lucy's good knee, and Donald lay on her foot. Great-Uncle Mario and Nonna Ferranti stood at the back, with Mr and Mrs Nicholas to one side of them. On their other side stood Nain Jones and Peter Pan.

Mr Everard checked the arrangement and the light and the distance. "Everybody smile!"

★

Dorothy had been excluded from the kitchen the day before the party. Mrs Nicholas had come over to help David, Lucy and Paul prepare the birthday tea. She had made the cake herself at home, and Paul had decorated it with sugar flowers. The wooden partition doors between the dining and sitting rooms had been folded back to create one enormous room, and the children had placed chairs in what they hoped were socially comfortable places. Bowls had been filled with winter berries and evergreen leaves, and a feast was spread over the dining-room table.

Lucy was surreptitiously poking the icing on her sugar buns to make sure it wasn't runny.

"Hey, stop that! It's unhygienic," said David. He was feeling deflated. Great-Uncle Mario had found him reading *How to Make a Million in Ten Easy Steps* and had said sharply, "Drop it in the bin." David had known he was right and did drop it in the bin, but the embarrassment lingered.

"Don't be bossy," said Lucy, and he managed a weak smile.

Paul had designed wonderfully coloured cards, inviting Dorothy's school friends for tea from half past three to six o'clock. She secretly hoped they wouldn't think the timing a little uncool, but she'd explained to them that she and Great-Uncle Mario were leaving for Rome very early in the morning, and he was anxious that they should have a quiet evening and go to bed early.

"It'll be hours before we get to the airport," he had said, "and although you may not need beauty sleep, I do."

Robin was back from Spain. It had been quite successful, the refurbishment. The *finca* was really classy. He'd had it fitted with piped music, a Jacuzzi, and a kitchen that looked like something from outer space. Nothing but the best. You could see from the sunbeds alone that money had been spent. No one could say he didn't have good taste.

The cave house was out of sight, just behind the main house, and it was well secured. Even Houdini wouldn't get out through all that wrought iron.

It was a pity that Paul's abduction had failed, but there you are, you can't win 'em all, and he still had enough money to get on with his marriage plans. He'd pop up to the kids' house tonight and wait outside to see if he could get a glimpse of Dorothy. Then he'd clear off back to Spain till after Christmas, maybe till the spring. This miserable climate was enough to polish anyone off. He'd got a couple of business deals to sort out and then he'd come back to fetch her.

★

At half past three on the dot the doorbell clanged and, within seconds, the room was full of Dorothy's friends and a pile of prettily wrapped presents had been heaped onto the hall chair. There followed half an hour of opening packages, thank-yous and hugs, and lots of chatter and shrieks of laughter.

Lucy felt an irrational pang of indignation as she watched that Izzy from down the road paying very special attention to David. Was that what people meant by 'flirting'? She tried to hide her annoyance by helping Paul as he dashed about busily, picking up discarded wrapping paper and putting it in the wastepaper basket. When she glanced up, Izzy had moved on and was talking to Jason. David caught Lucy's eye and winked, and they both laughed.

At last, Mrs Nicholas, beaming with sincere contentment, carried in the cake and David shouted, "Time to eat!"

"What a banquet!" exclaimed Great-Uncle Mario, rubbing his hands together. He took a plate and several sandwiches, and settled himself comfortably in a chair by the window. Outside, the sun was already setting, leaving streaks of brilliant orange over the sea.

"There is something about this place," he said to no one in particular. "It is a place where heavy burdens are lifted off one's shoulders."

The friends left at six o'clock, with much kissing on both cheeks, Italian-style, and promises to keep in touch and to visit Dorothy in Rome.

"Do you realise," she said when the last one had gone, "None of us has ever had a birthday party before – or even a present, let alone a birthday present!"

The others then put her to sit in the important carved chair, and brought her their presents.

Paul had drawn a picture of the four of them, standing facing the big house with their overnight bags on the pavement. Out of the front windows peered three faces. One was fat and smiling, the other was thin and sour, and the third was the whiskery face of a West Highland white terrier.

"It's beautiful!" said Dorothy bending down to kiss him. "When I get my pay from my new job, the first thing I shall buy is a frame to put it in, and I shall treasure it till I'm an old, old lady."

Lucy had bought her an almost-new Delia Smith cookery book from a charity shop, and David had carved her a little house out of wood that he'd found on the beach.

"Our house," he said.

She hugged them both. Her lovely, brown eyes filled with tears. "I'm so lucky," she said.

That evening, after Mr and Mrs Nicholas and Peter Pan had gone home and the children had cleared away the party food, they left the dividing doors folded back.

"I like all this space," said Great-Uncle Mario, throwing himself down into a large wing chair. "It's nice to have plenty of room."

Gwen placed a coffee table next to him and put a glass of port in his hand. "Try this and see if you like it," she said, "and then you can be comfortable."

He sighed with pleasure. "I'm already comfortable," he said.

"And I am too," said Dorothy, stretching herself out in her favourite place, on the window seat. "I've had such a lovely day, I don't think anything could have made it more perfect. Early to bed and then it'll be tomorrow and we'll be off to Rome first thing, so I'm going to savour this evening all I can." Her cheeks were rosy with pleasure.

Peace fell over the room. The two grandmothers chatted quietly. Dorothy turned over the pages of her new recipe book, and Lucy lay on the sofa reading, with her bad leg propped up over a cushion. David and Paul were on their stomachs on the floor, building a magnificent Lego castle.

Uncle Mario sipped his port. His eyes closed and opened several times, and he yawned loudly. "I'm ready for bed," he said.

The grandmothers stopped their chat and gave each other a little nod. Nonna Ferranti stood up and went quietly to the bureau in the corner. She pulled down the flap and took out a large envelope.

"Before you go up, my darling Dorothy, I want to give you my present, and it's with all my love."

Dorothy slid her long legs down from the window seat. She slowly opened the envelope, and pulled out a piece of paper and studied it hard with a look of puzzlement on her face. At last, she looked up at her grandmother. "What is it?" she asked.

Great-Uncle Mario stood up, wide awake now, and ambled over.

"Let me have a look," he said, taking the document from her. "Now, let's see. Here at the top it says Deed of Gift. So that means that something is being given. Here it says that the gift is from Nonna to you. So far, so good." He put his arm round her and gave her a hug, and then, his voice full of suspense, he said, "The mystery is, what is it that's being given to you. It's not just this piece of paper, is it?"

"I don't know," she said. "It's a lot of words."

"That's what's being given to you," he said, pointing.

"That's just our address," said Dorothy.

By this time David was looking over Dorothy's shoulder, and Lucy was struggling with her stick to get up off the sofa.

"For goodness sake, Mario!" exclaimed Mrs Ferranti. "Don't tease the poor girl!" She stepped over to Dorothy.

"You're right, my dear," she said gently. "It is your address, and I'm giving it to you. I bought this house from Mrs Nicholas and now it is my gift to you on your eighteenth birthday."

Dorothy gasped and sat down on the nearest chair. The others stood speechless.

"I can't accept," whispered Dorothy. "It's too much." She turned a troubled face to her grandmother. "You may need the money one day, for clothes, or for an operation, or to go to Rome or something. I'm going to look after you, remember?"

Her grandmother took her hand. "Darling, you have looked after me, all of you have, and you've done such a good job on me that I'm now as well as I've ever been. I'm back in the business with Mario. I've been through the books and the records, and caught up with it all, and I'll be back and forth to Rome from now on. I can assure you, I don't need the money. I have more than is good for me, so be kind to me and let me unload some of it on you."

"But how can I afford to run a house?"

"You will have the rent from two lodgers – me and Nain Jones. We'll manage the house for you while you're in Rome, and make sure that all the bills are paid."

The shock was absorbed slowly, the gift was accepted gratefully and its significance sank in. The children were too overwhelmed to go to bed. Lucy lay back on the sofa and dropped her stick onto the floor beside her. She tried to imagine what it would be like to stay in one place for years and years, with no more escapes and trials and foster homes.

David went to the kitchen. He was feeling doubly happy because, earlier on, Great-Uncle Mario had been explaining about investments to him. "I can show you how to make your fifty pounds grow and grow," he had said. "And, if you promise me you will never sacrifice your integrity for money, you can come to me in Rome when you're eighteen, and I will teach you how to become a successful businessman."

Lucy watched David as he came back with leftover sandwiches and hot chocolate and passed the tray around. She could feel his happiness. He really was the most handsome boy she had ever seen, now that he'd grown out his dyed-black hair. And he was the cleverest and bravest and nicest – as well as Paul, of course.

Great-Uncle Mario declined the sandwiches and asked if he could have another glass of port.

"A slightly bigger one this time," he said, as Gwen opened the bottle.

Everyone was busy with their own thoughts. Dorothy was back on her window seat gazing out towards the street. She didn't see the figure lurking in the doorway of the house on the corner. All she saw were the reflected colours of the room behind her and the blazing fire, and the peaceful faces of her family.

The evening slipped gently away. Lucy looked round the sleepy room. Her leg was aching, but she hardly noticed. Dorothy was studying her Deed of Gift, and the boys were clearing Lego off the floor. Nonna was quietly closing the flap of her bureau, and Nain had set aside her book. Great-Uncle Mario sat sipping his port, but his eyes were closed.

Could there be any greater happiness than this, wondered Lucy. She pulled herself up off the sofa and limped over to her grandmother. Gwen looked up and smiled. Lucy bent down and put her arms around her and kissed her soft cheek.

Paul climbed up onto the window seat next to Dorothy. Cupping his hands to exclude the reflection, he peered through them into the street. There was nothing to be seen but the grey shapes and shadows of trees and houses, and a dark figure with a funny walk making its way down the hill.

He hummed quietly to himself until the figure disappeared.

CPSIA information can be obtained
at www.ICGtesting.com
Printed in the USA
LVHW081723251019
635357LV00013B/574/P